UNBOUND
SPIRITS

PROJECT DEMON HUNTERS:
BOOK TWO

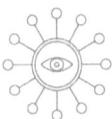

CHRISTINE POPE

This is a work of fiction. Names, characters, places, and incidents are either the product of the author's imagination or are used fictitiously. Any resemblance to actual events, places, organizations, or persons, whether living or dead, is entirely coincidental.

UNBOUND SPIRITS

Copyright © 2019 by Christine Pope

ISBN: 978-1-946435-21-7

Published by Dark Valentine Press

Cover art by Christian Bentulan

Print formatting by Indie Author Services

Michael Covenant stood in the tiny parking lot of the Thunderbird bed-and-breakfast in Tucson, frowning as he watched his sound technician, Susan Loomis, get out of her Subaru Outback.

Alone.

Without waiting for her to approach him, he walked over to her car, then demanded, "Where's Audrey?"

"She wasn't there."

Alarm lanced through him, although Michael tried to tell himself there were probably a hundred different reasons why Audrey Barrett hadn't been at Tucson's small international airport. Chief among those reasons was her current feud with him, but he pushed that concern aside for the moment so he could focus on the problem at hand.

"Was she on her flight?" he asked.

Susan shut the driver-side door of the Subaru and nodded. She was tall, bordering on thin, with sandy-blonde hair she always kept pulled back in a simple ponytail. "Yes, she was on the flight, and she also made it through baggage claim without any problems. But after that…?" Her words trailed off, and she shook her head. Although Susan was the sort of person who never seemed to get ruffled by much of anything, had kept recording his and Audrey's fight with the demons in the Whitcomb mansion's basement and hadn't batted an eye, she now looked troubled. "I talked to one of the attendants, just to make sure. He said he remembered Audrey getting off the flight, although she was one of the last to deplane. But since he didn't follow her into the terminal, he doesn't know what happened after that."

Damn it. Michael knew he should have been the one to pick up Audrey at the airport, despite the frosty relations they currently enjoyed. It had been Colin, their producer on *Project Demon Hunters,* who'd suggested that Susan run the errand instead, his reasoning being that the show might as well keep the "bickering lovebirds" apart for as long as possible. But Susan, while an eminently sensible person, was not the type to pick up on any strange vibes, or to be able to detect whether Audrey had somehow met with foul play. Michael's instincts weren't perfect, either, but they were far more tuned than Susan's.

"There's probably something on the airport's security cameras, although I don't know how we'd be able to access the footage," he said.

"Not without some kind of warrant," she agreed. "And I doubt we'd be able to convince anyone at the local police department to issue one."

No, probably not. Michael ran a hand through his shaggy hair, then turned and glanced back at the bed-and-breakfast. Its white adobe walls looked serene and spectacularly unhaunted under Tucson's impossibly blue skies, flowers blooming, the fountain in the courtyard splashing cheerfully away. Although he couldn't see them, he knew that Colin and Daniela, the show's hair-stylist/makeup artist, were probably settling into their rooms.

"Can you drive me to the airport?" he asked. "I want to take a look around for myself."

Susan sent him a dubious glance. "She wasn't there, Michael. I double-checked."

"I know. I just want to see if I can pick up on anything."

Although she still looked skeptical, she nodded. "All right. I suppose it's possible that she got lost, although Colin told her I was going to pick her up at the Southwest terminal. I had her paged, but that didn't seem to work, so I wandered around a bit, just to make sure we hadn't gotten our signals crossed."

"Let's hope that's all it is."

Michael went to the passenger side of Susan's Subaru, and she got back in the driver's seat. He didn't know Tucson at all, and so he refrained from commenting on the length of time it took to get from the bed-and-breakfast to the airport, although the drive felt interminable.

Once they finally got there, Susan parked in the short-term lot, and they both got out of the car and headed for the terminal that Southwest shared with several other airlines. For a smaller airport, there was plenty of hustle and bustle, although he didn't see how Audrey could have possibly gotten lost in a place this size. This wasn't LAX, or even the hub in Phoenix.

There was certainly no sign of her now, and in a place this busy, it was very difficult for him to pick out any traces of Audrey's energy among so many others. He thought he caught a single flash of her, wearing a fitted leather jacket and worn jeans, trundling along with a metallic teal rolling suitcase, but maybe he'd just imagined the image, conjuring it out of nowhere because he so desperately wanted to see her.

Maybe she'd simply turned around and gone home. Michael didn't want to think she would do something so cowardly as run away, although he was forced to admit that it could be a possibility. She might have gotten off the plane, claimed her suitcase…and decided she couldn't face another five weeks of filming opposite him. Maybe she'd realized she'd rather fight off a lawsuit than spend any more time with the man whose older brother had murdered her parents.

As much as he wanted to push that thought aside, Michael knew he couldn't completely ignore it. He'd really screwed up there, although, to be honest, of all the scenarios he'd tried to imagine where he finally faced Audrey and told her the truth about the connection between his brother Philip and her late parents, none of those scenarios had involved the two of them getting shit-faced drunk and sleeping together after the raucous wrap party that followed the successful conclusion of the first episode of *Project Demon Hunters.* The morning after, he'd been mostly concerned about how the shift in their relationship would affect their work. Well, that and having to confront the very real fact that he knew he felt something for her that he'd never felt for any other woman.

So he'd been completely blindsided when she showed him the book she'd found on one of his shelves, a volume with an old bookplate in the front displaying his given name. She'd demanded to know the truth, and he'd had no choice but to give it to her, even as he realized that his honesty would probably destroy any chance of a future together for them.

"Maybe she took an Uber or something," he told Susan, even as he realized he was grasping at straws.

Susan gave him a mystified look. "Why in the world would she do that? It's not as though I was running late—if anything, I was a little early."

Of course she was. Michael had worked with Susan off and on for the past four years, and he couldn't remember her ever being late for anything. Considering how shitty L.A. traffic tended to be, that was a minor miracle in and of itself.

"Let's go talk to someone in the Southwest office," he said. "I know you talked to one of the flight attendants, but it's possible one of the people actually working the counter saw something."

Judging by the way Susan's lips thinned, she didn't think that was going to help with anything. But they were here; they might as well try.

With her following dutifully a few feet behind

him, Michael maneuvered through the crowds to the ticket counter, where a man and a woman worked in tandem on the computer kiosks there. There was only one person ahead of him, so at least he wouldn't have to wait very long to try to get some information.

When it was their turn, he and Susan stepped up to the counter. The woman they approached— she looked to be around Susan's age, in her early forties—gave them an expectant look.

"Can I help you?"

"Hi," Michael said, doing his best to put on a winning smile. Whether it worked or not, he wasn't sure. Smiles didn't come as naturally to him as frowns. "We were wondering if you might have noticed a friend of ours come through the terminal here. She was supposed to have arrived on Flight 223 from Phoenix, but we can't seem to find her."

"You should check with one of the attendants —" the woman began, but Michael shook his head.

"We've already done that. He says she was on the flight. We're trying to find out if anyone here in the terminal saw her after she got off the plane."

The woman gave a helpless little shrug. "It's been busy on and off today, so I don't know if I would have noticed her or not."

"That's all right," Michael replied. "She's twenty-nine, tall, with long brown hair. She might have been wearing a dark blue leather jacket."

At that description, the man who'd been typing something into his computer looked up. He was a little younger than his coworker, with sandy hair and close-set eyes. Something about him immediately put Michael on edge, although he couldn't say precisely what it was.

"Oh, I noticed her," the man said.

Michael could guess why. Audrey would be striking in any setting, but here, among these travelers in their shabby sweats and jeans and general air of exhaustion, she would have stood out like a peacock in a flock of sparrows. "Did you see where she went?"

"Sure. She came from the baggage claim area"—the man sort of shrugged one shoulder in the direction of the baggage carousel—"and then went out through the doors at the front of the terminal. It looked like she was headed for the short-term parking lot there, but I can't say for sure."

"Thanks," Michael said. That was exactly where Susan had parked her car, and there hadn't been any sign of Audrey.

Still, at least now they had visual confirmation that she'd been here in the terminal, and that she'd gone outside. She hadn't stopped to rethink her life choices and then turned right back around.

"Yes, thank you," Susan said, although it was fairly obvious from her tone that she thought they were back to square one.

Which, in a way, they were. They went back out to the parking lot, both of them blinking at the bright sun and automatically putting their sunglasses on.

"Maybe she did take an Uber after all," Susan remarked.

Michael couldn't see why Audrey would have done such a thing, except as a way to tell Colin that she would come and go as she pleased, and not because he'd set something up for her. But no, that didn't sound like Audrey. If she hadn't wanted to drive with Susan, she would have told Colin straight out, and she certainly wouldn't have made her come all the way to the airport and waste her time.

Susan didn't exactly shrug, but Michael could tell she was nonplussed. Not quite worried yet, more puzzled than anything else.

While he, on the other hand, could only feel his own annoyance quickly fading into concern. Yes, it was good to know that Audrey had landed here in Tucson without incident, and that she'd been moving under her own power when she left the terminal, but where the hell could she possibly have gone?

Voice gentle, Susan said, "Michael, it's pretty obvious she's not here. Maybe it's more that we got our wires crossed—Colin says he told her that I was coming to get her, but it's possible he wasn't clear enough, and so Audrey decided to get her own transportation…a cab, an Uber…whatever. For all we know, she's back at the bed-and-breakfast, waiting for us."

That explanation sounded halfway plausible, although you'd think she would have called to let them know where she was. Or called Susan, anyway. Michael guessed it would be a cold day in hell before Audrey called him voluntarily.

"Well, we're not doing any good here, that's for sure," he said. "We might as well head back. If Audrey's not there…." He let the words trail off. Because if she didn't show up, they'd probably have to contact the police. The shoot would be postponed, and Colin would be climbing the walls, especially after having driven seven-plus hours to get here.

"She'll be there," Susan told him, her tone reassuring. Whether she believed what she was saying was an entirely different story.

They headed toward the space where Susan had left her Subaru. However, they'd only gone a few yards when Michael stopped, his entire body going cold, as if he'd just been pushed into an unheated swimming pool.

"What is it?" Susan asked, pausing as she looked at him with some concern.

"I don't know," he replied. His teeth wanted to chatter, and he clenched his jaw. "Something dark. Something evil."

"Here?" She looked around in bewilderment at the parking lot, at the rows of cars shimmering under the bright sun.

He could see that sun, but he couldn't feel its warmth. Even though he felt as if his legs couldn't move, they were so numb, he somehow managed to force himself to take a step forward, then another one. Slowly, the icy feeling dissipated until it was gone entirely.

Just to be sure, Michael began to retrace his steps. At once the cold surrounded him again, so tangible, it was like walking into a wall of ice. It seemed to emanate from a single parking space they'd passed. He went to it, and experienced a sharp shock of horror and surprise, gone quickly but still somehow thrumming in his bones.

Those weren't his emotions, however. Somehow he knew he was experiencing what Audrey had experienced in this very spot less than an hour earlier.

"Michael?"

He turned and looked back at Susan, who

stood at the edge of the parking space, her expression a study in confusion. Clearly, she couldn't feel anything, was only responding to his own reactions.

"I don't know where Audrey is," he said slowly. "But I'm fairly certain she's in very grave danger."

Chapter 2

EVEN THOUGH AUDREY DIDN'T KNOW WHAT the hell was going on—how a dead man could have gotten into the back seat with her—she knew enough to understand that she needed to get out of the car. Her fingers scrabbled for the door handle; they were still in the parking lot and therefore not moving very quickly, so she figured it would be safe to tuck and roll if she had to, but the door remained stubbornly unresponsive under her reaching fingertips.

"Oh, the driver made sure those were locked," Jeffrey Whitcomb said. "You had better put on your seatbelt, Ms. Barrett—it won't do for you to get injured if we come to a sudden stop."

Like she was going to meekly fasten her seatbelt. Instead, she grabbed her purse, thinking she maybe could use her heavy key ring as a tool to smash the back window in, but her companion tore it from her fingers and shoved it away somewhere beneath his feet.

"Now, now," he told her. "None of that."

Defeated, she slumped against the back of the seat and stared at him. Yes, that was the man she'd seen standing in Michael's backyard, but he looked subtly different, the shadows gone from under his eyes, his face not quite so gaunt. Younger, too, as if at least ten years had been erased from his appearance. But then, if he was a ghost, Audrey supposed he could alter his face... couldn't he?

"You're...you're dead," she said flatly.

"Some people think so," he responded. "Really, Ms. Barrett—I must insist that you fasten your seatbelt."

She wrestled the shoulder harness over herself and clicked the buckle. While doing so, she realized that being thus secured made her escape from the vehicle even less likely, but then, with the child locks on the back-seat doors engaged, she probably wasn't going anywhere anyway.

"There," she said. "Now, do you want to tell me how you can be here, sitting in the back of a Lincoln Town Car, when you died almost a hundred years ago?"

"No, I don't think I need to tell you that right

now," he replied, demeanor calm and unruffled. "It has no real bearing on why you're here."

She blinked at him. "It doesn't?"

"No." His expression darkened. "I suppose you think yourself very clever to have closed the portal in my basement last week."

Arrogant of him to call it "his" basement, when he hadn't actually owned the house since the early 1920s. But Audrey realized she had better let the comment slide. "It needed to be closed," she said. "Terrible things were coming through it."

"Terrible in your opinion, you mean," he corrected her. However, he didn't seem particularly angry, despite the way his black eyes glinted. "They were useful, and now I will have to utilize a different portal, one not as well proven, when that one was very stable and had served me well."

Audrey's head was swimming. Part of her really didn't want to recognize the fact that she was sitting here in the back seat of a Town Car, talking to a dead man. Of course, he didn't look very dead. She could see the way his chest rose and fell as he breathed, could detect a faint flush of color along his cheekbones, even though overall he was fairly pale, much paler than most men one might see in Southern California.

And really, how did she know for sure this was Jeffrey Whitcomb in the first place? She'd never seen a photo of the man in question, had only had

Michael confirm the resemblance when she described the specter who'd been standing out on his backyard lawn and staring at her through the kitchen window.

Michael....

Audrey sat up as straight as the seatbelt would let her, eyes narrowing in suspicion. "Did Michael put you up to this?"

One straight black bar of an eyebrow lifted slightly. "I beg your pardon?"

Triumph surged through her. That had to be what was going on here, and she was glad she'd figured out the ruse so quickly. Maybe it was only that she would much prefer this to be a setup of some sort, a way to get a rise out of her for the cameras, than to contemplate that she might actually have a dead man as her back-seat companion. "Michael hired you to kidnap me from the parking lot so he could get some good reactions for the new episode of *Project Demon Hunters.*" She paused and peered up at the roof of the car, at the dome light there. "Is that where you're hiding the camera?" she asked, pointing toward it.

Now Jeffrey—or whoever he was—actually laughed. "I had no idea you would be so amusing, Ms. Barrett. But no, I regret to inform you that the light you're pointing at is only a light, and I most certainly was not hired by Michael Covenant

—or Michael Stanek, if one wants to be precise about his actual identity."

The flush of triumph faded as quickly as it had come. Because as much as Audrey would have liked to believe this was all some sort of elaborate charade, she knew there was no way in hell Michael would have allowed anyone to know his real name, especially not someone he'd hired for a short part-time gig like pretending to be a kidnapper.

But the real Jeffrey Whitcomb…or the ghost of Jeffrey Whitcomb, to be more precise…might have known all sorts of things, even facts Michael would have preferred to keep hidden. Her fingers began to tremble, so she laced them together and held her hands in her lap. She desperately needed to stay calm. If she allowed panic to take over, then she might not recognize an opportunity for escape if one actually presented itself to her.

"All right, then," Audrey said. "How is it you're still alive?"

"'Alive' is possibly not the most precise term," he replied. A pause as he glanced out the window next to him; it was heavily tinted, but Audrey could still see that they were leaving the parking lot, the big Town Car easing its way out onto a wide, fairly busy street. It looked as though the car was pointed toward the mountains, which she thought meant they were headed east, although she didn't know the area well enough to tell for sure.

Once again, panic wanted to flare. She took a deep breath, willing herself to push back the sudden flash of fear. Not that she'd felt particularly safe in the parking lot of the airport, either, but if Jeffrey Whitcomb whisked her away to some hideout of his, how in the world would Michael —or anyone else—be able to track her down?

"What is the precise term, then?" Audrey asked. Thank God her voice sounded cool and clinical, as though she was talking to one of her research subjects back at the Rhine Institute rather than to a man who should have been dead for almost a century.

His head tilted to the side. Some silver glinted at his temples, although the rest of his hair was still very dark, almost black. "'Borrowed,' possibly. You see, the person everyone thought was Jeffrey Whitcomb ceased to be himself long before he moved into the mansion in Glendora."

Ice ran down her spine, a chill that had very little to do with the refrigerated air coming out of the Town Car's A/C vents. Audrey shifted as best she could with the seatbelt holding her in place, putting a little more distance between her and the…thing…that sat less than a foot away. "If you're not Jeffrey Whitcomb, then who are you?"

"I've had many names. You don't need to know any of them."

My name is legion. No, she didn't think this being sitting next to her was the Devil himself, but she also was beginning to realize that he wasn't exactly human, either. "I thought Jeffrey Whitcomb died in a sanitarium."

"No, Whitcomb's son Henry died in the sanitarium. A simple spell of illusion. I took on Henry's persona for many years, but once his life had run its course, I resumed Jeffrey's shape. It suited me better."

Dear God. No wonder "Jeffrey" had died raving in that sanitarium—he hadn't been Jeffrey at all, but his unfortunate son. Part of Audrey's mind wanted to reject the story in its entirety, but after what she'd seen in the basement of the Glendora mansion, she knew there were far darker forces at work in the world than she'd previously believed.

"You've been living as Jeffrey Whitcomb ever since?"

"No," the thing sitting next to her replied. "I've used several names during my time here, but it was easier for me to retain this form. There's no need for you to know which name I am using now."

No, probably not. He wore an expensive suit, and while the car could have been a rental, Audrey guessed it wasn't. Well, if he'd taken on Henry Whitcomb's identity for a time, then he would have inherited his share of the family fortune when Henry's mother passed away, even if said fortune was depleted from what it must have been at its height. Careful investments of that money over the next fifty years could have amassed considerable wealth. Of course, she was getting ahead of herself. She didn't know for certain that he…it…whatever it was…had done anything of the sort.

But she remembered how Michael had spoken briefly of Jeffrey Whitcomb's son, how he had lived a solitary life, had never married or had children. If his identity had been taken over by this being, if he truly had been possessed all that time, she could see why he'd remained so relentlessly alone.

"What do you want with me?" she asked, the faintest tremor entering her voice. She swallowed, then made herself add, "I'm no one."

"On your own, perhaps," he said calmly. "In combination with Michael Covenant…you are more dangerous than you know, Audrey Barrett."

Dangerous to demons, she guessed. She thought of how she and Michael had destroyed the spell circles in the basement of the Glendora house, how the demons had fought to keep them from taking away their portal to this plane. Could

Michael have done all that by himself? Hard to say. Audrey knew she would never have attempted such a thing on her own, wouldn't have even known where to begin.

Maybe it was crazy for her to even ask the question, but she had to know. "If I'm so dangerous, why kidnap me? Why not kill me and bury my body in the desert somewhere?"

Those questions earned her a thin smile. "Are you suggesting I should do that?"

"Well, no, but—"

He cut her off. "Murder is messy and leads to far too many questions. It's much easier to remove you from the equation instead. This foolish endeavor of Mr. Covenant's will fall apart with your continued absence. There will be no *Project Demon Hunters,* no further threat to my existence and my work. Once I know the show has been canceled, I will let you go."

"And you think I won't tell him what you did?" Audrey demanded.

"Possibly you could, if you remembered anything of it," he said, his tone careless. "I assure you that it will be very easy to ensure that all your memories of me will be gone. You will only recall that you realized you were far too angry with Michael Covenant to work with him, and so remained away until you knew the show would no longer be a viable project."

Thus opening her up to all those lawsuits Colin Turner, the producer, had threatened her with. However, Audrey doubted the being who sat in the back of the town car with her cared much about her finances, or whether she could lose her house in a lawsuit settlement.

Then again, being homeless was better than being dead.

The car turned onto a freeway onramp. Audrey caught a glimpse of a sign as they passed by it—*10 Freeway Eastbound*. That told her a little, but not enough.

"Where are you taking me?" she asked.

"A safe place."

"Safe for you, or for me?"

He'd been wearing a faint smile this whole time, as though he was pleased with himself for pulling off her kidnapping without any complications. Now that smile broadened slightly, deepening the lines around his eyes. Looking at that smile, Audrey felt more cold inch its way down her spine. She'd seen more human expressions on a shark.

"It is a place I own. You don't need to know anything more than that."

"But—"

Abruptly, the smile disappeared. Whitcomb's black eyes glittered, and he said, "Enough. I don't need your chatter distracting me."

Before she could move, try to pull away, he'd reached out and touched a finger to her temple. A bolt of searing pain went through her body, and she cried out. Immediately after the pain came darkness, and the world—and the thing living in Jeffrey Whitcomb's body—was gone.

Thank God Colin was nowhere in evidence when Michael climbed out of Susan's car. The last thing he felt like doing was trying to explain to the producer why their co-host was a no-show, especially since there was no real evidence to explain what had happened to her.

Something bad, though. Something wrong.

Michael murmured a thank-you to Susan for driving him to the airport and back, then slipped into his room. No need to press his luck by wandering around the grounds, even if they were quite beautiful, and might have offered him a quiet place to sit and try to figure out what in the world he was supposed to do now. However, avoiding Colin took precedence over any solace the fountain in the courtyard might have provided. While his producer would discover Audrey's absence sooner or later, Michael thought he might as well maximize his private time now while he had the chance.

His room at the B&B where they were filming the current episode of the show was actually a suite with a sitting area separate from the bedroom. He sat down on the couch, closed his eyes, and did his best to recall what he'd experienced in the parking lot at the airport. Cold, but localized, as if it had been connected to a car that had occupied the space where he stood. Had someone dragged Audrey into a car and then sped off with her? He supposed something like that could have happened, but he couldn't figure out why she would be in the parking lot in the first place. Even if she'd taken it into her head to rent a car rather than wait for Susan to show up, the car rental kiosks and parking lots were located in an entirely different part of the airport complex. It didn't make sense.

Michael would never have described himself as a true clairvoyant; he got impressions from places and people, but he didn't experience visions, didn't have the ability to conjure clear images of events that happened in separate places and times. Still, he strained for that kind of sight now, hoping against hope that the inner eye in his mind would suddenly open and grant him the information he so desperately needed.

Nothing, of course. He could still feel the cold of that one particular spot, the sense of evil that had pervaded it, but he couldn't pick up anything more than that. And the thing was, he had a hard time imagining Audrey being forced into a car against her will. She would have put up a fight, and there were enough people coming and going in the parking lot that surely someone would have noticed something, would have called security even if they didn't want to get involved themselves.

Which meant…what? That she'd known the person in the car?

That didn't make any sense.

Reluctantly, Michael opened his eyes, then got up from the couch and retrieved his laptop from where it rested in its case in the closet. He had basically nothing to go on, but he thought he might as well check to see if there had been any reports of human traffickers working in the parking lots at the airport. Again, though, if Audrey had been the target of someone like that, she would have fought back.

Unless she was drugged somehow….

He fought to clear that image from his head. The situation made him fear the worst, but he needed to stay sharp, to keep his wits about him as best he could. That was the only way he'd be able to figure out what had happened to her.

There was a small bistro set in one corner of the sitting area. Michael opened up his laptop and set it on the table, then sat down. Almost as soon as he logged in, he saw that he had more than a hundred unread emails in his inbox.

His first instinct was to ignore them and go on with the business at hand, but something stopped him, made him click on the icon for his mail program. Mostly junk, as he'd feared, but his gaze landed on an automated message from the contact form on his website. In general, he wouldn't have placed much importance on getting such a message, since he routinely received around a dozen every day, and yet this one seemed to jump out at him from among all the other unread emails.

He clicked on it, saw that the return address was rmcguire626@gmail.com. At first it didn't quite connect, but as soon as he began reading the message, he realized who the email was from.

I had to use your contact form because I don't have your phone number or email. Audrey said she would call when she got to Tucson, but it's after four now and I haven't heard anything. Her phone keeps going to voicemail. Please call and let me know if she's okay...626-555-2289.—Rosemary McGuire

At any other time, Michael might have been annoyed by what he viewed as interference from someone who really didn't know what they were dealing with. Now, however, he realized he probably could use Rosemary's help. They might have had their differences of opinion in the past, but she was a strong psychic, might be able to see where Audrey had been taken.

If she'd been taken at all. She still could have simply gone off on her own. As for not answering her phone, well, if she was still angry enough with him, she might have put her phone in "do not disturb" mode in order to avoid any intrusive calls.

But that didn't sound like Audrey. She was too responsible to indulge herself with those sorts of petty games, no matter what her personal feelings toward him might be.

He got his phone out of his pocket, called the number Rosemary had given him. It rang three times, and he worried it might go to voicemail. But then he heard her voice, and music in the background, quickly muted.

"Rosemary here."

"Rosemary, it's Michael Covenant."

A pause. Then she said, "Is Audrey with you?"

"No. We know she got off the plane, but she disappeared after that."

"Shit."

Exactly, he thought, but he only said, "We can't seem to find any trace of her. She left the terminal and just…vanished."

"Have you called the police?"

A logical question, but he had a feeling this

was something the police wouldn't be able to help them with. And besides…. "Not yet. They're not going to want to talk to me until Audrey's been missing for longer than a couple of hours."

"Oh. I hadn't thought of that." She seemed to hesitate, then said, "Do you need me to help?"

Trying to keep some of the relief out of his voice, he replied, "I was hoping you could."

"Of course. I'm on the road right now—I had a retreat in Idyllwild this weekend—but I'll do what I can when I get home."

"That would be a big help. I tried, but I couldn't see anything."

"The great Michael Covenant admitting failure?"

Obviously, she'd asked the question to get a rise out of him, but he was worried enough right now that he didn't want to waste energy by taking the bait. "Clairvoyance isn't my particular strength. I just figured I might as well make the attempt and see what happened."

"Got it. I should be home in another half hour or so. I can reach you at this number?"

"Yes, I'll be here."

"Okay. I'll call you then."

She ended the call, and Michael set his phone down on the table next to his laptop. It was a little disappointing that he would still have to wait a bit until Rosemary got home, but he supposed it could have been worse—she could have still been up in Idyllwild rather than halfway back to Glendora.

In the meantime…well, in the meantime, he might as well go over his notes on the bed-and-breakfast, get himself prepared for the upcoming shoot. He'd walked the grounds soon after he got here and hadn't seen or felt anything particularly out of the ordinary, but both ghosts and demons could be slippery prey, appearing at their own whim and no one else's.

As he pulled up the file on his laptop, he hoped that Susan had also been able to slip quietly into her room without encountering Colin…or Daniela, who was certainly friendly enough but who also had a tendency to gossip. There was also the added complication of her newfound relationship with Colin. Of course, Michael would never ask either of them outright, but he got the distinct impression that Colin and Daniela had also hooked up the night of the celebratory wrap party at The Bahooka.

Hooked up. Such a trite phrase to describe what he'd shared with Audrey that night. He'd been with enough women to know that what the two of them had experienced had been extraordinary, a connection he'd never felt with anyone else before. To have that promise before him, and then to have it snatched away so suddenly the next day....

He shook his head. Right now, the problem at hand was to locate Audrey and hope she was still well and whole. They could hash out their differences then...if she'd even allow him to. Hers had been a hard, bright, icy anger, difficult to work his way around. But he'd have to try. He knew it was impossible that they would simply work together on the show, then go their separate ways once shooting was done. If nothing else, their destruction of the circles in the basement of the Whitcomb mansion proved how well they worked together. He wanted to keep on working with her, wanted to be part of her life, and for her to be part of his.

Of course, they had to find her first.

Frowning, he looked down at his notes on the bed-and-breakfast. The main part of the house had been built in the 1870s, then added on to here and there as its various owners saw fit. Now it had five guest rooms in addition to the wing where its current owners lived, plus a common living room and dining area.

Supernatural phenomena had been detected in all the rooms in the place, although the activity had been most intense here in the room he'd taken for himself. He'd asked to stay here, wanting to see everything first hand if possible. When he'd walked in the room initially, he'd expected to get that strange thrill he usually experienced whenever he entered a space that had been touched by ghosts or demons. Here, though, he hadn't felt a damn thing.

While the lack of any strange vibrations had meant he probably would get a decent night's sleep, it didn't bode well for the upcoming shoot.

Colin had said it was no problem, that he could always find a way to "spice things up" if necessary, but Michael had no desire to go that route. Their first location had been a roaring success, and he wanted to keep that momentum going, not squander it on fake jump scares and breathy, over-sensationalized narration.

Although at the moment, he'd gladly shoot the fakest paranormal investigation to ever hit cable TV if it meant getting Audrey back safe and sound.

Then, out of the corner of his eye, he saw it.

The room was decorated in a mixture of Southwest and Mexican styles—oak lodge-pole bed, painted talavera pottery and punched-tin lighting fixtures and decorative items. One of these was a large cross that hung on the wall by the French doors which opened on the courtyard.

The cross was hanging upside down. It hadn't been like that when he entered the room twenty minutes ago. He was sure of it.

As he watched, the cross slowly described a half circle on the wall and then stopped, hanging once again in its normal position.

Now the hair on the back of his neck was standing up. Michael slowly shut the laptop, then went over to the cross. When he reached out to touch it, he had to pull his hand back, because the metal was scorchingly hot under his fingertips, as though someone had stuck it in an oven for a few minutes before they hung it back on its nail.

Wish I'd caught that on camera, he thought. The plan was to put motion-activated video cameras in most of the common areas of the bed-and-breakfast, but even though Colin had pushed to have them in the guest rooms as well, Michael had nixed that idea, saying they needed some privacy. Now, though, he was questioning his judgment in making that particular decision.

Either way…it seemed that the B&B wasn't quite as quiet as he thought.

Michael was about to sit back down and reopen his laptop when someone knocked at the door. Twice, though, not the three times that demonic presences liked to use, in a mockery of the Holy Trinity.

Praying it was Susan on the other side of the door—and guessing it was not—Michael opened it. Outside stood Colin Turner, his already ruddy complexion looking even redder from anger. As a nod to the Tucson weather, he'd replaced his usual long-sleeved chambray shirt for a plain gray T-shirt, but otherwise he looked much the same, sandy hair rumpled, blue eyes faintly bloodshot.

"She wasn't bloody there?" he demanded. "And just when the hell were you going to get around to telling me?"

Well, at least Susan had held him off for twenty minutes or so. Better than nothing.

"I didn't want to alarm you," Michael said mildly.

"Consider me alarmed," Colin shot back. "What the fuck are we supposed to do if Audrey's done a runner?"

"I'm trying to track her down."

"How? By sitting in here on your arse?"

"I have someone looking into it."

This vague reply only seemed to irritate Colin further. Arms crossed, he repeated, "'Someone'? Mind filling me in on who this 'someone' is?"

"A psychic I know. She's very good."

As soon as Michael said the word "psychic," Colin rolled his eyes. He might make his living producing documentaries about paranormal activities, but he was still far more of a skeptic than he would like to admit. "What about the police? A private investigator?"

"I'd rather let Rosemary give it a try first. The police aren't going to do anything this soon anyway. And Rosemary is willing to help us out for free, whereas I doubt a P.I. would be willing to extend us that kind of offer."

"Is she any good?"

"Rosemary?"

"Yeah, Rosemary."

"I know she's a very strong psychic. I just don't know how many missing persons cases she's handled. But it's worth having her try."

For a few seconds, Colin didn't say anything, only stood there with his arms crossed, looking simultaneously annoyed and baffled. Then his shoulders lifted and he said, "All right, we'll give her a chance. But what if she doesn't come up with anything?"

"Then I guess we go to the police. And while we're waiting, we can shoot some exteriors, have me give my introductory spiel. We don't need Audrey for any of that."

These suggestions earned Michael a grudging nod. "Okay. But you let me know the second you hear something."

"I will."

Another shrug, and Colin said, "Then I guess there isn't much we can do today. Daniela and I were going to go grab some food in a bit, if you want to come along."

Somehow, the way the invitation was phrased made Michael realize that Colin definitely didn't want him there, that he was only offering because he thought he should make the gesture.

"No, I'm good," he said casually. "I'm waiting to hear from Rosemary. Maybe Susan and I will get something a little later."

"Gotcha." Colin squinted past him, staring at the wall. "Your cross is upside down, by the way."

Michael turned and looked back at the cross. Sure enough, it had once more swung downward. Now he could see faint black marks on the wall behind it, probably from the dark metal rubbing against the room's pale yellow paint.

"Yeah, it keeps doing that," he said.

"Then film the bloody thing next time," Colin grumbled. "Might as well get some decent footage while we can."

"I'll do my best."

While that reply didn't exactly mollify the producer, at least he seemed willing to leave things there. He nodded, then let himself out.

Michael closed the door behind him. Almost as soon as it had shut, his cell phone started to ring. He hurried over to it, saw the number on the screen was from the 626 area code.

Rosemary.

"It's Michael," he said. "What have you got?"

"This is bad," she replied. Even over the phone, he could hear how shaky she sounded.

"How bad?"

"I—I don't know for sure. Just…she's there, but there's this terrible darkness swirling around her, almost as though she's caught inside some kind of horrible tornado. I don't know where she is. I can't see anything…just that darkness, and pressure, and cold."

Cold…yes, he could feel it, too, like some kind of terrible weight in his midsection. He forced himself to speak. "You really couldn't see anything at all?"

"No. But I got the impression she was someplace high, someplace out of reach. No details, though."

Of course there were no details, just as there apparently hadn't been any witnesses around when Audrey was taken. It could never be that easy.

"Well, it's a start," he said. "If she's someplace high, then at least we know she's not in New Orleans or Death Valley."

Rosemary made a scoffing noise. "This isn't funny, Michael."

"I wasn't making a joke," he replied.

A pause, and then she said, "Okay, fine. I'll keep trying, and I'll see if either Isabel or Cecily can pick anything up. But if they can't sense anything, either, then maybe I should come there to Tucson."

"Why?" Michael asked, surprised that she would even make the suggestion.

"Because maybe if I can come stand in the place where you think she was taken, I'll be able to pick up more than I would by trying to do this from five hundred miles away. That's all."

He had to concede that Rosemary had a point. But, with any luck, it wouldn't come to that. Maybe all it needed was for her to join forces with her sisters and bring all their powers to bear in determining where Audrey had been spirited off to—and by whom.

"We'll discuss that if and when the time comes," he replied. "But please work together with your sisters first. Then we'll see what we have to do next."

"I will." Once again, Rosemary hesitated, pausing for so long that Michael wondered if she actually intended to say anything else. Then she said, "Do you have any idea who might have done this?"

Several suspicions had begun to form, each of them worse than the last. But he didn't know for sure, and he didn't want to frighten Rosemary, not when he needed her as an ally. "No," he said. "I only know that when we do find out who it is, I'm going make sure they're sorry they ever pulled such a stunt."

Only time would tell whether those words were false bravado.

Chapter 3

SHE WAS LYING ON A SOFT SURFACE. HEAD aching, Audrey opened her eyes, looked up at a white plaster ceiling with a painted glass chandelier hanging directly above her. Since those particular details didn't give her many clues, she pushed herself upright and saw that she had been lying on a bed in a large room with dark moldings and walls painted a soft sage green. The architecture looked Victorian, as did the heavy carved furniture—a highboy, a pair of marble-topped tables that flanked the bed, a velvet-upholstered chaise longue in an alcove to one side.

Although she knew the haunted bed-and-breakfast in Tucson had been built in the 1870s, Audrey didn't hold out any hope that this was the same place. She'd seen the pictures on the B&B's website, and it looked nothing like this.

No, she must have been brought here by Jeffrey Whitcomb—that is, the thing occupying Jeffrey Whitcomb's body. But since she didn't know what else to call him, she guessed she would continue to refer to him by the name of the man whose life he'd stolen.

At least she'd been lying on top of the bed, whose heavy velvet patchwork quilt was a little disarranged but still more or less in place. And she was wearing the same clothes she'd had on when she was taken at the airport, although someone appeared to have removed her ankle boots. When she swung her legs over the side of the bed, she saw the boots sitting next to the bedside table, which cheered her up a little. She hadn't really looked forward to making an escape attempt in her sock feet.

As soon as she was standing upright, Audrey went across the room to one of the windows there. They were covered in lace curtains, which filtered out some of the light but definitely weren't room-darkening. As far as she could tell, it was still afternoon but later in the day, edging toward sundown.

She really didn't like the idea of being here — wherever "here" was — after night fell.

After pushing aside the curtains at one of the windows, she looked outside. The house was surrounded by trees, a combination of what appeared to be ponderosa pines and several bare-limbed varieties she couldn't identify. There was a flat lawn immediately under her second-story window, but it was level for only a few yards before it began to slope downward, indicating the house was probably built on the side of a hill.

And there was snow everywhere, telling her that she definitely wasn't in Tucson or anywhere else nearby. She could feel panic stir in her at the thought of being taken so far from where she was supposed to be, but she forced it back as best she could, telling herself that she needed to pay attention to her surroundings in case any stray detail might help her to figure out where she was.

The snow looked patchy and dirty, so it had probably been a few days since it had fallen. That made sense at the tail end of February, although she would be the first to admit that she didn't know much about weather patterns in places beyond the West Coast.

Still, she had to try to figure out where she'd been taken. Colorado? Maybe; the pine trees and the snow told her that she had to be someplace much farther north than Tucson or Phoenix, and she knew Colorado had its fair share of Victorian mansions, left over from the boom times of the gold mining era.

Why Whitcomb had brought her here, Audrey had no idea. Was this his nearest safe house? She could see why he might prefer someplace historic, a house that echoed some of the design cues of the mansion in Glendora, although she had a feeling this place was even older.

The bleak landscape outside told her one thing, though—this house didn't have any close neighbors. Although she scanned from side to side and strained to see what might be located off in the distance or past the edges of the building, she couldn't detect anything except acres and acres of trees and steeply sloped mountainsides. No wonder Whitcomb had chosen a property like this to hole up in. He would never have to worry about the next-door neighbors spying on what he was doing.

Which begged the question as to what exactly he was doing here…and what he planned to do with her.

Someone had left a pitcher of water and a glass on one of the bedside tables. Audrey eyed it warily, wondering whether it was really safe to drink. Then again, Whitcomb had already proven that he didn't need to drug her to knock her out. Hypnosis? Some kind of spell, or an innate power all demons possessed?

Because of course that had to be a demon inhabiting his body, even if it had played coy about telling her who—or what—it really was. Something far beyond possession…more like complete subversion of the personality and soul of what used to be Jeffrey Whitcomb. Was he still trapped in there somewhere, or was his soul as dead as the world thought he was?

Difficult questions, and Audrey didn't have the answers to any of them. She didn't even know whether an exorcism would work on him, because she supposed it was possible that only the demon's will held his borrowed body together at all.

Unfortunately, as much as she might pity that trapped soul, she had far more pressing matters to worry about. She needed to get out of there.

Right, she thought. *And then trek across God knows how many miles of snowy wilderness in a pair of ankle boots, a T-shirt, and a leather jacket.*

That prospect would probably have been daunting even for someone used to hiking in that sort of environment. A native of Southern California, Audrey had been in the snow exactly twice in her life, once when she was a child and her parents had taken her to Big Bear for the weekend, and then again in college when she and some friends rented a cabin for New Year's. Snow was pretty, but a week of having to trudge through it and scrape the windshields of their cars every morning was enough to convince her that she would never thrive in a climate that cold.

So climbing out the window and trying to escape on foot was basically out. She didn't even know whether she could open any of the windows, but that was easy enough to discover. The latch on the first window didn't budge, and neither did the second one she tried. The mechanisms could have been disabled somehow, or Whitcomb could have put the whammy on them. Since she didn't have much experience with demons, it was hard for her to say for sure.

All right, the windows were pretty much ruled out as an escape route, but she must have been brought here by car, which meant it probably had to be around the property somewhere. Audrey didn't know who had really been behind the wheel of the Lincoln; her mind had told her it was Susan, but that had to have been another illusion, similar to the one the demon had used to put Jeffrey Whitcomb's face on his son so he would be the one locked up in a sanitarium.

Was the driver still here? If he'd dropped off his passengers and left, then maybe the car was gone, too. Or maybe no one had been driving the car at all. Maybe it had been steered by the force of Whitcomb's will alone, and the "Susan" Audrey had seen wasn't an illusion cast on someone else's face, but nothing at all.

She shivered. The room was a little drafty, and she wished she could have blamed her chill on the temperature, but she knew better. The problem was, once you realized you were dealing with a demon, one who controlled all sorts of arcane powers, then almost any possibility remained on the table.

Her mouth was dry. Audrey looked at the pitcher of water with some longing and then decided the hell with it. Whitcomb had already said he didn't plan to kill her, only keep her out of the way.

The water was sweet and cool on her tongue. She didn't feel any different after drinking it, which seemed to indicate it was fine. A few more swallows, and again she waited, wondering if she were suddenly going to pass out, or double over with stomach cramps.

Nothing. Apparently, the Whitcomb-demon saw no need to get rid of her for now. As he'd said, murder was messy. If all he really needed to do was keep her out of the way for a time, then carefully rearrange her memories, there was no reason to kill her.

Audrey supposed that thought should have been reassuring. As it was, she found herself wondering exactly how he could eradicate her memory of being here, of knowing what he was. Hypnosis? Some kind of spell?

Who knew? Memory was an unpredictable thing at best. Humans suppressed painful memories all the time, so possibly the demon would use a similar mechanism to make sure any memories of being kidnapped were buried so deeply that she would never be able to access them again.

She thought of Michael. It had been hours and hours since Susan was supposed to bring Audrey to the bed-and-breakfast where they were shooting this week's show. Was he frantic, or did he think she'd skipped out on him intentionally? It wasn't that improbable, not after the way they'd fought. Of course, she would never do such a thing, but the two of them really didn't know each other very well, despite the physical intimacy they'd shared. He might very well believe the worst, think that she'd fled because she didn't want to be anywhere near him.

Which would play right into the Whitcomb-demon's hands. If she did manage to get out of here, she would have to find a way to convince Michael that she wouldn't back out on him or the show, although she thought that being kidnapped by a demon was a pretty good excuse for not showing up on time. Anyway, she needed to let him know that she could be professional about this.

If given the opportunity, that is. Imprisoned as she was, Audrey didn't have much of a chance to prove herself. Right then, she couldn't even be sure of how angry she still was. What Michael had done was wrong, but she knew what it felt like to want to be normal above anything else. To not be defined by her past, or her relatives and what had happened to them.

A large part of her therapy after her parents were killed was learning to forgive, to let go of her hatred so it wouldn't consume her. It had been a difficult battle, one that she'd had to revisit more often than she would have liked, but she believed it was a battle she had won…for the most part. And if she could forgive Philip Stanek for murdering her mother and father, then it stood to reason that she should be able to forgive his brother for trying to hide the connection from her. Like Audrey herself, Michael had wanted to be accepted for who he was, not who his brother had been.

And she'd be lying to herself if she didn't acknowledge how much she wanted him here with her right now, arms around her, his calm, resonant voice telling her that everything was going to be okay. In fact, she wanted him so much right then, it was almost like a physical ache.

But he wasn't there. She would have to do this on her own.

The room was growing slowly darker, telling Audrey her impression that sundown wasn't so far off must be true. The last thing she wanted was to sit in the dark, so she went to the door and flipped several of the switches in the light plate there.

A lamp next to the bed came on, as did a

torchiere-style lamp positioned behind the chaise longue. She couldn't help but let out a sigh of relief, because she really hadn't been sure whether or not the lights would even work. Demons could see in the dark, after all.

But apparently her captor wanted to keep up the illusion of being human, and that meant lights that really turned on. Audrey supposed it was possible that there were neighbors visible on the other side of the house. If they existed, then they probably would have thought it strange for this place to remain dark night after night.

Supposing that the Whitcomb-demon even lived here at all. He had called it a "safe place," and made it sound as though the house was only one of several different properties he owned. But even if he shuttled among them, he would still have to spend enough time here to make it seem as though there was nothing strange about his behavior.

Now that the world was rapidly darkening, Audrey went to the window again, thinking that she might be able to see a light from another house, something she wouldn't have been able to detect while the sun was still up. But no, an unrelieved darkness met her eyes, telling her she was utterly alone here.

The door to the bedroom opened with a faint squeak, and she startled.

All right, she wasn't quite as alone as she would have liked.

The Whitcomb-demon entered the room and paused near the foot of the bed. "Awake?"

"Obviously, or I wouldn't be standing here by the window," Audrey retorted. Somehow, knowing that he really didn't want to kill her had provided some much-needed courage.

Or had he told her that to put her at ease, and hadn't meant a word of it?

He seemed to ignore her tart tone. "There isn't much to see. If you're looking for neighbors—for help of any kind—you won't find it out there. The closest neighbor is nearly five miles away."

She'd gathered as much, but having the fact confirmed didn't help. Then again, he could be lying. Since his entire life was a deception, it wouldn't be much of a stretch for him to lie any time he found it expedient.

Audrey turned away from the window and crossed her arms. "Then what's this house doing in the middle of nowhere? It doesn't look like your run-of-the-mill cabin in the woods."

"It is not. There was a mining town less than a mile away, on the other side of the hill." A lift of his shoulders, one that looked subtly wrong to her, as if the gesture had been just a bit too exaggerated. Maybe even after all these years impersonating a human being, he still couldn't get everything quite right. "The mine was played out, the town abandoned. This house belonged to the mine's owner, who put it up for auction. The buyers thought to make it a resort, but the crash of 1929 happened and the bank seized it. I bought it a few years later and made sure it was kept in good repair. After all, it always helps to have a few sanctuaries scattered here and there."

She supposed it might, although she'd never had the kind of cash required to make that sort of setup remotely feasible. It seemed her earlier hypothesis, that he'd taken some of Henry Whitcomb's inheritance and invested it, was more or less true.

"You don't seem to mind answering my questions," Audrey told him then, and the Whitcomb-demon gave her another of those unnerving smiles.

"If there's nothing you can do with the information I give you, then why bother to withhold it? In this case, I thought it better to let you know something of your situation here, just so you understand that trying to escape would be utterly useless. Especially," he added, "since another storm is forecast for late tonight. The snow will be quite deep."

Even though she'd already discarded the notion of escaping on foot, this news still disquieted her. Because while that Town Car might have been big and plush, it sure as hell wasn't equipped with four-wheel drive.

Not that she'd ever driven a 4WD vehicle in her life…or driven in snow, since her college trip to the mountains had taken place between storms and the roads had been well-plowed. Even in the unlikely event that she somehow managed to find her way to the garage, steal the car, and get out of here without being intercepted, she would face the very real possibility of running right off the slick mountain roads. That kind of mistake wouldn't just be stupid…it might well be fatal.

"You seem dismayed," he said, sounding positively cheerful. "Possibly your blood sugar is low. Let us go downstairs and eat some dinner."

"'Dinner'?" Audrey repeated, not sure she'd heard him correctly. "You eat?"

"Of course," he replied. If she'd offended him, he didn't show it. "This is a human body, and so it requires fuel, just as yours does. Come along."

He gestured at the open door, and Audrey walked slowly toward him, mostly because she couldn't think of what else to do. The water hadn't been poisoned, and so she assumed whatever food he gave her would also be safe to eat. And, now that she'd been awake for a while, her headache had mostly subsided, replaced by a gnawing emptiness in her midsection. The last thing she'd had to eat was a packet of peanuts on her flight from Ontario to Phoenix.

So she followed him out into the hallway, which had magnificent dark wood wainscoting as high as her shoulder, topped by wallpaper striped in cream and wine. A patterned carpet covered the floor. The place was very Victorian, and obviously lovingly preserved. Audrey had a hard time imagining the Whitcomb-demon putting this much thought and care into a house, but maybe he'd done so in order to preserve his investment.

Down the sharply angled staircase, and through an entry hall with two-story ceilings and intricate stained glass on the double front door. The dining room was equally impressive, with more wainscoting and a fireplace at one end. A fire crackled away in the hearth, cheerfully oblivious to the fact that this home was owned by something not quite human.

Two places were set on the long mahogany dining table. Audrey glanced over at her "host." "Your driver isn't joining us?"

For a second, he only stared back at her, expression blank. Then he offered her another of those dead-eyed shark smiles. "Oh, I don't have a driver. I conjured the image of your friend to lure you into the car, but I was the one operating it."

Another hypothesis confirmed, although Audrey didn't feel particularly pleased about learning that she had been right once again. Just the thought of being in a car driven by no one was enough to send more shivers down her spine.

Maybe it was a good thing that she'd been out cold for most of the trip.

However, she also realized there was no way they could have driven all the way here in the space of a few hours. She'd never calculated the distance from Tucson to Denver—or wherever they currently were—but she guessed that kind of journey must take at least ten or twelve hours, depending on where in Colorado you were going. If they were even in Colorado. She knew the area around Flagstaff in northern Arizona was heavily forested, too, although she doubted that part of the world had many houses that looked anything like this particular mansion.

Had an entire day passed? That might explain her headache, and the empty feeling in her stomach.

"How long was I out?" Audrey asked.

The Whitcomb-demon didn't bother to ask what she meant. "We didn't drive the whole way. I took you out of Tucson, then went to a nearby municipal airport. We came the rest of the way in my plane...or at least, to the airport nearest here, then drove up the mountain."

"And you flew the plane the way you drove the car?"

"No," he replied. "I have a pilot on retainer. Flying a plane is considerably more difficult than operating a car."

Of course he had a pilot. "And your pilot didn't wonder why you were dragging a comatose woman into the plane with you?"

"No, because I allowed you to wake up enough to converse with him. You don't remember any of it because I made sure you wouldn't. After all, if you were able to recall the journey, then you would know exactly where this house is located." Another of those awful smiles. "I explained to the pilot that you were my girlfriend and were coming to spend the week with me at my mountain home."

Audrey couldn't quite hold back a shudder at that comment. Had he put his arm around her waist, held her hand? Leaned in for a kiss to make it seem as if the two of them really were a couple? The thought made her want to vomit. It was also disconcerting—to say the least—to realize she'd gotten on a plane and flown hundreds of miles, and didn't remember a single moment of it.

Clearly, his promise to erase her memories wasn't an idle threat.

"But sit down," he said. "No need to bother yourself with the logistics. You are here now, and no one has any idea where you are. That's all you need to know."

She wanted to retort that there was a whole hell of a lot more that she needed to know, but she realized there wasn't much point. He was in complete control of the situation, and it didn't really matter what she said or did.

With ill grace, Audrey pulled out the chair to the left of the head of the table and sat down. He took his seat as well, then spread his napkin— snowy white cloth—on his lap. She did the same, but then sent him a sideways glance.

"The table is very pretty," she said. "But I don't see any food."

The words had barely left her mouth before a bowl of some kind of creamy soup appeared in front of her. She was so shocked, she let out a gasp and slid backward in her chair.

The Whitcomb-demon chuckled. "You like my trick?"

"How…how did you do that?"

"It's lobster bisque from a restaurant in Denver. I merely 'borrowed' some."

While it was vaguely reassuring to know he hadn't been involved in the preparation of the food, Audrey still couldn't figure out how he'd been able to magically steal soup from a restaurant and have it appear in their bowls. "Are we near Denver?"

"Possibly." He lifted his spoon to his mouth, swallowed some of the soup. "Or not. It could simply be that I once visited this restaurant and enjoyed its food. You decide."

Which meant the real answer could be either of those possibilities…or neither of them. "I didn't know demons cared about fine cuisine."

"Since this body needs to eat, I might as well supply it with something worthwhile," the Whitcomb-demon said. "Just as it is better to have fresh air, since it needs air to breathe."

"And sleep?"

One heavy eyebrow lifted. "Thinking to catch me off guard, Ms. Barrett?"

Of course that was exactly what she'd been thinking when she asked the question, but now she shook her head. "No. It seemed a logical progression from eating and breathing."

"I have no need of sleep in the way you think of it," he said. "I…rest…from time to time. That is all."

So much for that idea. Audrey forced herself to swallow some of the soup, since she knew she wouldn't be much use without some food in her stomach. The bisque was, as he'd said, very good. And even though the way it had been brought here was unorthodox, to say the least, she was obscurely comforted by knowing that the soup had been made by human hands.

For a moment, they ate in silence. Audrey did her best to keep her attention on the food in front of her, because it was disconcerting enough to know her dinner companion wasn't really human without having to look at him. What was going through his mind, she had no idea. Maybe he was just pleased with himself for spiriting her away so easily. She also couldn't understand why he'd asked her to eat with him, unless it was another way for him to toy with her, to make her as uncomfortable as possible.

If that was his intention, he was succeeding.

Now she'd been missing for almost four hours, by her best estimate. Would Michael and Colin have called the police? Contacted her aunt to see if she knew where her niece was? Audrey had put her aunt's contact information down on the paperwork she'd had to fill out for Colin's production company since she was the closest relative she had.

If they'd done that, then Deb must be frantic. Even if Michael hadn't yet reached out to the authorities, she'd insist that the police be called in immediately. Not that it would do any good.

With an effort, Audrey pulled her thoughts away from those worries. She couldn't do anything about what any of them were doing. She could only focus on where she was now.

Who she was with.

"What do you use the portals for?" Audrey asked.

The Whitcomb-demon set his spoon down in the empty bowl and gave her an unreadable look. "I would think that was obvious enough."

"You bring things through," she said. "But for what purpose? To infest more houses, possess more people? It's not as if there's been a rash of demon possessions in the news."

"You know very well that people don't immediately ascribe abnormal behavior to demonic intervention. It's blamed on psychiatric problems, drug addiction…anything except addressing the root cause of the issue." He shrugged; the bowls in front of them disappeared, to be replaced by plates of grilled trout and rice and vegetables. Picking up a fork, he added, "At any rate, why I need the portals is nothing you need to know."

Audrey should have guessed that he wouldn't volunteer any valuable information. As she reached for her own fork, she had to wonder. This demon—whatever his true name was—had done a very good job of inhabiting Jeffrey Whitcomb's body. What if there were more out there like him, evil, unearthly intelligences exerting subtle influence on people who didn't even know they were possessed?

Her stomach churned, but she made herself take a bite of trout. It was excellent, and she wondered if it had been swimming in a cold mountain stream only a few hours earlier. The rice and grilled vegetables were very good, too. She imagined them all being prepared in a restaurant only a half hour away or so, even though she had no idea whether the food had really come from someplace in Denver. Still, she found a little comfort in believing that was the truth.

"How long have you been in that body?" Maybe it was foolish of her to keep asking questions, but she was a therapist and that was part of the job, although sitting and listening carefully comprised a good deal of what she did. She hoped he would answer her, partly because she was curious, and partly because it seemed as though he was willing enough to provide information as long as it didn't compromise whatever he was doing here.

"A very long time," the Whitcomb-demon said. He reached for his cut-crystal water glass and took a sip. Audrey noticed that he hadn't served any wine, which was probably just as well. Even so, she found herself wondering at the omission. Did alcohol somehow affect his ability to control the body he'd stolen? "Since even before Jeffrey Whitcomb arrived in California. He invited me in not long after he and Alice were married."

Audrey went still from shock, fork halfway lowered to her plate. Although Michael had never given her an exact timeline of Jeffrey Whitcomb's marriage, from the way he'd talked, it sounded clear enough that the two Whitcomb children had been born before the family relocated to California in 1911. Which meant....

"Oh, yes," the demon said with a slight lift of his thin lips. "I had my own taste of the delightful Alice. She was quite a beauty back in the day, you know. The children were of course Jeffrey's in a biological sense, but I like to think I participated in their conception."

Thank God she'd only eaten a few bites of her fish. The fork dropped with a clatter to her plate, and she pushed her chair away from the table.

The Whitcomb-demon's black eyes glinted up at her. "Going somewhere, Audrey?"

"I'm not hungry," she said flatly.

He smirked, then removed the napkin from his lap and stood up. "That revelation upset you, didn't it?"

Well, of course it had. Her research had turned up some disturbingly sexual components to many accounts of demon oppression and possession, but she supposed she'd been naïve enough to think that Jeffrey and Alice Whitcomb had grown apart by the time he started dabbling in the black arts.

And Audrey certainly didn't want to even contemplate the notion that the creature standing a few feet away from her had had sex with a human woman.

"Did Alice know?" she asked, and hated how her voice shook.

"Of course not. How could she? Jeffrey would never have told her the truth. Later on...after I'd taken full control...perhaps she began to suspect the real reason for the estrangement from her husband. Why do you think her children convinced her to put me in a sanitarium?"

Because clearly, they'd begun to notice something a little strange about Daddy. Audrey would have asked why he didn't try to stop them, but there was no need for that, since the demon already had a plan in place to make sure he remained free and that Henry, Jeffrey's only son, would pay the price for daring to institutionalize his father.

"I'm going upstairs," Audrey said, since there was no need to answer his question.

To her surprise, the Whitcomb-demon began to laugh. It was a horrible, high-pitched sound, at odds with the baritone of his speaking voice. In fact, it reminded her of the screeching laughter she'd heard at the mansion in Glendora, the first real sign that something was terribly wrong with the house. "Go ahead and hide," he said after he stopped laughing, "if it makes you feel better. Just know that you won't be able to stop me if I decide I want you. And also know that you won't remember a thing if I do."

She couldn't bear to hear any more. Without responding, she fled up the stairs, the heels of her boots clacking on the polished mahogany stairs. In some kind of dreadful counterpoint to the sound, he began laughing again, those shrill cackles tearing at her ears.

No point in looking back. Audrey ran down the upstairs hallway, then went into her room and closed the door behind her. It actually had a lock, although she didn't know whether it would really do any good. Still, she locked it, then went around the room and turned on all the lights, banishing every shadow, before she retreated to the bed and sat down there, hugging her knees to her chest, trembling so hard, she wasn't sure if she would ever stop.

She had to get out of there.

Chapter 4

AFTER SIX O'CLOCK, AND NO CALL FROM Rosemary. Michael knew he should probably try to eat something, but with the way his stomach was knotted up in worry, he didn't know whether that was such a good idea. Colin and Daniela were still out, and Susan had left as well, saying she wanted to poke around the neighborhood a bit.

That was probably his cue to say he would join her, but he knew he'd be rotten company, what with the way he kept checking his phone every five minutes. Luckily, Susan hadn't seemed to mind, had only said she hoped he would get some news about Audrey soon and then headed out to the parking lot.

He decided he might as well go out to the courtyard. Although the sun was nearly down, the temperature was still mild enough to sit outside for another half hour or so.

Unfortunately, he wasn't left alone to brood for very long. Less than five minutes after he'd sat down, a woman in her late fifties approached him. She was on the chubby side and wore her gray-streaked brown hair in a ponytail.

Michael recognized her immediately—Jackie Samuels, one of the owners of the bed-and-break-fast. Her husband Edgar helped her manage the place, although Michael hadn't seen him so far today. "Hi, Jackie," he said, figuring he might as well be polite. "Nice evening, isn't it?"

"Yes," she replied, although something about her manner seemed hesitant, as if she wasn't entirely sure whether the evening was all that nice. "Has everyone else gone out?"

He nodded. "They wanted to do a little exploring, but I figured I'd stay here."

"So you're going to set up tomorrow?"

Now he thought he had an inkling as to the reason behind her diffident manner. Maybe she wondered if they'd used the story about the TV show to get some free rooms here in Tucson, since there hadn't been much "official" activity going on today. "That's the plan," he replied. "We'll film the intro to the episode, and Colin will get various interior and exterior shots from around the B&B in addition to installing motion-activated cameras in the various rooms. Of course, we'll keep our eyes open for any supernatural phenomena during all that." In his mind's eye, Michael saw the cross slowly hang itself upside down and then trace a circle on the wall as it resumed its original position. Casually, he added, "I did notice the cross in my room."

Paradoxically, Jackie appeared more relaxed now after that revelation than when she'd first approached him. It was possible he'd set her mind at ease by detailing what the crew planned to do next...and that she felt better now after he'd seen for himself that everything was not as it seemed at the Thunderbird Bed and Breakfast Inn.

"Oh, yes, it does that all the time," she said. "For a while, I kept trying to put it back where it was supposed to go. But it never stayed put, so I just leave it alone now."

"It hung itself back in the correct position as I watched."

Her brown eyes widened slightly. "Really? It never did that for me."

Interesting. Was whatever spirit that lurked here trying to put on a special show just for him? Maybe even it wanted its fifteen minutes of fame. Putting that question aside for now, Michael said, "Do you have any other crosses here that display similar behavior?"

"We used to. I had a big wrought-iron and

wood one that was hanging in the breakfast room. But I couldn't get it to stay upright, either, so I ended up taking it down." She hesitated before asking, "What do you think is here?"

"I don't know," he said frankly. "I've seen the phenomenon for myself, so I know something's at work, but I'm not getting enough of an impression yet to make any kind of a judgment call. Our show is about demon hunting, and meddling with a cross is often a sign of a demonic infestation, but certain earthbound spirits have been known to mimic the work of demons to confuse the residents of the homes they inhabit." An idea occurred to him, and he went on, "I think I'll get out one of our EMF meters and take a walk around the property, see if anything registers."

To his surprise, Jackie nodded. "I've seen those on ghost-hunter shows. They really work?"

"They absolutely will record anomalous electromagnetic activity. If I find anything, then that would point to ghosts being involved here, not demons."

This statement seemed to worry their hostess more than reassure her. "If you think it's ghosts, will you still film your episode?"

"Of course," Michael said. "I think it might help to show what a haunting looks like as opposed to an infestation. And we can still help you to clear the building."

Not quite sagging with relief, she said, "Oh, good. Because this thing has been killing our business. We've had some curiosity-seekers, but most people just want to have a nice, peaceful stay while they're on vacation and not have to worry about ghosts or demons or whatever they are interfering with their sleep."

"One way or another, we'll get to the bottom of it," he assured her. From inside his pocket, his phone began to ring, and he sent her an apologetic smile. "Sorry, I need to get this."

"Of course," Jackie said. "You just come knock if you need anything."

He gave her an abstracted nod as he pulled out his phone and looked at the screen. Rosemary McGuire's number. "This is Michael."

"Hi," Rosemary responded. She sounded tired and discouraged, and his heart sank.

"You couldn't make contact."

"No. And it wasn't for lack of trying. Izzie and CeeCee and I made a circle, reached out to Audrey—we used the key to the guest house, since it was the only thing we had that she'd recently touched—and couldn't come up with anything. It's like she's been sucked into a void or something."

"Shit." With his free hand, Michael reached up to rub his forehead. It felt like a headache was coming on, probably a combination of stress and hunger. "You didn't get anything?"

"Just that same darkness and cold." Rosemary paused for a second or two, then said, "I really think I should come to Tucson. I looked up the flights. There's one leaving at seven fifty-five from Ontario that I could take. I have to connect in Las Vegas, but I'll still be in Tucson around ten."

He wanted to tell her no, that he had this handled, but the sad truth was that he didn't have it handled. Rosemary could be sending herself on a wild goose chase, true, and yet if there was even the slightest possibility she might be able to do something in person that she couldn't do remotely, they had to try.

"All right," he said. "I'll be there to pick you up. You can stay here at the room that was supposed to be Audrey's." Even as he made the suggestion, though, he winced inwardly. Although it was a practical enough solution to providing Rosemary with someplace to stay, he hated the sound of it, as if he didn't expect Audrey to be here any time soon. To cover his unease, he added quickly, "You might have to put up with a few ghosts, though."

"Just ghosts? That doesn't sound too bad." A forced chuckle, and she said, "I'll go pack. Izzie already offered to drive me to the airport, so that's handled. I'll be"—a pause as she apparently stopped to look something up—"on Flight 792. Southwest, arriving at ten-fifteen from Las Vegas."

Michael reached for the pen he always kept in his jacket pocket, and extracted it and a receipt from Starbucks. Scribbling quickly, he wrote down the information Rosemary had just given him. "Got it," he said when he was done. "I'll be there."

"Okay." Another hesitation before she added, "We can do this. We'll find her."

God, he hoped so. "I know. I'll see you at the airport."

They ended the call, and he slid his phone and his pen back in his pocket. Jackie had slipped away while he was talking to Rosemary.

Well, this seemed to provide him with an opportunity to check the property with the EMF meter, as he'd promised. He got up from the table in the courtyard and headed back to his room, then rummaged through the duffle that held several of the meters, along with a couple of spare motion-detecting cameras. Even though he knew Colin planned to set up a series of the cameras the next morning, Michael figured it couldn't hurt to get a few of them out there now.

Besides, the more things he could do to keep himself busy while he was waiting for Rosemary's plane to arrive, the better. He couldn't stop thinking about the darkness she'd described, the way she hadn't been able to feel even a hint of Audrey's presence.

What if the darkness she'd felt was death? What if Audrey was already lost to them?

No, he refused to believe that. They'd only made love the one time, but he wanted to think that he'd still somehow feel it if she'd died. Some people might call that crazy, magical thinking, and yet Michael had seen enough phenomena that people would call crazy to realize there was far more to this world than most wanted to admit.

He set up one of the motion-activated cameras in the walkway outside his room, then headed into the common area that had once been the living room of the original adobe house. The email Jackie had sent describing the otherworldly activities in the B&B indicated that quite a lot of disturbances had taken place in this room as well, so he figured it was as good a spot as any to position the other spare camera.

Once he was done with that task, he pulled the EMF meter out of his jacket pocket and turned it on. It was tuned to filter out manmade electromagnetic fields, and so if he picked up anything, it should be ghostly in origin, rather than a "noisy" cable box or electrical panel.

By this point, the sun was gone, and a bluish twilight hung over the desert town. Michael glanced up at the sky, thought he saw Venus clear and bright a few degrees above the western horizon. It was a beautiful evening, still mild and pleasant, and yet he couldn't stop thinking about Audrey…where she was, if she was all right. She should have been here with him, exploring the grounds of the B&B, enjoying the desert air.

No, he was painting too rosy a picture there. The way they had left things suggested that she probably would have done whatever she could to stay out of his orbit, except for those times when Colin was actively shooting the episode and she had no choice but to interact with him.

He should have apologized right away. That had been his biggest mistake—well, after concealing the truth from her in the first place— and now he cursed his stubbornness in believing that he hadn't done anything terribly wrong. Lies of omission were still lies.

Well, he couldn't do anything about any of that now, but if—*when*—they found her, he'd have to make sure that he told her what a screwup he'd been. Anything less, and he wouldn't have done fairly by her.

The courtyard and pathways that wound in and around the main house and various outbuildings that made up the Thunderbird Bed and Breakfast were all picked out in solar landscape lights, so he had no trouble making his way around the property. While he walked, he kept glancing down at the meter he held, but so far it hadn't emitted a single beep.

Which could either mean that whatever presence lurked here really was demonic after all, or the ghosts had taken the night off. Just because a place was haunted didn't mean you'd necessarily get consistent readings from day to day. It was part of the reason why these investigations tended to span days or weeks—the researchers involved had to get some kind of baseline they could use to measure abnormal activity against.

Well, the upside-down cross in his bedroom had been pretty abnormal. Something was here, even if it had decided to play hide-and-seek tonight.

He crossed the courtyard once again and then cut over to the tiny five-space parking lot, where the Jeep Grand Cherokee he'd rented for the trip stood in lonely splendor. Colin's rented white van was gone, as was Susan's Subaru Outback. Michael stood there for a long moment, feeling the gentle desert breeze ruffle his hair, staring up at the sky as the stars began to come out one by one, hard and bright, clearer than they could ever hope to be in Southern California.

The EMF meter was quiescent in his hands. He angled his left wrist so he could squint through the darkness at his watch, the glowing hour markers telling him that it wasn't quite seven-thirty yet. Once again his stomach growled, but he ignored it. He was in the middle of something here. He could always get a bite from a drive-through as he was driving to the airport to meet Rosemary, although that would make for a very late dinner.

What did it matter, though? What if Audrey, wherever she was, hadn't eaten anything? What if she was hungry and cold and frightened?

He didn't want to think of her that way. Despite the losses she'd suffered in her life—or maybe because of them—she was tough and strong, someone who would continue to fight even if she was scared out of her wits. Michael knew he'd never forget the way she'd kept working on erasing those spell circles in the Whitcomb mansion's basement, even with demons attacking on either side. How many other people could have managed to do what she'd accomplished there?

That was the image of her he held now, of her forging ahead no matter what. Whoever had taken her had very likely underestimated their prey.

Now he was walking past the parking lot, to a gravel-paved area that separated the main part of the bed-and-breakfast from a small building, probably a storage shed of some kind. As he approached it, the EMF meter suddenly went wild, the needle swinging all the way to the right as it emitted a series of high-pitched beeps.

Something was hanging in the air in front of the storage shed.

Not the dark shape of a demon, but an amorphous blob of hazy, pale light, so insubstantial that Michael could see the outlines of the building through it. His pulse immediately accelerated, but he'd experienced enough of these encounters that he was able to ignore his atavistic response to such an apparition, could say calmly, "I'm Michael. What are you trying to tell us?"

It remained floating there. For a second, it seemed to grow more solid, and then it was nearly transparent again, its edges attenuating into nothingness. And then, before he could even blink, it seemed to shrink down into a ball of brilliant white light before racing past his head and disappearing.

Colin's going to be really pissed he didn't get that on camera, Michael thought.

As unnerving as the encounter had been, he hadn't gotten any sense of evil from the ghost, or entity, or whatever it was. If anything, it had seemed almost benign, as though it had wanted to communicate with him but didn't know how.

His gaze moved to the storage shed. Was there a particular reason why the ghost had decided to manifest here?

He reached into his pocket and pulled out the super-bright penlight he always carried with him.

After he turned it on, he shone the beam on the small building in front of him. It had brown wooden siding and white trim around the door, and didn't match the historic B&B at all. In fact, the shed looked like the sort of thing you often saw sitting in the parking lot of a big-box home improvement store. Probably Jackie and Edgar hadn't worried too much about whether it fit in with the architecture of their property, tucked away back here as it was.

Definitely not the sort of place you'd think was haunted, unless the ghost was attracted to the location itself, and not the portable structure that had been placed on it.

Frowning, Michael walked all the way around the storage shed. It didn't have any windows, no way in or out except the door in its front wall, which was secured with a padlock. Tomorrow he'd have to ask Jackie if she could open it up so he could look inside. Whatever was in there—if anything—could wait for the next morning, when Colin would be here to film the thing in case it turned out there was something interesting inside.

Still, at least the apparition he'd seen seemed to prove there was some kind of presence here on the property, even if he couldn't quite determine what it might be. That might cheer Colin up a little. Michael wouldn't allow himself to get too excited about what he'd seen—he was still far too worried about Audrey to take any particular satisfaction in learning the B&B did seem to be haunted.

He looked down at his watch again. Almost eight now. He supposed he could hang around here and wait for Colin and Daniela or Susan to return, but he realized he didn't actually feel like dealing with any of them right now. Probably better to just head off to the airport, which was about twenty-five minutes away. He could get something to eat there while he was waiting for Rosemary's flight to arrive. At least that plan would get him away from here for a few hours. Right then, he didn't want to deal with any more ghosts, or upside-down crosses, or whatever other distractions might come his way.

As he walked over to his rented vehicle, his thoughts again went to Audrey, wherever she might be.

He hoped she was hanging on.

Chapter 5

Audrey couldn't stop staring at the door, thinking that at any moment the handle would turn, and he…it…whatever you wanted to call it…would come into her room.

All right, it wasn't really her room, merely the place the Whitcomb-demon had dumped her. But right then, it was the only sanctuary she had.

All remained quiet, though. An antique clock ticked on the mantel, but otherwise she couldn't hear anything at all. Maybe the demon had sat back down at the table and calmly finished eating his meal, since he knew she wasn't going anywhere.

Even though she knew the effort would be futile, Audrey went back to the window again and tugged in vain at the latch. About all she accomplished was to chip her supposedly chip-proof gel manicure.

"Damn it," she muttered. In the grand scheme of things, a chipped fingernail was certainly not the end of the world, but she'd already experienced enough setbacks today. She needed to feel as if she had control over *something*.

Unfortunately, she didn't have any control over that window, her manicure, or her overall situation. Shapes seemed to move in the darkness, and the skin crawled on the back of her neck. As her eyes strained to see something of what was going on out there, she realized that all she'd seen were flakes of snow falling.

So the Whitcomb-demon had been right about the weather. Somehow, knowing that fresh snow was piling up outside made Audrey feel even worse about her predicament. If it got deep enough, neither of them would be going anywhere.

With a sigh, she pulled the curtains closed again, then went back over and sat down on the bed. She had to hope this was only a passing flurry, and that the snow wouldn't be too bad, but she couldn't count on that, not with the way her luck had been going lately.

Once again, she glanced over at the door, but there were no footsteps in the hallway outside, no unseen fingers fiddling with the knob. For all she knew, the demon had made those revelations about Whitcomb's wife exactly because he'd wanted to mess with her head, wanted to have her imagine the worst.

Well, so far he'd succeeded, because Audrey couldn't stop thinking about how he'd threatened to do the same to her, and how she wouldn't even remember because he'd make sure those memories were erased. Although she'd really eaten very little, her stomach felt acid with worry.

She took a deep breath. *If you let him get to you like this, he's won,* she told herself. *Do something constructive!*

Exactly what, she didn't know. But she made herself get up off the bed and look inside the closet. It was completely empty except for an extra blanket folded on the top shelf. She wasn't even sure what she'd been expecting to find—a new wardrobe?—but it was obvious this room had never been used for much of anything.

Likewise with the drawers in the dresser and bedside tables. Once she was done checking in all those, Audrey went into the *en suite* bathroom and poked around as well. At least in there she did find a few useful items—a travel-size tube of toothpaste and a toothbrush still in its packaging, a little pack of facial wipes, and a package of small black combs, the kind a guy might slip into his back pocket, just as unused as the toothbrush.

Had the Whitcomb-demon put all these items here, or had the previous owners left them behind?

No, that didn't make any sense. From what the demon had told her, he'd owned this place since the early 1930s, and the items she'd found in the drawer were new, with modern packaging. She was pretty sure that no one had any Burt's Bees facial wipes in 1932.

So he'd put them there for her, but hadn't bothered to supply a change of clothes? Or was she not the first victim he'd brought here? She supposed she could see that as a possibility, although she really didn't want to think about what might have happened to those other women.

Maybe if Michael were here, he'd be able to tell whether the house was haunted or not. Audrey didn't think she had that ability, despite the few odd psychic flashes she'd experienced over the years, or the way she'd been able to work so closely with Michael to shut down the demons in the Glendora mansion.

That memory got her thinking, though. It seemed that the two of them shared some kind of connection, and so maybe instead of sitting there and stressing about whether her captor was going to come in here and assault her, she should try to reach out to Michael and see if she could give him any sort of clue about where she was being held.

Just a few days earlier, that would have sounded like an insane plan, but Audrey had seen enough recently to know that the universe encompassed far more than she'd previously believed.

Once again, she went over to the bed. She paused to take off her boots and set them down in front of the nightstand, then sat in the very center of the mattress and crossed her legs. Not quite a real lotus position, but hopefully close enough that she'd be able to maintain it for a while. Her hands resting on her knees, palms up, she closed her eyes.

It had been a while since she'd meditated, and that wasn't really what she wanted to accomplish here. However, she cleared her mind as best she could—no easy feat, considering what was still downstairs, eating the rest of its dinner—and focused on Michael, on the piercing gray eyes with their flecks of gold, the shaggy dark blond hair, the wide cheekbones and straight nose. More than that, she thought of the sound of his voice, the way his lips had felt when he kissed her…the strength of his body as it pressed against hers in the darkness.

No anger for him anymore, only need. Only her soul reaching out to his, hoping against hope that his spirit would recognize hers, would realize that the miles between them were really nothing at all. She didn't have much information to give him, but she provided everything she could—a Victorian mansion somewhere in the mountains. Snow falling. And her very real fear that if he didn't find her soon, she might die here, no matter what false promises the Whitcomb-demon had made her.

Michael…Michael….

The pizza didn't look half bad. Actually, as hungry as he was, probably a lukewarm burger that had been sitting on the back of the grill at McDonalds for most of the day would have seemed delicious. He hadn't ordered a beer, because he had to drive Rosemary back to the B&B, but he'd been tempted. Now that it was past nine-thirty, the day felt as though it had dragged on forever. He couldn't really look forward to bed, however, because he had a feeling his worry for Audrey would prevent him from getting any real rest.

He picked up one slice of his pepperoni pizza, took a bite. Yes, that was pretty decent, and not as greasy as he'd feared. Good thing he'd bought two slices, since he could tell he was going to devour this first one in record time.

Just as he'd taken another bite, then reached for his bottle of water to wash it down, an image appeared in front of his eyes, so real that for a second he thought he must have suddenly teleported out of the Tucson Airport terminal and reappeared in another century.

Long velvet drapes framing a tall window. Heavy Queen Anne–style antiques, the kind his mother used to sigh over every time she got a new issue of her beloved *Victorian Home* magazine. A high ceiling with a painted glass fixture in the center. Outside the window, snow was falling.

And then, clear as a flash, he saw Audrey, her expression pleading, her hands outstretched.

Michael…Michael….

"Audrey!" Almost at once, he realized he'd blurted her name out loud, and the other patrons of the food court in the Southwest terminal were staring at him like he'd just lost his mind.

Maybe he had.

"Sorry," he mumbled. "Thought my girlfriend was calling." He tapped his jacket pocket with his free hand, as if to indicate the cell phone in his pocket, and the people around him seemed to shrug and return to their meals.

But the image was gone. He closed his eyes for a moment, trying to reach out, but the connection —whatever it had been—appeared to be gone for good. Still, he'd gotten a few pieces of useful information.

Audrey was all right. Somehow, he knew the vision had come from her, wasn't something that his own worry and fear had conjured out of nothing. The details had been too sharp, too distinctive. She'd been trying to tell him where she was.

Quickly, he set down his slice of pizza, pulled a pen out of his pocket, and began listing everything he'd seen—the dark Victorian antiques, the tall window, the light fixture. Dark molding framing the ceiling, a crystal knob on the door.

And outside, snow falling.

He set down his pen and got out his phone, went to one of his weather apps. Most of the country was clear on this late February day, except for a storm system pushing its way through the eastern half of Colorado before moving on to Wyoming.

Colorado....

That made sense. A lot of quite impressive mansions had been built there in the latter part of the nineteenth century, spurred by the boom of the mining years. And Colorado, while a ten-hour drive from Tucson, would have been easy to reach by air in just a few hours.

None of this answered his questions about who had taken Audrey, or why. But he could look for those answers later. The important thing was that he had someplace he could start searching.

Relief made him even more ravenous, and he finished his first slice of pizza and ate the second one in record time. Just as he was swallowing the last of the water in the bottle he'd bought, he heard the announcement for the arrival of Rosemary's flight.

Perfect. He picked up his tray and dumped his trash in the can, then dropped the empty water bottle in the recycling bin next to it. After that, he went to wait in the baggage claim area, figuring that was where Rosemary would emerge.

And there she was, wild hair nearly hiding the jean jacket she wore over her tank top. Sequins glittered from her long skirt, and she was the recipient of several stares as she walked up to meet him. Michael couldn't tell whether she noticed or not; with her decidedly bohemian way of dressing and her elfin prettiness, she was probably used to attracting attention.

"What is it?" she asked as soon as she got near him.

While he knew she was a strong psychic, he was still a little startled by how she'd been able to easily detect that something paranormal had just happened to him. "A vision," he said. "I'm pretty sure it was from Audrey." Briefly, he explained what he'd seen, and Rosemary nodded.

"She's trying to reach out. I'm kind of surprised she was able to get past the darkness that's been surrounding her, trying to hide her. She must be a stronger psychic than either of us thought."

"It seems that way," he agreed. "But now, let me take you to the place in the parking lot where I'm pretty sure Audrey was kidnapped. I'm parked nearby, so we can put your luggage away first. In fact, why don't you let me take that?"

He reached for the rolling suitcase Rosemary had been lugging behind her, and she sent him a wry grin, obviously not quite sure what to do about this show of chivalry.

"Sure," she said. "Lead on."

They left the terminal and took a quick detour to where his rented Grand Cherokee was parked. After they'd stowed her suitcase and the duffle she'd used as a carry-on, he closed the lift gate.

"Over here," he told her. "It's just in the next aisle."

Other than that, he didn't want to say much about the location of the parking space in question. He wanted to see if Rosemary would pick up on it, would be able to sense that something bad had happened there.

Clearly, she wasn't faking her psychic credentials, because as soon as she got within a few feet of the spot, she stopped dead, hands going to her mouth as if to prevent herself from letting out a cry of dismay. In the weird, bleached illumination from the lights of the parking lot, it looked as though she'd gone dead white.

"Oh, God," she said at last, the words almost a

moan. "He took her…he came here and took her and they drove away."

"He who?" Michael demanded.

"He wore the face of a dead man, but he's not dead. Not really. He's…other."

Cold worked its way down Michael's spine, but he made himself ask calmly, "Who did you see, Rosemary?"

She shifted her position, taking a step with her hands outstretched before she stopped again. "A man, tall, with black hair and eyes, heavy brows."

Whitcomb, Michael thought. *I don't know how, but it sounds like him.* "I think you saw Jeffrey Whitcomb."

Rosemary stared at him. "Hasn't he been dead for decades?"

"Yes."

She was silent for a moment, eyes half shut as though mentally reviewing what she'd just seen, then nodded. "It's a mask. He's wearing him like a suit."

"Who is?"

Her eyes shut, and she shook her head. "He won't let any of us know his name. But he's like the ones infesting the Whitcomb mansion, except older and smarter. He took her because he needed to stop you two."

These revelations made Michael go even colder, but at the same time, he felt a certain grim satisfaction. At least now he knew who Audrey's kidnapper was, although that knowledge only sharpened his fear. Why the demon had decided to wear the face of a man who'd been dead for decades, Michael wasn't sure. That didn't matter right now. What mattered was figuring out where Audrey was being held.

"Let's go," he said, then added, "You're amazing, Rosemary. Now we have a real lead we can work with."

"Well, it sounds like Audrey gave you one, too, but sure." Rosemary's face was still pale, but she smiled, looking relieved that she'd been able to help in such a concrete way.

She followed him to his rented SUV, and he backed out of the spot, then paused to pay the attendant at the booth before they headed north toward the heart of Tucson and the Thunderbird B&B. For a few moments, they were both silent. Then Rosemary spoke.

"I wonder how he got her to go with him. I mean, he would have tried to avoid a physical confrontation—that would have attracted too much attention."

Michael shook his head. "I don't know, but then again, if we're dealing with a demon who's taken on a human form, then he has a much bigger arsenal to play with than an ordinary man."

"Why do you think he looks like Jeffrey Whitcomb?"

Again, Michael had no idea. However, a suspicion began to form in his mind. He replied slowly, gathering his thoughts, "I'm not sure, but the evidence seems to suggest that Whitcomb was messing around with dark magic long before he moved to Glendora. If he'd opened himself to demonic forces, then they might have taken control early on. Maybe it's just that the demon controlling him is used to using that disguise. It's not as though there are many people left alive who would even know what Whitcomb looked like."

That was the simple truth, as far as Michael knew. Somehow, he had a feeling that Jeffrey's daughter would have done what she could to shield her own daughters from the truth about their grandfather, and any information still floating around probably wouldn't have been passed down to their children. It was easy enough to lose track of those sorts of things, especially if the parties involved wanted to make sure the facts were safely buried.

"I hadn't thought about that," Rosemary said. She shifted in her seat and gave him a hard look. "Sort of like what you've done, right?"

The non sequitur might have taken most people by surprise, but Michael knew all too well that Rosemary picked up on things others would never have detected. He wasn't sure she could read minds directly...but, on the other hand, he wasn't sure she couldn't.

Still, he had to deflect as best he could. "I'm not sure what you're talking about."

She tilted her head to one side, dangly silver earrings glinting in the illumination from the street lights they passed. "Come on, Michael. It's so obvious that you're hiding something...that you've been hiding something for a long time. I'm not sure what it is, but I bet I'll be able to figure it out after spending a bit more time with you."

That was the last thing he needed. He'd brought Rosemary here to help with the search for Audrey, not to pick his brain.

Since he hadn't answered right away, she apparently took that as a cue to continue. "And it's what made Audrey so mad at you, isn't it?"

Damn. Sometimes psychics could be a real pain in the ass.

He found himself clenching his jaw, then relaxed it enough to reply, "What went on between Audrey and me is none of your business."

Rather than be offended, Rosemary just laughed. "Oh, come on, Michael. Get that stick out of your ass. I like Audrey—I think we could be good friends—and she doesn't deserve to have you messing with her head."

No, she didn't deserve that. She didn't deserve

anything of what had happened to her since he'd come into her life, but here they all were.

"I wasn't messing with her head," he said. "It's just…complicated."

"You'll have to do better than that. Life is complicated. Deal with it."

This pithy advice did nothing to improve his mood. The last thing he'd needed was for Rosemary to assume the role of Audrey's protector, but he would also be the first to admit that she probably could use more friends in her life. She seemed to live a pretty solitary existence—it hadn't escaped his notice that she'd only talked about having to make accommodations for her clients in order to film the show, hadn't mentioned anything about plans with friends.

Besides, he knew he'd screwed up.

And he was getting very, very tired of having to hide the truth from everyone.

"If I tell you, it can only be between us," he said, wondering if he was making the biggest mistake of his life. "You can't say anything to your sisters, you can't say anything to anyone filming at the B&B or post it on Facebook or whatever. Understand?"

"Yes," she said, the flip tone gone from her voice, as if she realized this was something far bigger than a simple lover's quarrel. "I know how to keep a secret. It's only…I could tell how upset

Audrey was, and it wasn't just about whatever is going on inside her house."

Michael pulled in a breath. He hadn't willingly offered this information to anyone—not even to Audrey—and for a moment, he wondered whether he had the courage to tell Rosemary the truth, even though he'd promised her he would.

"You know how her parents were killed in the Waikiki Massacre?" he asked.

Rosemary nodded, although her expression was somewhat puzzled. Tone guarded, she said, "Yes."

"The gunman was named Philip Stanek. My real name is Michael Stanek."

Realization spread across Rosemary's delicate features. "Oh, my God."

"Exactly," Michael said, his voice grim. "My big brother. No one in the family knew what he was up to. He'd said he was going to Hawaii for a few weeks with some friends from college, and none of us thought there was anything strange about that, since he'd been working and saving up. My parents got a postcard…everything seemed just fine with him. And then…we saw it on the news."

Rosemary's blue eyes looked as big as saucers. "Damn."

"Basically, yes." Michael paused for a moment, wondering how much more he should say. There were things he'd wanted to tell Audrey about his brother and hadn't had the chance. Better to wait until he saw her again, could speak to her. Rosemary had already heard far more than anyone else he knew. "Anyway, I changed my name, moved out of state to go to college. I did everything I could to hide my connection to Philip, and of course my parents helped in every way they could. They didn't want that stigma following me for the rest of my life."

He stopped there, mostly because talking about his family was painful. Neither of his parents had been able to deal with what their son had done. His father started drinking heavily, although he did a good job of hiding his addiction from his family and his coworkers. A heart attack took him just days before his sixty-fifth birthday, and Michael knew that booze had been the culprit, even though the death certificate only said he had died of natural causes. His mother retreated into Xanax and sleeping pills and basically fried her brain. She was now in an assisted-living facility in Florida. Michael paid her bills, but he knew he used the distance between her current home and his house in Pasadena as an excuse to stay away.

And his sister Anna had also changed her name, gone to college in upstate Washington, married a Canadian guy she'd met in between semesters. Now she lived in Vancouver...or at least, Michael assumed she was still there. They hadn't spoken in almost three years.

"But Audrey found out," Rosemary said softly.

"Yes," he replied, doing his best to tear his thoughts away from the ruin of his family. "She found a book at my house that had my real name written in it. 'Stanek' isn't a very common name, and she knew that Philip's younger brother was named Michael. She confronted me, and I told her the truth."

"No wonder she was so angry." Rosemary hesitated, as if she knew that what she wanted to say might offend him, then went ahead and commented, "You should have told her before you slept with her."

How Rosemary knew that he and Audrey had had sex, Michael had no idea. Her psychic abilities again, or just the insight to know that Audrey wouldn't have been nearly so upset if she hadn't been intimate with him?

"I wanted to tell her," he said. In a way, it was good that he had to concentrate on Tucson's unfamiliar streets, because then he didn't have to look over at the woman who sat in the passenger seat. "I was going to, after we were done shooting. It's just...life sort of intervened."

"That's for sure."

"She was going to back out of the show, but

Colin threatened to sue her," Michael went on. That sounded so ugly when spoken out loud, but he figured Rosemary might as well know the worst about the situation. "That was the only reason she came here. It's all my fault."

"Yes, it is," Rosemary said, her tone frank. "What the hell were you thinking?"

"I don't know. I guess I was thinking in the back of my mind that if she was here and we were working together, I'd at least have the chance to talk to her, to try to explain." Once again, worry and guilt knotted his gut. This was all his fault, just as he'd said. "Only I never got that chance. Our demon disguised as Jeffrey Whitcomb took care of that."

"We'll fix it," Rosemary told him. She seemed less irritated now that he'd admitted to making such a hash of things. In fact, she even smiled slightly. "We have the clues we need to track her down. It's just a matter of time."

He wanted to believe her. He had to, because he already had far too much on his conscience. He couldn't let anything else happen to Audrey.

They'd reached the driveway that led into the B&B's parking lot. Michael pulled in, noting that Susan's Subaru Outback was parked there now, although Colin's van appeared to be MIA. Maybe he and Daniela had decided to make a night of it, which didn't seem like that wise an idea if they were going to be filming the next day. Then again, possibly Colin had decided that he could cut loose a little bit, since Audrey was missing and the most they'd be able to do was shoot some exteriors and Michael's intro.

Anyway, it wasn't really his problem. He parked the Grand Cherokee and got out, while Rosemary did the same on her side of the vehicle. They met at the back, and he opened the cargo area and pulled out her rolling suitcase as she grabbed her duffle.

"Here we are," he said unnecessarily. "I'll show you the room where you'll be staying. It's just off the courtyard."

"Okay," Rosemary replied, looking around with some interest even though there wasn't that much to be seen in the darkness.

He began to lead her along the path, but she stopped quite suddenly, her gaze moving toward the storage shed a few yards from where they stood.

"Something's there," she said.

Michael knew that all too well. Still, when he looked at the spot that seemed to have her transfixed, he couldn't see anything. "What is it?"

"A presence…." The words trailed off, and she shook her head. "I don't know. I could feel it, but now it seems to be gone."

"Well, there's a reason why we chose this spot

for our second episode," he told her as they resumed walking along the path. "The place is definitely haunted by something—I saw it as I was out here earlier this evening."

"An apparition?" She sounded far more eager than frightened.

"Yes. Fairly standard sort of blob of foggy light. It disappeared, though. I was planning to take a look in the storage shed tomorrow to see what's there."

Rosemary sent him a sideways look. "What about Audrey?"

"That's what we're doing tonight. Unless you wanted to go straight to bed."

That comment made her huff out a breath of contempt. "Before midnight? Hardly."

Exactly what he wanted to hear. Every second that passed was one where Audrey was alone, certainly frightened and possibly in pain.

His resolve would keep him going. "Let's put your things in your room, and then we'll get started."

Chapter 6

Had her silent plea worked? She had no way of knowing, but Audrey felt a little better now that she at least had tried.

All was still in the house, except for the faint *tick-tick* of the clock on the mantel and every once in a while a strange, keening sound that she guessed must be the wind whistling through the pines. For a moment, she thought to go to the window and look outside, but since the property didn't appear to have any exterior lights—or at least any lights that were turned on—she doubted she'd be able to see anything.

She unfolded her legs, which felt a little stiff after sitting in that not-quite lotus position for more than twenty minutes, and leaned against the headboard. In that moment, she realized how utterly bone-tired she was. It had been a long and terrible day, but she wasn't sure she could allow herself to sleep. Not with that thing downstairs, possibly waiting for that moment of vulnerability.

The problem was, she didn't see what she could do to keep herself awake. She didn't know what had happened to her purse while she was out cold; evidently, the Whitcomb-demon had spirited it away someplace, since it wasn't anywhere in this room. They were so far out in the middle of nowhere that Audrey doubted her phone would have even gotten a signal, but she at least could have played games or read on her Kindle app to keep herself awake.

Well, one thing she could do was use some of the supplies she'd found in the bathroom. The lobster bisque had left a bad taste in her mouth… or maybe that was just the taste of frustration. Either way, she could get down off this bed, walk in there, get herself prepped for the night.

Brushing her teeth and using the facial wipes to get the minimal makeup she wore off her face took a little over three minutes. But it did help to get up from the bed, to walk around a bit. She still felt dead tired, but her eyelids weren't quite as droopy.

Should she try to reach out to Michael again? After all, she had no idea whether her first attempt had even been successful. Something in her mind told her no, that she'd done what she could and it was up to him to take the next step.

All right. She went to the closet and got down the spare blanket she'd found, then laid it across the foot of the bed in case she gave up and decided she needed to sleep, despite the inherent dangers of being out cold with a demon roaming around the house. Although if he was roaming, he was being very quiet about it. Old houses like this, no matter how well-maintained, always managed to creak somewhere. She'd heard a few odd noises coming from the roof, but nothing from the hallway outside her door.

Maybe he'd left her here while he attended to business elsewhere. That would be the ultimate irony, wouldn't it—that she'd been left unguarded this whole time?

Unfortunately, she wasn't quite brave enough to leave her room and venture downstairs to check.

After pacing the room for about fifteen minutes, Audrey realized there was no way she could keep this up all night. Eventually, she'd drop where she stood. So she shrugged out of her leather jacket and hung it on one of the bedposts, then turned back the covers and climbed in.

She was definitely leaving all the lights on, though.

The funny thing was, once she'd lain down

and resigned herself to sleep, she found she couldn't. Her eyes shut, but they flared open at every sound, every howl of the wind, every time the clock on the mantel made a tick that wasn't quite in time with the others.

Well, at least she was lying down, and comfortable. The room felt a little chilly now that she'd taken off her jacket, but Audrey reached down to the foot of the bed and retrieved the blanket she'd placed there, then spread it out over herself. At least this place had some kind of central heat, although the air temperature was colder than she would have liked it, probably somewhere in the low sixties.

But yes, with the blanket covering her, that was better. She could close her eyes and pretend she was at the bed-and-breakfast in Tucson, that Michael was in the room next to hers, there in case she needed him for anything. She wouldn't even bother to act as though she wasn't speaking to him, because she knew she'd already forgiven him.

The light outside her closed eyelids grew dimmer and dimmer. And just like that, she was asleep.

She walked in her dreams, on a low, rounded hill covered in dry grass. In the dream, it was as if she was both inside herself and observing from outside, as though watching a movie. The wind was brisk and pulled at her hair, and clouds scudded across a lowering sky. Strangely, though, she wasn't cold…or at least, her dream-self couldn't feel the cold.

Somehow, she knew she wasn't alone. She turned and saw a tall man walking up the hill toward her. The same breeze that tugged her hair played with the hem of his long coat, making it blow in black tails behind him.

As soon as he drew closer, Audrey knew who was standing there. Jeffrey Whitcomb, in the same clothes he'd worn when he appeared in the backyard of Michael's house, rather than the modern business suit he'd had on when he kidnapped her from the airport parking lot in Tucson.

For some reason, she wasn't afraid. The man who faced her now was not the Whitcomb-demon, although she couldn't have said how she immediately knew the difference.

"Can you help me?" she asked.

He shook his head. "I was going to ask you the same thing."

"I don't think I'm in a position to help anyone," she said.

"You might be surprised." He was quiet for a moment, during which she studied his face, his expression. This man looked older than the possessed version of himself, as if the demon that now inhabited his body wanted to present a younger, more vigorous face to the world. His dark eyes were sad, filled with deep melancholy.

"Can you tell me why you did it?"

Whitcomb didn't ask Audrey to explain what she meant. He studied her for a moment before replying, "I wanted everything I didn't have. I was born a poor man and didn't want to die that way. I had some early success, but I knew it wouldn't be enough. So I…took a shortcut."

"Summoning demons is a shortcut?" she asked. Her dream-self looked skeptical and crossed her arms.

"You always think you're going to stay in control, that you'll be able to manage the situation. At first, that was the case. My investments yielded profits beyond my wildest dreams. I married a beautiful woman. But…."

"But it didn't last."

"No. I started to hear strange voices in my sleep, in my dreams. There were days when I couldn't recall whether I was awake or asleep, when something else was guiding my actions, speaking with my voice. That was when I realized it had all gone horribly wrong."

"Why didn't you try to send them back, like Michael and I did? Or reach out to a priest for an exorcism?"

"Because the demon already controlled me to the point where I no longer had enough free will to take the necessary action to save myself. It was as though my body had become a prison, and I was locked away in a forgotten cell, ignored while something else lived my life."

Audrey couldn't help shivering. She remembered how the demon had boasted of putting Whitcomb's face on his son's body, forcing Henry to endure years in a sanitarium while his possessed father was free to roam the world in his child's form. Watching the anguish in the dream-Whitcomb's face, she couldn't help but feel sorry for him, even though she knew he'd brought all this on himself.

"But you can free me," he went on. "You know how, don't you?"

His expression was pleading, but she could only shake her head. "No, I really don't."

"Kill the body, and the demon will have no place to live."

She stared at him. "Why not exorcise the demon from your body?"

"Because if you kill my body, the demon will die with it. If you only banish him, he will find some way to come back. He's wily like that. He is older than time, and his name is—"

A hand clamped down on her throat. She gasped, eyelids flying open, and stared up into the face of the Whitcomb-demon, whose black eyes glittered down at her.

"Now, now, Audrey," he said. "Hasn't anyone told you to be careful about the company you keep?"

Michael and Rosemary sat at the small table in his room, his laptop positioned between the two of them so they could both get a good view of the screen. For the last twenty minutes, they'd been surfing through sites dedicated to old houses, trying to find one that closely matched what he'd seen in the vision Audrey had sent him. So far, they'd seen one or two that were similar in architecture, but both were located in towns, not built up on a mountainside somewhere.

"What about searching in county assessors' websites?" Rosemary suggested after she took a sip of water. "Wouldn't there be a record of Whitcomb owning property in Colorado?"

"Maybe," Michael said. "Although I think he probably would have done what he could to keep his name hidden…using a trust or something like that."

"Oh, right," Rosemary replied. Disappointment was clear on her face. "I'm not used to all the maneuvering rich people do to hide their money and assets."

Once upon a time, Michael hadn't been,

either. But after spending ten years making sure no one would have an easy time figuring out who he was, he knew a good many of the tricks. Not all of them, of course, because although his books and DVDs and speaking fees all added up to a comfortable income, he wasn't exactly at the level where he needed to create a shell corporation in the Cayman Islands or something.

"It's all right," he said. He leaned back in his chair and rubbed at the scruff on his chin, considering the problem. Of course, there was always the chance that the house Whitcomb was currently holed up in had never been photographed, but there had to be a record somewhere. "Maybe we're going at this the wrong way."

"How do you mean?"

Michael leaned forward and opened another tab in his browser. "Maybe what we need to do is look for former mining towns that were prosperous enough to support the construction of that kind of mansion. Then we can poke around in those records and see if we can narrow things down."

"All right," Rosemary said, her eyes shining. "That sounds like a good idea."

After running a few searches, however, he began to wonder whether it was really that good an idea after all. Colorado had been dotted with both silver and gold mining towns, many of which flourished wildly before collapsing when the mine was played out. A few of them he could dismiss immediately, because the terrain wasn't anything close to what Audrey had sent him in her vision. Even so, he still had about five viable candidates to choose from once he'd gone through that first round of eliminations.

He brought up a map of Colorado again. "Could be Silverton," he said. "Or maybe Idaho Springs."

Rosemary squinted at the map. "Of course they have to be on opposite sides of the state."

There wasn't much Michael could do about that, so he only shrugged. "I know it's frustrating. Let's start with Idaho Springs and see if we can come up with anything."

For a moment, she didn't reply. Then she leaned forward, one hand reaching out to touch the laptop's screen. Voice dreamy, she said, "Yes, Idaho Springs."

"You can see Audrey there?" The question came out sharper than he'd intended, but Rosemary didn't seem to mind.

Still looking far away, she shook her head. "No, I don't see her. It's just…a feeling."

Since Rosemary was a person whose feelings you generally didn't question, Michael nodded, taking her statement at face value. "Let me see if I can find anything."

He angled the laptop toward himself so it would be easier to type, then quickly ran an image search on Victorian houses in the Idaho Springs area. As usual, he had to wade through a lot of chaff, but as soon as he opened up one particular image, he somehow knew it was the one.

"That's it," Rosemary said, confirming his suspicions.

"You're sure?"

She nodded.

Hardly daring to hope they were right, Michael enlarged the image to fill the laptop's screen. The house was quite large, with a tower on one wing and what looked to be three stories, along with multiple fireplaces. A large brick walkway led up to it, and the house appeared to be surrounded by a dense ponderosa forest.

"The Bridger House," he read aloud. "Built in 1892. It says it was sold at auction in the early 1930s, but there's no mention of who bought it."

"That would be our demon friend covering his tracks, right?" Rosemary sent him an inquiring look, and Michael nodded.

"Probably. But let's see if we can find anything else."

Since he now had the name of the house, it didn't take too much work to get the parcel number from the assessor's website for Clear Creek County. No address, though, which meant he wouldn't be able to simply plug a street number into the nav on his phone and find the place that way. And unfortunately, the information for the parcel itself didn't tell him very much.

"The property is currently owned by something called the Underhill Trust," he told Rosemary. "I have to assume that's what the demon uses to hide his investments. I could try to see if I can dig up any information about it, but I have a feeling it's probably owned by another trust."

"It's all right," she said. "We don't really need to know that right now. The important thing is to get Audrey out of that house. Where's Idaho Springs located, anyway?"

"About thirty miles west of Denver, looks like."

"Well, that makes it easier. We can fly to Denver and then rent a car. It would be faster than driving, wouldn't it?"

"Probably." Michael brought up another tab, then did a quick search to locate that information. "Driving, it would take almost thirteen hours. Let me see what's available in flights from Tucson to Denver." Another search, and he frowned. "There isn't anything leaving until tomorrow morning. The earliest direct flight is on Southwest. It would get us there at a quarter to nine."

Rosemary looked troubled, but then she nodded, as if affirming something to herself.

"That's still better than driving. Even if we left now, we wouldn't get there until noon at the earliest."

Plus, there was the bad weather he knew covered most of Colorado right now. By morning, it would have moved on to the east, and they would have an easier time getting from Denver to the small town of Idaho Springs. He could only hope the roads would be plowed; it looked like the old gold mine was still a tourist attraction, so maybe keeping the highway open would be a priority.

"I'll go ahead and book a pair of tickets, then," he said, even as he worried that this was too little, too late, that something terrible was happening to Audrey while they wasted time with airplane tickets and internet searches. Still, what else could they do? Call the local authorities? Michael knew that he and Rosemary were going on pure instinct here; if he tried to explain to the Clear Creek County sheriff's office that a demon was holding a colleague hostage at a mansion outside Idaho Springs, they'd probably hang up on him…if they decided to go easy and not try to bust him for filing a false report.

From outside the door came the sound of laughter, incongruous compared to the way he and Rosemary practically vibrated with tension. Then someone knocked at the door.

Michael wished he could ignore the knock, but he'd recognized the laughter and knew it was Colin and Daniela, coming back from wherever it was that they'd spent their evening. Luckily, he was almost done with his purchase, and he paused to hit the final "accept" button before he went to answer the door.

As he'd thought, Colin and Daniela were outside, looking a little worse for wear. Daniela's usual sleek black ponytail had some long strands that had managed to escape it, and the cat-eye liner that emphasized her big dark eyes was smudged. Clearly, the two of them had decided they could party the night away since all they were doing was a few exterior shots the next day.

Good thing he doesn't need me for those, Michael thought. *Although we're going to have to skip the introductory speech until I get back with Audrey.*

"Hey, Colin," he said evenly, although he was irritated by the interruption…and by the way Colin's gaze slid right past him to focus on Rosemary, who'd turned in her seat so she could see what was happening in the doorway of his suite. Because he knew his producer was going to ask, Michael added, "This is Rosemary McGuire. She's a friend of Audrey's and came here to help with the search."

"I didn't know we had a search going on," Colin replied.

Well, you might have if you'd bothered to stay in touch at all. However, although Michael could feel a frown digging at his brow, he kept that particular thought to himself. No point in getting into an argument this late in the game. "We've been checking some leads," he said. "We're pretty sure she's in Colorado. I just got the tickets—our flight leaves tomorrow morning."

At least one word in all that got through to his producer. "Tomorrow? We're supposed to start filming the episode tomorrow."

"You were only going to do exteriors anyway," Michael pointed out. "We should be back sometime in the afternoon, so you can still shoot my intro when we get here."

This was, of course, being extremely optimistic. He really had no idea what he and Rosemary might be facing when they reached Idaho Springs and the Bridger House. Their instincts could be failing them utterly, and they'd get there, only to find out they'd gone on a wild goose chase. Even if their psychic abilities had brought them to the correct place, he didn't know what it would take to free Audrey from the demon who'd kidnapped her. This wasn't some kind of simple minion like the ones that had tried to stop them from erasing the spell circles in the Glendora house—this was a being with the cunning and intelligence to hide himself in a human body for decades.

But Michael didn't see the point in trying to explain any of that to Colin. Better to feed him some sunshine now and hope that it would all turn out for the best.

Daniela, who'd been hanging back behind Colin, peered over his shoulder. In addition to the smudged eyeliner, her lip gloss was smeared, but she sent him a bleary smile. "That sounds like a good plan," she said. "Come on, Colin—we all need to get to bed."

"Right," Michael said, thankful for her intervention. "Rosemary and I will have to be up by five to catch our flight. Don't worry—we'll still have plenty of time to get everything done here."

And before Colin could protest, Michael closed the door. About all he could do was hope that his producer would give up the fight and head back to his room, mostly because Rosemary needed to get settled in her own room here at the B&B.

He heard some grumbling from outside the door, but then it subsided. Rosemary was standing now, one hand resting on the back of her chair.

"He's gone," she said. A quick grin, and she added, "He seems like a lovely person."

"Not really, but he knows what he's doing

when it comes to putting shows like this together." Michael reached up and rubbed the back of his neck, and hoped he didn't have a headache coming on. After the day he'd just put in, it wouldn't be all that surprising.

"Well, then," she said, suddenly brisk. "I'll head off to bed, too. When do we need to leave?"

"We should be out the door a little before six," he said. "I don't know what morning traffic is like around here, so I think we should give ourselves some extra time."

"Not a problem," she replied, although he thought he saw her wince a bit at the early hour. She didn't strike him as a morning person, but they were already taking a big hit by having to wait for that nonstop flight. No way would they have left later in the day.

"You can meet me out in the parking lot," he suggested, figuring it might be easier than showing up on her doorstep first thing in the morning.

"Sounds like a plan." To his surprise, she gave his shoulder a reassuring pat. "It's going to be fine, Michael. We'll find her, and we'll kick some demon ass."

About all he could do was nod. He hoped Rosemary was right…

…but he desperately feared she was not.

Chapter 7

AUDREY WRITHED UNDER THE DEMON'S GRASP as her breath rattled in her throat. His fingers were cold, and felt as though they had been forged from steel. "Let me go!" she gasped, surprised that she had even enough air to get out those three syllables.

"Eventually," he said. "I don't want you talking to people who tell tales out of school, especially a weak-minded fool like the man who once owned this body. Understand?"

All she could do was nod. Her heart pounded, and sweat glued her T-shirt to her body, even though it was chilly in here, drafts finding their way past the casement windows that overlooked the snowy yard. How the demon had even been able to tell she was speaking with Jeffrey Whitcomb, Audrey had no idea.

But…that was only a dream, wasn't it?

Maybe not. She most definitely hadn't been awake, but perhaps her soul had walked on the astral plane, rather than being lost in REM sleep. She'd never tried astral projection, had never been entirely sure it was even a real phenomenon, and yet….

It didn't feel like a dream. She could remember every detail of Jeffrey Whitcomb's appearance, from the heavy, straight black brows to his thin lips to the long, dark coat he'd been wearing. One might say that was easy enough, since the demon had stolen his body, but the Jeffrey she'd met in that otherwhere was not the same one who glared down at her now. His clothing was different, his demeanor was different.

And he'd still been wearing a gold band on the ring finger of his left hand. The demon holding her captive certainly bore no such sign of marital fidelity.

As frightened as she was, Audrey knew she had to fight back somehow. She didn't want to cower here, have him think he'd beaten her. Suddenly, she recalled the words of the prayer Michael had taught her. It had helped to drive back the demons in the basement. Maybe it could help her now.

"The light of God surrounds me;
The love of God enfolds me;

The presence of God watches over me;
Wherever I am, God is!"

The words came out in a roar, even though just a minute earlier, she'd barely been able to gather enough breath to push out three simple syllables. At once, the demon's grip on her throat loosened, and he staggered backward a few paces, dark eyes blazing with fury and pain.

That was the only opening she needed. He stood between her and the hallway, but there was an open path to the bathroom. She ran for it, then slammed the door behind her and turned the lock.

For a long, long moment, she only heard an ominous silence. Then there came the sound of heavy footsteps approaching. They stopped. The doorknob turned, but only part of the way before the lock prevented it from going any further.

A low, evil chuckle. "Do you really think this will keep me out?"

She honestly didn't, but there hadn't been any place else for her to run. A quick, frantic look around the bathroom told her there wasn't much here in terms of items she could use for defense. Tucked away next to the toilet was a plunger, and that was about it. Audrey supposed she could use it to hit him over the head or maybe poke him in the eye, but mostly likely that wouldn't do any real damage and would only make him angrier.

"You're not in here yet, are you?" she returned, even as she bent to open the cupboard under the sink to see if there was anything useful there. Unless you could count spare rolls of toilet paper as an offensive weapon, she was definitely out of luck.

The door rattled again. Then, to her horror, it began to bulge in the center, as if some kind of horrible pressure was being exerted on the wood. Even as she stared at it, the door seemed to contract, then bulge outward again. The overall effect was of something huge and inhuman breathing, inhaling and exhaling, and cold sweat began to drip down her back.

Once again, she sent a frantic look around her, but there just wasn't anything useful here.

Except....

Audrey's gaze fell on the brass sink faucet. She thought of how Michael had flung those vials of holy water at the demons, had made them shriek, their skin smoking from the impact of the blessed liquid. No, she wasn't a priest or a nun or an ordained minister like Michael, but her words had some power, or she wouldn't have been able to use the prayer to get away from her captor.

It was worth a try. And if it didn't work, maybe the Whitcomb-demon would be so busy laughing at her feeble attempts to resist him that he wouldn't retaliate. After all, he'd said murder was messy. She didn't think he would kill her.

But he might do something worse. Her stomach clenched as she imagined what that "worse" might be…the same "worse" that had happened to Alice Whitcomb, only she hadn't realized the thing in her bed wasn't actually her husband.

Pushing that thought out of her head, Audrey picked up the plastic tumbler that sat next to the sink, then filled it with water. Under her breath, she recited the words of the Lord's Prayer, since she had no idea what else to say.

A horrible creaking sound filled her ears. She turned away from the sink to see the door bulging and contracting again. This time, fine cracks began to appear in the old wood, telling her that it wouldn't be able to hold up against this treatment for much longer.

She sucked in a breath, sent another prayer heavenward for good measure, then reached out with her free hand and unlocked the door. For one brief second, the demon's black eyes met hers, flaring with surprise.

No time to stop to think. She shouted, *"The light of God surrounds me!"*, and flung the cupful of water she'd blessed right in the Whitcomb-demon's face.

He didn't exactly scream, "I'm melting!", but

the effect was nearly as dramatic. His hands clawed at his face, leaving deep gouges behind. Dark blood welled up from those gouges, even as he wailed in pain.

Staggering backward, he tripped over the edge of the Persian carpet and fell down with a crunch that made Audrey wince. "You bitch!" His voice sounded different, deeper, rasping with anger.

"I've got plenty more where that came from!" she shot back. Her whole body shook, as though it couldn't quite recognize that, against all hope, she'd somehow prevailed against the inhuman bastard. "So leave me alone!"

She slammed the bathroom door and engaged the lock. After that, she went back over to the sink and refilled the cup with water, performed the same ritual over it that she'd done previously. Hands trembling, she clung to the cup, waiting for the demon to come back.

But he didn't. Or rather, she heard a terrible, harsh breathing, followed by scraping noises, as if he was hurt badly enough that he couldn't stand, had to drag himself across the floor to escape the bedroom.

And then the bang of a door.

Audrey remained where she was, fingers curled around the cool plastic of the cup. There was no way to know when he'd be back...*if* he'd be back.

But for now, she'd bought herself some time.

The runway had been plowed, of course, but it was easy enough to see that Denver had gotten a good coating of fresh snow overnight. Michael only had the leather coat he'd brought with him to Tucson, and clearly Rosemary was faring even worse in the cold, judging by the way she held her arms around herself.

"Damn it," she said, teeth chattering a bit before she climbed into their rented Jeep Wrangler. "I packed for Tucson weather, not Denver!"

"Sorry," Michael replied, reaching at once for the climate controls so he could turn the heater up full blast. "I didn't know I was going to have to take this kind of field trip, either."

She shrugged. "I know. Good thing I packed some boots at least." Under the long gypsy skirt she wore, she wriggled her feet, briefly revealing the low-heeled slouch boots she wore. "Could have been worse."

He supposed it could have. Right then, he was just grateful for the three cups of coffee he'd drunk on the flight here, since he'd passed a restive night, unable to fully fall asleep, his brain overloaded with worry for Audrey. Probably he'd gotten two or three hours of sleep at the most, but he figured he could crash after this, after she was safe.

The nav system guided them away from the

airport, then west on I-70, which should take them directly to Idaho Springs. It was clear, thank God, and not even that slick, thanks to the bright sun shining in the clear blue sky overhead, which helped to dry out the asphalt.

There was still a good bit of traffic, though, the tail end of the morning rush hour. Michael clung to the steering wheel and told himself it could have been worse. At least they weren't in L.A.

Eventually, though, they passed through the outskirts of Lakewood and were heading toward the mountains. Seeing them, their peaks capped with fresh snow, he felt his heartbeat speed up a little. They weren't there yet, but at least now they had less than a half hour to go before they reached their destination.

"Are we crazy for doing this?" he asked after they passed a sign that said they were five miles from Idaho Springs. While Michael knew the general direction they were supposed to go, he hadn't been able to find any kind of a street address for Bridger House, which meant the nav on either of their phones or in the Jeep was of no use to them. About all they could do was follow their instincts and hope for the best.

Rosemary, who'd been staring out the window —presumably at the pine trees passing by, since there wasn't much else to look at—stirred and glanced over at him. "No," she said at once. "In fact, the closer we get, the surer I am that we're on the right path. If anything had felt off, I would have told you."

Her words cheered him a little. Still, he wouldn't be able to relax until he saw Audrey again, knew she was all right.

Actually, to be completely honest, he didn't think he could really relax until they were back in Tucson, and possibly not even then. They still had a haunting—or an infestation—to investigate and solve in only four days.

However, he only commented, "Good," and returned his focus to the road.

Within a few minutes, they were pulling off at 13th Street and began to cruise through the town, which seemed to have preserved many of the houses from its boom days, albeit interspersed with restaurants and grocery stores and gas stations.

"Up that way," Rosemary said suddenly, and Michael started.

"Virginia Canyon Road?"

"Yes, that one."

He followed her instructions and pointed the Wrangler down the street she'd indicated—or rather up, since it wound away from town and into the hills. However, it had also been plowed, so the going was smooth enough…for now. He remembered how wooded the area had been around the house in his vision, how high up it had seemed. Somehow, he doubted the roads would be in this good condition wherever they ended up.

Which turned out to be the case, because they'd only been driving for about a mile before Rosemary once again told him to turn, this time onto a rutted, muddy forest road, not much more than a track. Michael didn't have time to check whether it even had a name or just a number, and hoped her instincts would be strong enough to guide them safely back out to the main road once this was all over with.

If anyone had been here recently, the snowfall overnight had covered any signs of their passage. He slowed down and selected the "Snow" function for the Jeep's four-wheel drive, rather than leave it in "Auto" mode. Luckily, he was used to driving an off-road vehicle, although his ancient Land Cruiser bore about as much resemblance to this brand-new Wrangler as a bass boat did to an ocean liner.

However, despite the four or five inches of fresh-fallen snow, and despite the bumpy and rutted track they were currently traversing, the Jeep soldiered on as stolidly as though they were still driving on the highway's smooth asphalt. Because the trees were so thick, Michael couldn't really see much of where they were going, could only trust that if he continued to follow this track, eventually he would come out somewhere near their destination.

If not, they'd just have to turn around and try again.

In the passenger seat, Rosemary was looking a little queasy as she hung on to the door handle and watched the snowy woods pass by.

"You've never been off-roading before?" he asked.

She managed a wan smile. "No. I never really saw the point in tearing up the wilderness in a truck." They jounced over a particularly deep rut, and she winced. "Right now I'm not really seeing where this is supposed to be fun."

Despite the urgency of their mission, he couldn't help grinning at her comment. "You don't think it's beautiful out here?"

Rosemary looked out the window at the snow-frosted trees and gave the slightest lift of her shoulders. "Oh, it's beautiful. But I'm fine with someone sending me a postcard."

He shook his head. "I guess I can understand that. I always liked it…getting out and away from other people."

For a second, she didn't say anything. Then she remarked, "You've done a lot of that in your life, haven't you? Getting away from other people, I mean."

Michael wanted to deny the mild accusation, tell Rosemary she didn't know what she was talking about. However, deep down he had to admit she was right. His work required him to be around people, but he interacted with them on a surface level, dispensing his knowledge at conferences and workshops, then leaving immediately afterward so no one got a chance to get too close. There had been women, but he'd let them flirt with him, chat him up, then made sure they were out of his life before anything could get serious. If they'd even wanted to get serious. He was sure that some of them just wanted the chance to sleep with Michael Covenant, and weren't expecting much more than that.

"I guess so," he said. Something in his tone must have told Rosemary that he didn't want to pursue the subject, because after sending him another penetrating look, she pursed her lips and returned her attention to the scenery outside the Jeep's window.

Just as well, because after they came around a slight bend, the forest opened up into a snowy clearing, and at the far end of that clearing was the house he'd found during his internet search. The roof was now covered thickly in snow, and the aspens planted to either side had long since lost their leaves, but it was definitely the same place.

As much as he wanted to floor it and get inside as quickly as he could, Michael knew he still needed to be cautious in his approach. He glanced over at Rosemary. "You feel anything?"

"Not really," she replied after pausing for a moment, probably to reach out with her extrasensory abilities and get a read on the property. "But I tend to do better at this sort of thing if I'm actually inside a place instead of a hundred yards away."

Well, clearly, but he hated the idea of going inside without any sort of intel about what might be waiting for them. Rosemary was a strong psychic, but he didn't know whether she possessed the same warrior spirit that had shown itself so unexpectedly in Audrey. Whatever they came up against, he had to be prepared to handle it on his own.

"Okay," he said briefly. There wasn't much point in pushing her, so he kept driving across the clearing, his destination a *porte cochère* on one side of the house. As he got closer, he could see one set of tire marks in the snow, marks that led away from the building. Had someone dropped off the fake Whitcomb and his captive, then left this morning after the storm had finished dumping its snow?

They must have, because there definitely wasn't a car here now. As far as he could tell, the house didn't have a garage, unless it was tucked away out back somewhere in the pine trees that came within a few yards of the back porch.

The Wrangler's tires crunched on gravel once they were in the shelter of the *porte cochère*; if snow had blown in here overnight, it must have melted fairly quickly. Michael turned off the engine and looked over at Rosemary. "Are you ready to do this?"

"Probably not, but I'll try to keep up."

For a moment, he wondered whether he should tell her to stay here in the vehicle, to wait until he'd done a sweep of the house and—hopefully—found Audrey. However, he doubted Rosemary would agree to that plan, and besides, splitting up was always a bad idea.

"Here," he said, and pulled out one of the vials of holy water he always kept in an inside pocket of his jacket. That was part of the reason why he wore a coat almost all the time—it was easier to carry all the items he found necessary for his work and still have his hands free. He handed Rosemary the vial. She took it, expression skeptical.

"Holy water? I'm not Christian."

"No, but I am, and since I'm the one who

blessed it, I know it works." He reached for the door handle and said, "Come on."

Although she still looked doubtful, she slipped the vial into a pocket in her jean jacket, then opened her door and got out of the Jeep. He followed suit, sucking in his breath a little at the iciness of the air. The temperature was probably above freezing…but just barely.

A path wound from the *porte cochère* toward the back of the house, and he headed that way, feeling the snow already begin to seep through the soles of the shoes he wore. Behind him, Rosemary muttered something under her breath that he couldn't quite catch, probably a complaint about the cold.

It was uncomfortable, but at least it wasn't icy…yet. He hoped they would be out of here long before the snow really began to melt and create nasty little patches of black ice along this path.

"How are we going to get in?" Rosemary asked.

Michael patted his jacket pocket. "Lock picks."

She let out a little huff of a breath. "Is there anything you don't have in that Swiss Army jacket of yours?"

"A gun." He had a knife, but it was only a

utility model, not something that would do any real damage in a fight.

"Thank God for that. Guns make me nervous."

"They're not much use against demons, so there isn't any real point to having one."

Now they were standing in the relative shelter of the back porch, which was brick like the rest of the ground floor of the house. Little eddies of snow covered the pavers, showing that the wind had been strong enough to create a few small drifts. Luckily, though, the snow seemed to be confined to the corners of the walled area, and wasn't much in their way.

Michael looked at Rosemary once again. Now she was standing just slightly behind him, arms hugged around her midsection in an attempt to protect herself from the freezing air. "Do you feel anything now?"

Almost at once, she shook her head. "Still nothing."

What if the demon had taken Audrey and left? That would explain the tire marks in the snow. Michael really didn't want to entertain that thought, however, not after coming so far to save her.

"All right," he said. "Let's go in."

The lock on the back door was a simple Schlage deadbolt. Easy enough. He put his hand on the latch and gave it an experimental jiggle, just to see how much play there was in the lock. To his surprise, the door latch pressed down all the way, and the door swung inward slightly.

Rosemary let out a surprised little gasp. "It wasn't locked?"

"Apparently not," Michael replied.

"That doesn't make any sense."

No, it didn't. If the house had been owned by a regular human being, rather than a demon masquerading as one, then maybe it wouldn't have been so strange for the owner to leave the back door unlocked. After all, they were out in the middle of nowhere here. Most thieves weren't dedicated enough to go off-road for miles to rob a house, especially during a snowstorm. But this?

He didn't know what to think.

About all he could do was shrug, then tell Rosemary, "It saves us some time, though. Just keep your eyes open."

"Believe me, I will."

They went inside, and he quietly shut the door behind them. A quick glance told him this was a mudroom of some sort, with an indoor/outdoor carpet, hooks for hanging jackets, and a little cabinet he thought might be for storing boots. Immediately beyond the mudroom was a large kitchen, one that looked like a time capsule from decades ago, with its chipped tile counters and ancient appliances. Clearly, the demon who owned this place didn't care much about updating his property.

Michael paused, and Rosemary stood quietly next to him. The house was nearly silent, except for the humming of the antique refrigerator. It was also extremely cold in here; if the house had central heat, it wasn't being directed toward this room.

"I don't feel anything evil," Rosemary said in an undertone. "But I think there might be someone up on the second floor."

If the psychic could detect a presence that wasn't evil, then maybe what she was feeling was Audrey. *Please, God, let her be okay....* "All right," he said, also in a low murmur. "Let's go upstairs and see what we can find."

They exited the kitchen and made their way down a hallway toward the foyer. The light in here was dim, all the heavy velvet curtains pulled tightly shut, but Michael knew better than to open any of them. While it seemed the demon hadn't yet detected their presence, there was no need to advertise that trespassers roamed the house.

The bottom step creaked slightly, and Michael winced but kept on going. He wished he could take more time to inventory his surroundings— old houses had always fascinated him—but they weren't here to sightsee, but to get Audrey away as quickly as possible.

At the top of the stairs, he paused for a second, waiting for Rosemary to catch up with him. Immediately to his right was a door that stood open, revealing what must be the master suite. He caught a quick glimpse of a large bed with a velvet bedspread, more dark wood wainscoting, a huge and clearly expensive Persian rug.

Then Rosemary whispered, "Down the hall. The last door on the left."

He nodded and began moving in that direction. It was hard not to tense up, to wonder if the demon had laid a trap for them and was waiting behind that mahogany door. But they'd come this far, and he certainly wasn't going to stop now.

Unlike the back door off the kitchen, this one was locked. However, since it was a simple pushbutton, he didn't even have to truly pick it, but simply used one of his tools to push on the button from this side, forcing it to release. Hand still resting on the glass doorknob, he glanced over at Rosemary. She didn't say anything, but nodded. A faint gleam from inside her clenched fist told him that she held the vial of holy water, ready to lob it at anything that attacked them.

He turned the knob, took a step into the room. It was large, with a somewhat rumpled bed off to his right, a tall window nearly opposite where he stood, and a fireplace with a marble surround over to the left. The hearth was swept clean, and clearly hadn't been used in a very long time. Just like downstairs, the room was very cold, but with the rawness of an unheated house, not the unearthly chill that accompanied a haunting.

As far as he could tell, the room was empty. But then he saw a pair of lace-up brown boots next to the bed, and a dark blue leather jacket hanging from one of the bedposts. Although Michael knew he hadn't memorized Audrey's wardrobe, he was fairly certain those items belonged to her, and hope stirred within him. If she'd been able to put her things there in such an orderly way, that had to mean she was all right…didn't it?

His gaze traveled toward the same wall where the fireplace was located. A few feet away from it was a door. Bathroom? Closet?

Only one way to be sure.

He went over to the door, Rosemary immediately behind him, vial of holy water still clenched in her hand and waiting to be deployed. Just as he was reaching for the knob, that door opened, and Audrey stared out at him. She was pale and her hair was a mess, but as far as he could tell, she seemed to be fine.

For some reason, she was holding a plastic bathroom cup in one hand, half-raised as though she'd been about to throw its contents at him. As soon as she seemed to realize who stood in front of her, she lowered the hand and somehow, impossibly, smiled at him, although that smile looked a little trembly around the edges.

"Thank God," she said, her voice breathy, not really sounding like herself. "Let's get the hell out of here."

Chapter 8

ALTHOUGH AUDREY HAD HOPED MICHAEL would somehow be able to find her, she still couldn't quite believe her eyes when she saw him standing there outside the bathroom door. As soon as she'd heard the footsteps outside that door, she'd thought for sure that must be the Whitcomb-demon returning to enact some form of revenge for the injuries she'd inflicted on him, and she'd grabbed the cup of holy water she'd made to replace the first one.

But then she saw it was Michael—somehow with Rosemary McGuire standing next to him— and Audrey realized that her improbable rescue truly had happened. Still, that didn't mean she intended to stay there a single minute longer than she had to.

"Let's get out of here," she told him, and he

nodded. If Rosemary hadn't been standing there, Audrey might have gone and flung her arms around his waist—and probably shocked the hell out of him, since he had no way of knowing that she'd already decided to forgive him. But since Rosemary was there, Audrey thought it better to wait. They'd have plenty of time later.

She hoped.

"What happened?" Michael asked as she hurried over to the bed and pulled on the boots she'd left there, then put her jacket back on as well. It was very cold in here, colder than it had been the night before. She wondered if the Whitcomb-demon had shut off the central heat as a final act of retaliation before he vanished.

"Too much to tell you now," she replied. "But I brewed up some homemade holy water and threw it at the demon, and it hurt him enough that he disappeared. I've been hiding in the bathroom all night, just in case he came back." She sent them a frightened glance. "Did you see him? Is he here?"

Michael shook his head. "We haven't seen any sign of him…whatever that means."

"Can she really do that with the holy water?" Rosemary asked, glancing from Audrey to Michael. "I mean—"

"Holy water is all about the intent in your

heart when you say a prayer over it," Michael told her. "That obviously was enough."

"Whenever he does come back, I want to make sure I'm miles away from here," Audrey said.

"Sounds like a plan," Rosemary remarked. "We have a Jeep out back."

Perfect. Michael led the way, and they all clattered down the stairs, none of them bothering to keep quiet. It seemed obvious enough that the demon was nowhere around, so haste was far more important than stealth right then.

As they hurried through the kitchen, though, something sitting on the counter caught Audrey's eye. Recognition clicked, and she realized it was her purse. Probably the Whitcomb-demon had dropped it here when he brought her into the house from the Town Car, but since she had been out cold at the time and had no idea what had happened to her bag, she'd thought it was gone forever.

"Just a sec," she told Michael, and ran over and picked it up, slinging it over her shoulder.

He gave a nod of understanding, but then they were all back on their way again, out through the mudroom and onto a large covered back porch. Snow gleamed on the brick surface, and Audrey's breath came out in little puffs of white smoke. She'd thought it was cold inside, but the frigid air out here seemed to penetrate her leather jacket as though it was made out of thin silk.

Luckily, she was moving quickly enough that she didn't have too much time to worry about the cold. The three of them made their way along a path that led to a *porte cochère*, and parked beneath it was a mud-splashed but very new-looking white Jeep Wrangler. Even as she grabbed the door handle to haul herself into the passenger seat, Audrey kept thinking that the Whitcomb-demon was going to appear in a puff of smoke and haul her away again. Where the hell was he? Had she really hurt him badly enough to drive him off permanently?

No one stopped them. Rosemary climbed in the back, and Michael got in behind the wheel, foot on the gas as soon as his door slammed shut. He backed out of the *porte cochère,* pausing for a moment to turn the vehicle around. Then he followed the tracks he'd made coming here, out across the clearing that surrounded the house. In less than a minute, the vehicle was hidden within the woods, ponderosa pines and bare oak and aspen trees on either side.

Finally, Audrey felt as though she could let out a breath. She looked over at Michael, whose gaze was intent on the rough forest road they were following. The Jeep bounced around a good bit, but since he'd gotten out here in one piece, she figured he knew what he was doing.

"How did you find me?"

In the back seat, Rosemary leaned forward slightly. "A little process of elimination and a lot of intuition. And that vision you sent of your surroundings here."

"That worked?" Audrey asked, startled. At the time, she'd sent out that thought because she had no idea what else to do. Even with Michael telling her that she was a stronger psychic than she believed, it hadn't been much more than an experiment, a way to tell herself that she was doing something to help herself out of a horrible situation.

"It did," Michael said. For just the barest second—all he could spare, thanks to the rough terrain they were driving through—he looked over at her. His gray eyes held a warmth she hadn't been expecting. A flush of heat touched her cheeks, and she realized she wasn't the only one who'd been reconsidering the harsh words they'd exchanged the last time they saw each other. "I was at the airport, waiting for Rosemary's flight to get in, and there it was. I told you that you were stronger than you thought."

Because she'd never been very good with compliments, Audrey gave a little shrug and instead focused on his mention of Rosemary's flight. "How did that happen, anyway? You coming to Tucson, I mean."

"I got in touch with Michael when I didn't hear anything from you," she said. "And then I convinced him that I could help track you down."

"Which she did," he added, "so I'm very glad she wouldn't take no for an answer."

Although she'd been smiling before, now her expression grew sober. "What happened, anyway? In the parking lot at the airport, I mean."

Audrey did her best to explain how she thought it was Susan picking her up, and then found out later the woman she'd seen was only a terrible illusion. "I don't know how the demon did it," she said. "But I really thought it was Susan. So I got in the car, and that's the last thing I remembered until I woke up in the bedroom here."

"It sounds like you two really rattled this demon," Rosemary said.

"He was not very happy with Michael and me, that's for sure." Audrey recalled how the Whitcomb-demon's eyes had glittered with spite, how he'd spoken of the way they had interfered with his plans. "It sounds as though he used the portal in the Glendora mansion a good deal."

"But for what?" Michael asked. His tone was musing, but she saw the way he frowned, and she guessed that his grim expression only had a little to do with how he was focused on the road.

"I don't know," she replied. "He wouldn't say."

Rosemary shook her head, wild curls bouncing as the Jeep jounced its way along the rutted road. "This is all beyond me. I thought demons only infested houses and occasionally made people speak in tongues and throw up pea soup. What is this guy doing with Lincoln Town Cars and big Gold Rush mansions out in the wilds of Colorado?"

"So we are in Colorado," Audrey murmured.

"Yes," Michael said, "a little outside Idaho Springs, which is about a half hour from Denver. Anyway," he went on, "the simple answer, Rosemary, is that I don't really know. I've investigated probably thirty cases of demon infestation or possession by now, and this is the first time I've come across an instance where the demon doing the possessing has basically taken over the life of the possessee…become them, to all intents and purposes. And this case is even stranger because the demon is inside the body of a man who's well over a hundred years old."

"He definitely doesn't look that old," Audrey said. "In fact, he looks younger than the ghost I saw of him in your backyard."

Rosemary's eyes widened. "Wait…you saw Whitcomb's *ghost?*"

"I think so," Audrey replied. "And I met him again in a dream…or maybe it wasn't really a dream. I don't know. But both those versions of Whitcomb looked about ten or fifteen years older than the one with the demon inside him." For a moment, she considered telling them that Jeffrey Whitcomb had been possessed for years before he even moved to Glendora, then decided to leave it alone for now. At some point, she'd have to tell Michael everything she knew, but she didn't see how that particular tidbit couldn't wait. The rush of relief at getting out of there had faded somewhat, and now she was just tired as hell. Sleeping on a bathroom floor while wrapped up in spare towels to keep from freezing to death could take a lot out of a person.

"Interesting," Michael said…but that was all he said, as if he knew she was holding a few things back and also preferred to wait until they could talk in private. It wasn't that they didn't trust Rosemary, but that it might be better to hash these things out together on their own. Audrey was still a little shocked that the two of them had been able to put their differences aside in order to track her down…although she was very grateful to the psychic for lending her assistance. It was good to know that she'd somehow had a very unexpected friend enter her life.

Yes, it had taken all three of them working

together—even if they hadn't known it at the time —to effect Audrey's escape. She wondered where the demon had gone. Did he need to be some-place secure to heal from the wounds he'd given himself? Did demons heal faster than humans?

Because he certainly wouldn't be fit to be seen in public until the gashes he'd torn open in his cheeks had disappeared.

They were all quiet for a minute. Then they came to another road, a real road with asphalt, and Michael turned off onto it, relief clear in his face. It had to have been nerve-wracking to maneuver the Jeep along that forest track with the snow still thick on the ground. Now that they were traveling on a paved road, the rest of the drive should go fairly quickly.

Then Michael exclaimed, "Shit!" and took his foot off the gas.

A black Lincoln Town Car was stretched across the road, blocking both lanes. He hit the brakes, but the road was slick with melting snow and Audrey could feel the tires start to slip, to squeal on the wet asphalt. Their vehicle began to spin, hurtling closer and closer to the car in the middle of the road….

She wasn't sure exactly what happened. Some-how, Michael managed to maneuver the Jeep onto the shoulder, just sliding past the Town Car, which still seemed to loom at them, looking as big as a tank. And then, just as suddenly as it had been there, it disappeared, melting away like mist.

"Holy shit," Rosemary whispered from the back seat. "What the hell was that?"

"A deterrent," Michael said grimly. He gave the Jeep a little gas, began to move forward again, going slowly until they were back on the road itself. Even then, Audrey noticed that he stayed about five miles an hour below the speed limit, just in case he encountered another supernatural obstacle. "A little parting gift from Audrey's host."

"Why didn't he try harder to stop us?" Audrey asked. "If he knew I was getting away, why not do something at the house itself?"

"He probably didn't know," Michael replied. "That could just have been a trap he left, something that was automatically triggered as we came through. Demons aren't gods, you know. They have abilities greater than a mortal's, true, but they're definitely not all-seeing and all-knowing."

"Thank God," she said, her voice shaking a bit. "Because they're bad enough as they are."

"I think that was his last-ditch effort to prevent us from getting away," Michael said. Now his tone was more reassuring than anything else. "Creatures like this don't like to operate in bright daylight. I think he'll go off and bide his time, and wait to see what we're going to do next."

"Which is?" Audrey asked. She thought she

might already know the answer, but even so, his reply calmed her nerves a bit.

"Go back to Tucson and shoot this episode before Colin has a complete panic attack," Michael said. "After that…we'll figure out what to do about Whitcomb."

Because she'd been able to retrieve her purse and therefore still had her I.D., getting back to Tucson was a fairly straightforward process. The three of them went to the Southwest kiosk at Denver International and bought a ticket for the same flight that Rosemary and Michael already were on, thanks to the round-trip fares they'd purchased in Tucson.

"But you can take my seat, and I'll take yours," Rosemary suggested. She didn't seem too put out by the prospect, but then, sitting by yourself on a flight that barely lasted an hour and a half probably wasn't that big a deal.

Still, Audrey was thankful for the offer, because even though she knew she was safe now, she also realized it would probably be some time before she could completely shake off the events of the past twenty-four hours. And she was equally thankful after they all boarded the plane and she saw that the row in front of them was empty, which meant she and Michael could get caught up on what had happened after the Whitcomb-demon kidnapped her.

He seemed of the same mind, because almost as soon as the plane had taken off—only fifteen minutes late—he leaned closer to her and murmured, "You're sure you're okay?"

She nodded. It felt good to be sitting here on this 737, surrounded by the commonplaces of air travel…and it felt even better to have Michael next to her. He looked tired but also calm, as though he knew they'd surmounted one hurdle and would have a little breathing space before the next.

Hopefully, he was correct in that assumption. Now that she could lean back in the padded seat and finally allow herself to relax, she could feel every bruise, every knotted muscle she'd picked up during her sojourn in the demon's Colorado mansion. Also, she felt warmer now; that bathroom floor had been icy cold, and the chill had felt as though it penetrated her bones. She really hadn't warmed up much on the drive to the airport in Denver, even though Michael was blasting the heat from his rented Jeep's climate-control system.

"I'm fine," she said. Would it be weird to reach over and rest her hand on his? She wanted to, desperately. Now that she'd forgiven him in her heart, she wanted him to know that things would be different between the two of them from now on.

You've got to start somewhere, she told herself, and went ahead and lifted her right hand from the armrest and set it on Michael's left. He started, just a little, and then shifted in his seat so his gaze could meet hers. For a few seconds, they both sat there in silence, watching one another, and then the corners of his mouth lifted, and the golden glints in his gray eyes seemed to grow warmer, like little shards of sunshine. Something hard and tight and frightened in her began to relax, as if she somehow knew this was going to be okay.

His fingers tightened on hers, strong, reassuring. "I'm so glad you're safe," he said.

"So am I. It was…frightening." There was an understatement. Now she was away, though, the whole ordeal had begun to feel like something out of a nightmare, a nightmare that was slowly fading the longer she could see the sun and know that Michael was here next to her. She shook her head. "It was worse than that, really. I didn't know how you would ever be able to find me, and I didn't see how I could escape on foot. I didn't know how close to the road the house really was."

"Not that close," Michael said. He didn't seem inclined to let go of her hand, instead held on, as if making sure she couldn't possibly get away again. "About four miles. That's a long ways to walk in the dark and the snow. And from there it would have been another three miles into Idaho Springs itself."

Audrey had walked that far on day hikes, but the two situations weren't remotely similar. Those hikes had been undertaken on sunny, mild days, with the proper footwear and a GPS unit in her backpack in case she really got turned around. "I suppose so," she allowed. "Anyway, about all I could do was hold on and see if I could come up with some way to get out of there on my own."

"The holy water was a nice trick," he said with a smile.

Even though she'd long ago told herself that she didn't need anyone else's approval to feel good about her accomplishments, she had to admit that Michael's smile was a nice reward, especially since he didn't seem to deploy it very often. Maybe that was because of all the years of keeping the truth of his history to himself, of making sure he never let anyone get too close.

She had to hope he'd let her get close...again.

"I was desperate. But I used the prayer you taught me on him when he was trying to attack me, and when that worked, I figured trying some holy water couldn't hurt."

At once Michael's smile disappeared, replaced by a furrowed brow and an angry glint in his eyes.

"He tried to attack you? I thought you said he didn't hurt you."

"He didn't hurt me. Or at least, he held back until he thought I was getting too close to something important." Quickly, she related the strange dream she'd had with the much older-looking Jeffrey, the way he'd been about to reveal the demon's name. "And that was when he attacked me," she said. "Obviously, he must have had some inkling of what was going on in my head, or he wouldn't have interfered that way."

"Yes," Michael said, his tone musing. "Demons never want you to learn their true names, because then you can effectively banish them. The astral Jeffrey must have been trying to make amends by passing that information on to you."

"So you really think I was on the astral plane, that it wasn't just a dream?" Yes, Audrey had considered that possibility, but it felt strange to say those words aloud now, even though she and Michael didn't have an audience that could overhear them.

"I'm almost positive. Not that you couldn't have simply been experiencing a very clear, very lucid dream, but because of the demon's reaction to it. If it had only been a dream, you would have known somehow, would have known the information the dream Jeffrey had given you wasn't true and was only something your subconscious had filled in because you desperately wanted it to be true." Very gently, he let go of her hand, but only because the flight attendant was now bumping along the aisle with her drink cart.

Audrey eyed the mini wine bottles longingly, but she hadn't eaten anything more than a few swallows of soup for more than twenty-four hours now. Drinking alcohol didn't seem like a very good idea.

But Michael got them both some bottled water and a few packets of peanuts. He handed both of them to her, saying, "I'll get you a real breakfast when we get to Tucson. Or maybe brunch…it'll be past one by the time we land."

"Brunch sounds great," Audrey replied. She'd have to duck into the bathroom to tidy her hair and put on some lipstick, but she knew it probably wouldn't be smart to go by the B&B to change and freshen up. Knowing Colin, he'd pounce the second she and Michael appeared, and would demand they start shooting immediately. "But the peanuts will hold me."

She tore open one of the packets and ate a few of the nuts, then washed them down with large swallows of water. Even this simple snack made her feel better, made her think she was going to survive this whole ordeal after all.

Since Michael had remained silent while she

ate her peanuts and drank her water, Audrey figured she might as well ask a few questions of her own. "Does Colin know?"

"Not the whole story," Michael replied, clearly understanding the unspoken part of her question. "He knows you never showed up, and he knows that Rosemary and I were coming to Colorado because we had a lead as to where you might be, but he doesn't know anything about Whitcomb's dopplegänger."

"That's going to be hard to explain," Audrey said. "I'm not sure I understand all of it myself."

"Tell me what he told you."

She sipped some more water, took a breath, and then did her best to recount everything the demon had said—how he had lived as Jeffrey Whitcomb's son, fooling the surviving members of his family and, apparently, the rest of the world…dooming poor Henry Whitcomb to a miserable life locked up in a sanitarium. How the demon had owned the Colorado house for decades, using it as a sanctuary.

"Whatever that's supposed to mean," she added. "I would have thought he could pretty much come and go as he pleased."

"Maybe," Michael said. He steepled his fingers together and rested them against the dark gold scruff on his chin, clearly pondering everything she'd just said. "I keep coming back to the part about the portal in the Glendora mansion being his 'main one.' That seems to indicate he has them in a number of different places. Did you see anything in the Colorado house?"

"No," Audrey replied. "But I was still blacked out when he brought me to the house, so I didn't see anything until I woke up in that bedroom. Even afterward, I went down to the dining room and saw a bit of the foyer and the downstairs hall, but that was it."

"And you didn't feel anything?"

She shook her head. "It wasn't like the Glendora house at all. Almost as soon as I walked in there, I started to get the heebie-jeebies, but I didn't get that sort of feeling at all in Colorado. That doesn't mean I wasn't frightened, but it was the company that frightened me, not the house. Did you feel something there?"

"No." Michael was silent for a moment, a slight frown pulling at his brows. "That is, I was more focused on finding you than picking up any vibes in the house, but even so, if it had been strong enough, I should have noticed something. And even if I didn't, Rosemary probably would have, but she didn't mention feeling anything out of the ordinary."

In a way, Audrey supposed it was a good thing that the house itself had felt neutral, because she was already overloaded enough dealing with her demon host. So did it mean that there really wasn't a portal in the Colorado mansion, or that it wasn't in use and therefore not sending out any bad vibes, or…what?

She really didn't know. How those things worked was still something of a mystery to her. They connected this world to the world of the demons, but maybe, since the Whitcomb-demon had adopted a human disguise, it was easier for him to get around like a regular human while living and functioning in this world.

"We came in a car," she said slowly. "If he was using portals to get around, why not have one in this house?"

Michael's answer seemed to confirm her suspicions. "Because that's not how they work. They're not a mode of transportation, but a connection between this world and the dimension where the demons live. I suppose a physicist might say they fold space and time, but in a very particular way. Understand?"

She thought she did, or at least, she thought she could intuit what he was saying as long as she looked at the problem sideways and didn't try to attack it head-on. "If he has other portals in other places, what would he be using them for?"

"To bring more of his kind here," Michael said without hesitating. "That's always been their goal… to subsume as many humans as they can, to increase their influence here. I don't have any idea how many people might already be affected, but they're here."

A shiver trickled its way down her spine. There had been a sort of hard, unflinching conviction in his voice, something that told her he had personal experience with these sorts of possessions. "How do you know?" she asked softly.

He glanced across the aisle to the sole passenger sitting in that row, but the man had his eyes closed and a set of earbuds on, which meant he probably couldn't hear anything of what they were saying. Still, Michael lowered his voice before answering, "Because of my brother."

She raised her eyebrows but waited for him to go on.

He hesitated for a moment, then gave a very small lift of his shoulders before sipping from his bottle of water. Finally, he said, "I'd thought he seemed different when he came home from college at Christmas that year, but I couldn't really put my finger on it. Like…he didn't laugh when someone told a joke, while at other times I'd catch him with a creepy smile but no real reason for why he'd be smiling in the first place. I didn't say anything to my parents, mostly because it was just a suspicion that something was wrong. After all, he was just about to finish college. People change when they go away to school."

Audrey remained silent. She knew what was going to come next—or at least, she knew how this story ended, because she'd lived through its horror as well, only in a very different way.

"We—we had to fly to Hawaii to visit him in jail. My mother was crying during the whole flight." Michael rubbed his hands on the knees of his dark trousers, a nervous gesture that surprised her a little, just because he usually seemed so controlled. "He hadn't really spoken since his arrest, although it was clear he'd done it—he hadn't made any attempt to get away, and they found his fingerprints all over the assault rifle he used. The authorities were hoping he might say something to his family. But he wouldn't talk to my parents, either. I begged them to let me try— Philip and I had been pretty close when we were younger, although that changed after he went to college. Finally, they gave in. I went and looked at him through the glass, and said one word: 'Why?'"

"Did he answer?"

She could see the way the muscles tightened in Michael's jaw. "Not at first. He just stared at me, and even though I really hadn't had any experiences with demons before then, I could tell there was something terribly wrong with him. That wasn't my brother staring back at me…that was something else. Something inhuman was living behind those eyes."

It would have been easy for her to give him a pat explanation, to say that mental illness often manifested in ways that were highly disturbing to those close to the person in question. However, Audrey didn't bother, because she'd learned over the past week that sometimes there were no rational explanations for the horrors in people's lives, that sometimes you had to understand that the universe worked through the inexplicable, the paranormal.

"You think he was possessed?" she asked, the words barely a murmur.

"I know he was." Michael wasn't looking at her, but at the screen set into the seat back in front of him. It was blank, because of course he hadn't ordered an in-flight movie, and yet he seemed fascinated by its flat gray surface. "No human being could have looked at me like that. And then he began to laugh. He said, 'Less room for you. More room for us,' and kept laughing and laughing. They finally took me out of the visitation room and hauled him back to his cell. And that was where they found him dead, three days later."

"No mark on him, no obvious cause of death." Audrey remembered that part of the story very well; more than once in the intervening ten years, she'd pondered that mystery, wondering how it was that a young, healthy man of twenty-two could simply drop dead like that. "What are you trying to tell me, Michael?"

One corner of his mouth twisted, and he turned in his seat so he could face her. "I'm saying the demons used him to kill those people. Once the deed was done, they had no further use for him. What else could he have meant when he said, 'More room for us'? There are beings who want this world, want to take it from us."

His gray eyes latched on hers.

"We have to make sure we can stop them."

Chapter 9

TUCSON WAS BLESSEDLY WARM AND SUNNY, and Audrey could feel her spirits lift as they left the terminal and headed out to the place where Michael had left his rented SUV in the long-term parking lot. His words on the plane haunted her, but she tried to tell herself the situation wasn't quite as bad as he made things seem. Obviously, the demon inhabiting Jeffrey Whitcomb's body wasn't omnipotent, or the world would have been overrun with possessed people by now. It took work to get those spirits to this plane, and they'd dealt him a serious blow by destroying one of his main means to do so.

For now, it was enough for the three of them to go to a restaurant not too far from the airport, where they sat down and had enormous South-west breakfasts, even though it was now almost one-thirty. Michael invited Rosemary to stay longer—"your instincts could really help us on the show"—but she demurred.

"I think you'll do fine with Audrey," she said after taking a large bite of her chilaquiles. "Her powers are growing by leaps and bounds. I'm not really the TV type."

"Neither am I," Audrey protested. "I just sort of fell into it."

"Okay, but really, I'm not interested. I need to get back home, get back to work there. Besides," Rosemary added, looking thoughtful, "I can keep an eye on the Glendora mansion for you, let you know if anything starts rearing its ugly head again."

"God, I hope not." The last thing Audrey wanted to hear was that their work at the Whitcomb mansion in Southern California wasn't yet done. She'd be happy if she never saw the inside of that place again.

"It's not likely," Michael said, but then added, quashing her hopes, "but it's not impossible, either. It'll help to have someone on the ground there, just in case Whitcomb decides to go back and try to reconstruct the portal we destroyed."

"He's not really Whitcomb," Audrey pointed out, but Michael only shrugged.

"Shorthand. We don't know his demon name, so it's just easier to call him that. I know someone in L.A. who's really good at sifting through old records. I think once we get back to the B&B—and before Colin pounces and expects us to start shooting—I'm going to drop my friend Fred Peñasco a quick email and see if he can start digging, find any other properties our demon friend has purchased. If anyone can locate that information, it's Fred."

"Do you think those properties are where Whitcomb's set up his other portals?" Rosemary asked, pausing with a forkful of chilaquiles halfway to her mouth.

"Probably," Michael replied. He fiddled with the straw in his glass of iced tea, obviously thinking over her question. "I mean, it just makes more sense to own the properties where you're conducting that kind of magic, because then you don't have to worry so much about anyone interfering. The Glendora mansion is an outlier... maybe he felt attached to it because it was the place where he opened his first portal. I can't say for sure."

And solidified his hold on the man he'd possessed, if the demon's comments to her were to be believed. Audrey had always heard that it was a spectacularly bad idea to dabble in that kind of magic, and Jeffrey Whitcomb's fate served as an object lesson as to exactly why that sort of thing could go horribly wrong. Had

Michael's brother done the same thing? Was that why a demon had invaded his consciousness, made him commit such a heinous act of violence?

She really didn't know. Because obviously, not all demons committed mayhem the second they had possession of a human's body, or Whitcomb would have gone on his own killing spree.

Or maybe he had. Maybe he'd just never gotten caught.

The restaurant was warm, almost stuffy, and yet she still felt cold. She couldn't help wondering how she'd managed to survive, the demon's comments about not killing people notwithstanding. Obviously, the demon who'd possessed Michael's brother didn't have the same scruples.

His hand touched hers under the table, and Audrey startled. "Sorry," she said. "I guess I'm having a hard time wrapping my head around all this."

"You and me both," Rosemary said with a strained sort of chuckle. "Because if the demon inside Whitcomb has managed to walk around and mingle with normal humans for this many years, it makes me wonder how many others like him are out there."

"Probably not too many," Michael remarked. "He's a rarity."

Audrey raised an eyebrow at him. "What do you mean?"

He shot a quick glance at the booth next to theirs, but the people there were in the process of getting up and leaving, and didn't seem to be paying any attention to them. "There are hierarchies of demons, just like there are hierarchies of angels. The lowest form of demon—the most numerous—doesn't have a lot of native intelligence. They're mostly good at causing mayhem. The farther you go up the rungs, so to speak, the more sophisticated the demons become. There aren't as many of them, though. So I don't think we have to worry too much about there being armies of possessed human beings, biding their time until they can take over. That doesn't mean Whitcomb isn't extremely dangerous."

Not exactly what Audrey wanted to hear, but she'd already known that about him. "Dangerous how, exactly?"

"He can let in lesser demons, like the ones we battled in the basement of the Glendora house. They can cause a lot of damage."

"But why?" Rosemary asked. She'd set down her fork and didn't look as though she intended to pick it up again. "I mean, what's the *point?*"

He gave her a weary smile. Something about the expression made Audrey want to take his hand and tell him everything was going to be all right, although the smile hadn't even been directed at her. "Don't bother to ascribe human motivations to the beings we're dealing with. They delight in destruction for its own sake. Remember, this world was made by God, and if they can do anything that wreaks havoc on His creation, they're all for it."

Rosemary's mouth twisted. "I don't believe in God."

Audrey wasn't all that surprised by the psychic's revelation—she seemed to be fairly nonreligious—but she was a little startled that Rosemary would state her position so boldly. However, Michael didn't seem fazed.

"That doesn't matter," he said. "And when I say God, I really mean the Creator, the motivating force in the universe, not some white-bearded representative of the patriarchy."

His comment made Rosemary grin. "Ah, okay. Well, then, we're probably a little closer in spirit than I imagined. And I guess I can see why the demons would want to disrupt that."

"Exactly. Their whole reason for being is chaos. Which is why we need to make sure to keep a close eye on Whitcomb and what he's doing with them."

All while shooting a television show. Audrey wished they could go back to the B&B and tell Colin *Project Demon Hunters* was on hold indefinitely, but she knew that wasn't how these things worked. They had a schedule they had to stick to, or risk having the show canceled…which was exactly what Whitcomb wanted. Besides, right now they didn't even know where to look for him. Locating the demon was going to take time…and a lot of digging. She'd just have to suffer through these next episodes, no matter what happened.

On the upside, after being held captive by the Whitcomb-demon, she figured it was going to take a lot more to scare her going forward.

"If we can even figure out where he—it—is," she said.

Michael gave a resigned lift of his shoulders. "Which is why I want to get in touch with Fred. He can work on that angle in the background while we're filming."

"While *you're* filming," Rosemary replied. "I checked, and there's a Southwest flight from Tucson to Ontario this afternoon at 4:45. I was hoping one of you would give me a ride, since I still need to go back to the bed-and-breakfast and pack up my stuff."

"Not a problem," Michael said. "That is, Colin might make it a problem, since it'll cut into our shooting time, but I'll make sure we get you to your flight."

She didn't quite smile, but she did look relieved, as though she was worried that he might try again to convince her to stay in Tucson and help with the shoot. "Thanks."

After that, they finished what was left of their meals, then paid the tab and left. Once they were inside Michael's rental and headed back to the B&B, Audrey asked, "What're you going to tell Colin?"

Michael looked vaguely surprised by the question. "The truth, of course. He won't like it—he may not even want to believe it—but I'm sure as hell not going to let him blame you for losing a day's worth of work when none of this is remotely your fault."

She supposed she should have expected him to reply in such a way, but she could still feel some of the tension begin to leave her neck. No, none of this was her fault, but Colin seemed to be the kind of person to sling blame, if for no other reason than to make himself feel better. No doubt the tactic had worked for him in the past, or he wouldn't still be doing it. However, she felt better knowing that Michael would be there to deflect if necessary.

As she watched the streets of Tucson pass by, bright and clear and sharp under a blazing sun, it was hard to remember that she'd been trapped, cold and hungry, in a snowbound mansion only two states away from here. It felt like another world, one she had no desire to visit ever again.

When they pulled into the parking lot of the Thunderbird bed-and-breakfast, Audrey had a difficult time believing this place could possibly be haunted, let alone infested by demons. It was a cheerful mishmash of colonial pueblo architecture and Victorian accents, and was surrounded by lovely grounds, lush and green even now, in late February.

"This place is haunted?" she asked, looking around her as she clutched a little bag of necessities they'd bought at a Walgreens on the way over. Her clothes were gone, but at least now she had toiletries, makeup, and a package of new underwear to get her through the next few days. Michael had suggested that she borrow the clothing she needed from the wardrobe that had been brought for the shoot, and she'd gone along with the plan. Right then, she was just too tired to worry about doing any real shopping.

"Oh, yes," Michael said. Neither he nor Audrey had taken any luggage along with them on their rescue mission, so there was no need to get anything out of the trunk. He pushed the Grand Cherokee's remote to lock the vehicle, then gestured toward a path that led away from the tiny five-space parking lot. "Come on—let's see if you can pick up on anything."

That sounded vaguely ominous, but, after all, this was what they'd come here for. She walked next to Michael, with Rosemary a few paces behind them, and almost at once her attention was caught by a storage shed a few yards away from the path. Why she'd looked in that direction, she really couldn't say, since the little building was really very ordinary, one of thousands of prefab structures just like it.

The outline of the shed looked hazy, as though something was partially obscuring it. Audrey stopped and stared, realizing after a moment that the haze was a blob of pale, glowing light, almost invisible in the harsh glare of the sun overhead.

"You see it?" Michael asked in a murmur.

"Yes," she replied in the same undertone.

Rosemary had paused next to them. Now she smiled, one hand lifted to shield her eyes from the bright sunlight. "I told you, Michael. You don't need me here. Audrey's perfectly capable of doing the heavy lifting."

She wasn't so sure about that, but it seemed clear enough that she was witnessing some kind of apparition. And it wasn't in a dark hallway or basement, but right out here in the open with the sun blazing down overhead.

"That's our ghost?" she asked.

"We don't know for sure yet," Michael replied. "That is, I know it's a spirit of some kind, but I haven't been able to determine whether it's the only entity we're dealing with here. We had to leave to come find you before I had a chance to really start investigating."

Now she really did feel guilty, even though it wasn't her fault that Michael hadn't been able to dive right into ghost hunting or demon hunting, or whatever it was that they'd end up doing here. Well, they'd remedy that lack soon enough. They still had a little time before they had to take Rosemary to the airport.

And then…it was gone. Audrey wanted to blame what she'd seen on the glare of the sun, or a simple visual hallucination brought on by lack of sleep and extreme stress, but she knew better. It had been there. Both Michael and Rosemary had seen it, too.

He touched her arm. "It'll come back. This is the second time I've seen it, but I doubt it'll be the last. And I want to get in that storage shed. There has to be a reason why the apparition keeps showing up in that spot."

"Sounds like a plan," Audrey said. "But I want to change first. I'm starting to feel like these clothes have grown on me."

"You should let Colin know about it," Rosemary suggested. "Maybe that way you guys could film something today. It might make him a little less crabby about Audrey's disappearance."

"But we need to take you to the airport —" Michael began.

"No biggie," Rosemary cut in. "I'll pack my stuff, and you can have what's-her-name—Susan —drive me."

"Because that worked out so well last time," Audrey remarked.

Rosemary didn't look too worried. "Well, I assume you have the real Susan here, don't you? I mean, the one at the airport was just an illusion created by Whitcomb, right?"

"That's what he said." Although she knew intellectually that Rosemary was correct, Audrey still didn't like the idea of someone else driving her to the airport. She'd feel safer if she and Michael took Rosemary, and stood and watched until her plane was in the air and getting farther from Tucson by the second.

However, Michael didn't seem all that concerned. "She's right," he said. "It would go a long way to keep Colin from going on a rampage if we got some footage today, even if our ghost doesn't show himself again."

"All right," Audrey said. She was feeling too tired right then to argue with the both of them. "But Rosemary—please text us when you land in Ontario."

"Of course I will."

By this point, they'd reached the little bungalow that apparently was Rosemary's room here at the B&B. She ducked inside, saying, "It'll only take me a few minutes to pack. If you could ask Susan about driving me, that'd be great. Otherwise, I'll need to call an Uber."

"We will," Michael promised. A flash of a grin, and the door closed. He went on, "Your room is over here, next to mine. I hope that's okay."

Audrey slanted a glance up at him. There were so many things she wanted to say, and yet now really didn't feel like the right time. Maybe they'd have a chance to talk privately later, once they got their filming done for the afternoon.

"It's fine," she said lightly. "I'm going to slip in and take a shower. I guess you can go let Colin know that I'm back."

"Will do." His gaze lingered on hers for a moment, and she also got the sense that he wanted to talk to her more in depth at some point, even if now wasn't convenient for a number of reasons. "Daniela put your wardrobe in the closet, so it's waiting for you."

God bless Daniela, for her quick efficiency… and for not chickening out the way their wardrobe supervisor Kathleen had, leaving them high and dry. The clothes would be a huge help—and so would Daniela's skills with hair and makeup. Audrey had a feeling those skills would be put to the test covering up the aftermath of the hideous night she'd just spent.

She murmured a thank-you to Michael, who reached in his pocket and dug out the key to her room before handing it to her. Why he had it, she wasn't sure, although she figured he must have gotten it from the B&B managers the day before, hoping that he'd be able to give it to her as soon as she was back in town.

A quick, grateful squeeze of his fingers as she took the key from him, and then she went inside the room and closed the door, locking it behind her. Not because she didn't trust Michael to stay away, but because she wasn't sure Colin would have the restraint to keep from barging in once he learned she was back.

The bathroom was small, but cheerful with its Mexican tile in bright shades of green and red and yellow. *Talavera,* she reminded herself. She'd admired the gaily painted pottery when she'd seen it in specialty shops before, but it didn't really fit the more traditional style of her Craftsman house, so she'd never bought any.

Aside from that, it felt heavenly to get out of her rumpled and stained clothing, to stand under the stream of hot water and let it wash away some of the fear and worry and discomfort of the past twenty-four hours. She'd bought travel-sized shampoo and conditioner, and she scrubbed her hair right down to her scalp, wanting to make sure there wasn't a single trace of the demon's Colorado house left on her.

Afterward, she moisturized her face and blow-dried her hair, and thought she looked better than she had any right to, considering what she'd just experienced. For just a few seconds, she'd been afraid to look in the mirror, worried about what might be peering back at her, but there was nothing but her own reflection.

Then to get dressed in new jeans and a crisp black cotton jacket over a white tank top. Low black boots—and, thank God, Daniela had also supplied some jewelry, just a simple silver chain and matching hoop earrings, but enough for Audrey to feel dressed, and not as if something was missing.

Someone knocked at the door, and she jumped a little. Maybe it was silly to be starting at shadows like that, but then again, she had just seen an apparition out by the B&B's storage shed. Something was going on here, although she hadn't experienced any of the creeping sensations of dread that had assaulted her in the Whitcomb mansion in Glendora.

It wasn't Michael outside but Daniela, who had her makeup case with her.

"So glad to see you safe and sound!" she exclaimed. "Michael told us about what happened —are you really okay?"

"I'm fine," Audrey replied. "Now that I'm back here with all of you."

"You seem very calm," Daniela went on as she laid out her brushes and various pots of color on the dresser. "I think I'd still be a nervous wreck."

"Well, I know we have to get some work done today." Audrey hoped that sounded like a reasonable enough explanation. Truth was, she could still feel how shaky she was inside, but if the demon managed to turn her into a basket case, he would have won, and she absolutely did not plan to have that happen.

Daniela let out an exaggerated sigh. "True. As soon as Colin found out you were here—and that there was a ghost Michael wanted to investigate—he wanted to get started right away. But Michael told him you needed to get cleaned up and that you'd be ready when you were ready, and not a moment before."

Her knight in shining armor. Well, maybe not exactly, but Michael had definitely done a lot to take care of her during the last twenty-four hours. Once upon a time, she might have grown indignant at the supposition that she couldn't handle on her own anything that was thrown at her, but that was before the demons came on the scene.

"Well, let's get me ready," Audrey said. "Then we'll see what we can find."

Daniela nodded and set to work. This time,

she worked even more quickly than before, as if all too aware that somewhere on the property, Colin was probably tapping his foot and checking his watch every other minute.

"I'm just going to pull your hair back," Daniela said after she was done with Audrey's makeup. "It'll still look polished, but I won't have to spend all that time on curling it."

"That's fine." Personally, Audrey didn't really care what she looked like, as long as it was passable enough for her to not appear like death warmed over in front of the cameras.

But—once Daniela was done and Audrey was able to take a quick look in the mirror to inspect her work—it was clear that she looked better than she had any right to. Once again, Daniela's artistry hid flaws and accentuated highlights, and the sleek ponytail she'd created looked very brisk and no-nonsense, but not at all like what Audrey tended to refer to as "gym hair."

"Thanks so much," she told the makeup artist, who only shrugged as she put her things away.

"That's what I'm here for. Now, go ahead—I'll close up here once I'm done packing my stuff. The less time you make Colin wait, the better."

Since Audrey couldn't really argue with that sentiment, she only nodded, straightened her jacket, and headed out the door. She didn't know the grounds here at all, but she figured she'd follow the path until she got to something that looked like the main building. The other B&Bs she'd stayed in had had a central living space where people could relax, often connected to the dining area, and she hoped the setup here was more or less the same.

Her hunch proved to be right, because she crossed a courtyard and headed toward a set of French doors that opened on the patio, doors connected to a large building with two stories. Even as she approached, Michael and Colin emerged through the French doors, pausing when they caught sight of her.

"I told you she'd be ready soon," Michael said, and Colin hitched his shoulders but still looked less than pleased with her.

"Right," he said. "You all squared away now?"

"Yes," Audrey replied calmly. It was clear enough that he didn't care anything about what had happened to her, what kind of trauma she'd suffered, only that she'd caused enough of a delay and he didn't want to deal with any more drama. That realization made anger stir within her, but she knew she had to do her best to keep this professional. "Michael told you about the apparition we saw by the storage shed?"

Colin nodded. "And we got the key from the owners, so let's all go over there and take a little look-see, shall we?"

"Your camera?"

"It's in my room. We'll swing by and pick it up as we go."

That seemed like a logical enough plan, so Audrey followed him and Michael as they went back the way she'd just come, this time to another bungalow, one that seemed bigger than the building where she and Michael had back-to-back rooms.

While they were waiting for Colin, she murmured to Michael, "Rosemary?"

"She's gone already," he replied. "Susan drove her to the airport, as we'd planned."

"And Susan seemed…okay?"

Michael touched her hand briefly, but even that light touch was immensely reassuring. "She's fine, Audrey. The real Susan had nothing to do with what Whitcomb did to you. Actually, she was horrified when she heard the story."

She managed to smile. "Of course she was. Don't mind me—I'm still a little jumpy."

"With cause. But you're safe now."

"As safe as anyone going ghost-hunting can be, you mean."

He didn't bother to contradict her. "This setup seems pretty harmless. And it's still broad daylight. I don't think we have much to worry about."

She hoped he was right.

Colin emerged from his room, camera with its

Steadicam setup clutched in one hand. "Since Susan's not here, I'm just going to use the mike on the camera instead of the boom mike. Shouldn't be too much of a problem, since we'll be in a quiet spot out back. But lead on."

The three of them headed back to the storage shed. Sitting there in the afternoon sunlight, it looked completely innocuous—no sign of any apparitions, no sign that anything at all was out of the ordinary about it. Already, Colin was frowning, but Michael didn't look too concerned. Either he knew something Audrey didn't, or he was so used to Colin's frowns that they simply didn't register anymore.

Once they were a few yards away from the door to the shed, Colin paused. "I'm going to shoot from here. You two go ahead. Act natural."

Easier said than done. Audrey wasn't picking up anything unusual at the moment, but she couldn't forget what she'd seen here less than an hour ago. Michael gave her the slightest of nods, and she tilted her head in reply, indicating she was ready...or at least as ready as she would ever be.

He turned toward the camera. "The Thunderbird Bed and Breakfast Inn. Maybe the last place you'd expect to be haunted...or worse. But the owners came to us for help, told us they'd experienced strange phenomena here, paranormal occurrences that couldn't be easily explained away. I myself saw a cross on the wall in my room turn upside down, and then do this." With a finger in the air, he drew an arc showing how the cross had resumed its regular position. "No one else was in the room. There were no wires or strings or anything else that might explain its bizarre movements. And then last night, I saw an apparition by this shed." His gaze turned toward Audrey, and she did her best to stand there looking brisk and professional, and not as though she'd spent the night before huddled on a tile bathroom floor, hiding from a demon. "You saw the same thing earlier today, didn't you?"

She nodded. "It was an amorphous shape, not quite transparent, hanging here near the door. A fairly typical apparition, when you think about it."

Michael took up the thread from her, obviously glad that she'd provided the opening he needed. "The thing is, when the owners of the B&B called us to come investigate their inn, they said they didn't think it was a ghost. After seeing the upside-down cross in my room, I was inclined to agree with them. But, as Audrey pointed out, what we've witnessed in the vicinity of the shed doesn't seem to be anything demonic." He reached into his pocket and pulled out a key, held it in his palm. It glinted silver in the afternoon sunlight before his fingers closed on it once again. "The owners gave us permission to check in the shed. So…let's see what we can find."

Although Colin had maintained his distance while the two of them were speaking, now he moved slowly forward, focusing the camera on the door. Michael inserted the key in the lock, then turned the doorknob.

In contrast to the bright sun outside, it looked pitch black in there. Audrey sent Michael a quizzical glance. "Colleen said the building has electricity," he told her. "The switch should be just inside the door."

Obviously, that was a cue to step in and turn on the lights. While Audrey wasn't too happy to be the first inside, she knew she had to play along. At least she still wasn't feeling anything evil here, wasn't really sensing anything at all.

She moved forward, acutely aware of the camera focused on her, and paused in the doorway so her fingers could brush against the wall immediately to her right. At once she felt the hard protrusion of a light switch under her fingertips, and she turned it on.

Inside was a jumble of boxes, unused yard equipment, and large, brightly painted plywood figures that seemed to be part of a Christmas display. She turned back toward Michael—and the camera—and said, "I don't really see anything in here."

Brows drawn together in concentration, he stepped into the shed and took a look around. For just the briefest moment, he looked puzzled, as if he also couldn't understand the significance of the shed and its contents. Then he froze, his lean form tense. "There," he said in a murmur. "Back wall, over to the left."

Audrey followed his gaze and realized the same gauzy entity was hovering in the spot he'd indicated. It looked darker now, more of a pale gray than pure white. Strange little sparks of light seemed to appear deep within it, not white, but a washed-out pink.

"What's it doing?" she murmured, and Michael shook his head.

"I don't know."

Neither of them had any time for conjecture, because in the next second, the ghost seemed to shiver apart where it was floating, as if unseen hands had grabbed hold of it somehow and pulled it apart. A high-pitched, terrible screech assaulted Audrey's ears, and she raised her hands to cover them, only to find that the sound had already died away.

"What was that?" she demanded.

Michael didn't reply, instead moved toward the spot where the ghost had been floating only a few seconds earlier. Reluctantly, Audrey followed, knowing that they needed to get this on camera no matter what happened.

The back corner in question had several boxes stacked there, along with a black trash bag sitting on top of the stack. Michael went toward it, then paused, hand resting on top of the bag.

"The apparition seemed interested in this," he said, addressing the camera again. "I guess we'd better see what's inside."

After picking up the trash bag, he came over to where Audrey stood, then dumped its contents on the floor of the storage shed. The objects appeared to be a random assortment of items that probably had been left behind in the B&B's rooms or on its grounds—a couple of coffee mugs, several compact umbrellas, a lone flip-flop, several bottles of sunscreen.

And on top of all of them, a thin board about a foot and a half wide and a little less than half that tall. Michael turned it over, and the familiar alphabet and "yes/no" of a Ouija board stared up at them.

"Well, he said grimly, more to Audrey than to the camera, "I think I know why the Thunderbird B&B has been having a demon infestation problem…."

Chapter 10

"I FOUND IT ON THE GROUNDS A WHILE back," Edgar Samuels said as Colin stood in the corner with his camera, filming everything. They sat at one of the tables in the dining room, since that seemed like the most logical place to gather. "I planned to toss it at some point, but I guess I forgot about it. Usually, we go through the discards and donate what we can and throw out the rest, but we were having the place re-roofed this past spring, and it must have slipped my mind."

He frowned, and his wife patted him on the arm. They were both in their late fifties, pleasant-faced, Edgar balding and his wife Jackie with brown gray-streaked hair she wore plainly in a ponytail. Now they looked over at Michael with some concern, as though they were worried he was going to chastise them for being so careless with something so potentially dangerous.

"But it's just a toy, isn't it?" Jackie asked. Her worried gaze slipped from Michael to Audrey, who did her best to offer a reassuring smile in return. "I mean, I remember playing with one of these things when I was a little girl and not having any problems."

"It depends on the situation," Michael said. The Ouija board lay on the table in front of him. Audrey guessed that it must have been outside in the elements for some time before Edgar found it, because the board was warped, the edges worn, the laminated cardboard on its face water-stained. "A lot of the time, nothing goes wrong, mostly because the kids playing with the board don't have any ill intentions. The problem is that Ouija boards were marketed as toys, but they're really devices for communicating with the other side. When untrained people reach out to those energies, anything can answer...and sometimes does."

Some of the cheerful rosiness in Jackie Samuels' cheeks seemed to fade, and her voice faltered as she asked, "But why would anyone bring one of these things here?"

"I honestly don't know." Michael reached out to touch the board, but carefully, by the edge, his fingers staying safely away from any of the letters or numbers printed on one side. "Best guess?

Someone probably brought the Ouija board to your B&B because they'd heard it was haunted and wanted to have some kind of a seance here. It is haunted, isn't it?"

Husband and wife exchanged a glance. "The previous owners told us it was, but we never saw much evidence of it," Edgar said. "Once or twice, items were moved around—or at least we thought they were—but that could have just been absentmindedness on our part and nothing supernatural at all. We never felt anything bad, so to speak."

"Not until about six months ago," Jackie added. "But maybe that was when the Ouija board was left behind."

"I doubt it was a coincidence," Michael said. "Maybe you should check your records and see who was staying here at that time."

"Even if we find out who it was, what good will that do?" Now Jackie sounded plaintive and a little scared, as though she feared that Michael expected her and her husband to confront the people who'd brought chaos into their lives. "We can't prove anything."

"No, and leaving Ouija boards lying around someone's property isn't a prosecutable offense." He rubbed a thoughtful thumb over his chin. "But still, if you're able to track them down, then you would have the chance to ask them what they were doing with the board. It might help us figure out what they attracted here."

Edgar asked, "What about the ghost?"

Audrey had been pondering that problem, and now she thought it was a good time to jump in. "I think it was the ghost who showed us the way, so to speak. It probably would have taken a long time to find the bag with the Ouija board in it if the apparition hadn't been hanging around the storage shed, or hadn't gone to the spot inside where we found the bag with the board."

From the light of approval in Michael's eyes, she thought she'd just impressed him a little. "A ghost who's dwelled in a place for a long time would find a new intrusion by demons extremely disruptive. While the ghost couldn't intervene directly, he—or she—could work to attract our attention and get us to help out."

"Which is exactly what we're going to do," Audrey said, hoping she sounded proactive…and that Michael would know what steps they needed to take next.

He nodded, picking up the thread as he remarked, "Cleansing the property should be pretty straightforward. While I've seen some activity here that indicates it's demonic in origin, and not the work of your ghost, the demon doesn't seem too entrenched. It probably won't be a battle royal like our last encounter with demons."

Audrey hoped he was right, that his assertions weren't false bravado. True, she hadn't felt anything particularly strange here, but neither had she gone looking for it.

"What's the procedure, then?" Jackie asked.

The question earned her a smile. "There really isn't a set procedure," Michael said. "We'll smudge the house, just because that's good for an overall cleansing. I doubt it'll drive the demons out, but it'll put them on edge, make them more likely to act out."

"And that's a good thing?" Edgar sounded skeptical, to say the least.

"Better the enemy you can see," Michael told him. "Right now, they seem pretty quiescent, like they're content to only lash out every once in a while. But if they're agitated, trying to come after us…then we can mount a more coordinated defense and get rid of them for good."

Jackie and Edgar looked at one another. Neither one of them appeared all that happy about the plan, but Audrey could almost feel their frustration and knew they would end up agreeing. Ghosts might be an added attraction for the B&B's guests, but demons were something else entirely, and definitely bad for business.

"All right," Jackie said at last. "Let us know what we have to do."

Night had fallen. Luckily, Colin had pronounced himself pleased with the footage they'd gotten that day—the apparition in the shed had shown up remarkably well—and so he hadn't pressed them to continue shooting after dark.

"Besides," Michael told him. "I need to formulate a plan."

"A plan?" Colin repeated, looking unimpressed. "This seems like the sort of thing you could do in your sleep."

"Maybe, but I don't want to make any mistakes—and I also want to come up with something that'll read well on camera and keep Edgar and Jackie Samuels safe at the same time."

To Audrey's surprise, Colin appeared mollified by Michael's explanation, and said he'd be ready to get to work the next morning at ten. He invited the two of them to join him and Daniela and Susan for dinner, but after Michael shot her a quick glance from under his lashes, Audrey had begged off, saying she was tired after her ordeal in Colorado and that she planned to get something delivered.

That was why she and Michael now sat at the

little table in his suite, eating pizza and sharing a bottle of chianti. Maybe it was unwise for her to be alone with him here like this…but, on the other hand, she couldn't think of anywhere else she'd rather be.

The room had come with a set of vanilla chai–scented candles, and they flickered cheerfully from on top of the dresser, casting a warm glow around them. Audrey cocked an eye at the cross on the wall, the one Michael had said turned upside down even as he watched, but for now it seemed quiescent.

"Can we talk about it?" he said then, fingers resting on the tabletop next to the stemless wine glass that held his chianti. Because the room was a suite, it had come equipped with all sorts of handy items—the plates that held their pizza, the glasses for their wine.

"Talk about what?" Audrey asked, although she thought she knew what he meant. This was the first chance they'd really had to discuss the situation in private, and while she was glad of it, she also felt almost nervous, as if she wasn't quite sure whether Michael would really accept any of her explanations. Yes, they'd held hands on the flight back to Tucson, and it seemed as though everything was getting smoothed out, but….

"When we last spoke in Southern California, you were less than happy with me," he said. "Now it seems as if everything has changed. Don't get me wrong—I'm very glad about your change of heart, if that's what this is—but I still want to know what happened."

He was facing her directly, expression frank, open. And his eyes were fixed on hers, telling her that he was going to pay very close attention to everything she said.

She reached for her glass of wine, let herself have a healthy swallow. "I suppose I had time to think. A lot—a lot of my therapy after I lost my parents had to do with forgiveness, with letting go and moving on. I couldn't understand why your brother did what he did, Michael, but I realized at some point that if I held on to my hate and my anger, then I'd never have a chance to truly move on with my life. The same thing here...although of course what you did isn't remotely close to your brother's crimes. I was angry with you, of course. But then I understood that my anger would only get in the way if I let it."

"Get in the way of what?" he asked. His tone was soft, though, as if he already knew the answer to the question.

"Get in the way of us," she replied truthfully. "I don't know exactly where we're going with any of this, Michael, but I do know that it's probably foolish to try to run away from it."

He'd been sitting across from her. Now he

stood up and came over to her seat, held out a hand. Audrey let herself take it, let him help her up to a standing position. His arms wrapped around her waist, and he pulled her closer. How warm he was, how strong and right and perfect.

She'd said earlier that she was tired and she hadn't even been lying, but now her weariness was gone as if it had never existed. Had anyone ever had this effect on her before, made her heart beat faster and her limbs feel warm and flushed and yet somehow weightless at the same time, as if his very nearness was enough to bring a lightness to her soul she hadn't even realized was missing.

"I don't want you to run away," he said, his voice almost harsh, as though he could no longer hide his need for her, had to let it escape somehow. "I want you to always be here next to me. The two of us together, in all ways. Do you want that?"

About all she could do was nod. Funny how she'd always prided herself on how articulate and in control she could be, and now she only had to have Michael Covenant holding her and telling her he wanted her for all rational thought to somehow flee. When she'd agreed to have dinner in his bungalow, she'd somehow known where this was going to end up, but she didn't mind. Let Colin and Susan and Daniela think what they wanted. She wasn't about to let their opinions interfere with her and Michael, with what was building between them.

At last, Audrey found her voice. "I want that, Michael. I want to be with you. I'm not going to let the past dictate our futures."

"Neither am I," he said, and now he bent down and kissed her, his lips warm, his body pressed against hers.

She clung to him, needing the reassurance of his strength right then, even though she knew she was safe. Well, relatively safe. The Thunderbird B&B had issues of its own, and the Whitcomb-demon was still lurking out there somewhere, but all that could wait. Right now, she only wanted to be with Michael, think of Michael.

They stumbled together toward the bed, then fell down on it together, lips still locked. She felt her fingers grasping his belt buckle so she could unfasten it, realized that he was tugging her T-shirt free from her jeans. Was their urgency now born of the realization that they could have lost this, that their connection might have been destroyed if the Whitcomb-demon had had his way?

Audrey didn't know for sure. She only knew she needed to show Michael that her anger was a thing of the past, and that she wanted him with her no matter what happened.

His hand closed on her breast, and she

released a soft moan, body already anticipating what was going to come next. But then she heard an odd scraping sound and she opened her eyes, realizing that the cross on the wall had moved, was now hanging upside down.

No, it wasn't simply upside down—it was swinging back and forth against the wall, almost like the pendulum of a clock.

She lifted her mouth from Michael's, then whispered urgently, "Michael!"

He blinked at her, obviously confused. Understandable, since his back was to the wall where the cross hung, and therefore he couldn't see what was happening.

"The cross," she said, and he shifted to look over his shoulder at the object in question.

Now the sound of it scraping against the plaster was obvious, a horrible *scritch-scritch* noise that made the flesh on the back of her neck crawl. Even though they hadn't turned on all the lights, the black marks it was leaving behind were plain to see, a strange half-circle about a foot wide.

Frowning, Michael said, "I've never seen it do that before. Maybe—"

He didn't finish the sentence, because in that same second, the cross tore itself from the wall and hurtled toward them, pointed end headed straight for his head. With a curse, he grasped one of the pillows from the bed and held it up like a shield. The sharp iron drilled into the fabric with such force that feathers went everywhere—and it showed no signs of stopping. With a grunt, Michael flung the pillow and the cross embedded in it across the room, then quickly reached for his jacket and one of the vials of holy water he always kept in its pocket. Almost before Audrey could blink, he'd strode over to the pillow and splashed the blessed water all over it and the cross.

At once, the object went still. It had all happened so fast, she had remained where she was, T-shirt pushed up, baring her stomach as she half-lay on top of the bedclothes. Now, though, she scrambled to a sitting position and tucked her T-shirt back into her jeans, her heart still going about a mile a minute.

"What the hell was that?" she demanded.

Michael turned back toward her, empty vial clenched in his hand. "It seems the demons who've taken up residence here didn't much like us getting intimate."

"Puritanical demons?" she inquired, and he almost smiled.

"It looks that way. Or rather," he went on as he came over to her and took her hand in his, letting her know he was all right, "they don't appreciate the positive energy we were creating." He sat down next to her on the bed. "I'm afraid we had better hold off until we're done here."

More good news. Audrey released a frustrated huff of a breath and leaned her head against his shoulder. "It's really not fair."

"No, it's not," he agreed. He still held her hand and showed no sign of letting go. Maybe this was the only intimacy he'd allow between the two of them. "Especially since I'm pretty sure Colin and Daniela didn't suffer any similar interruptions."

"You really think they're sleeping together?" Audrey asked, a little startled by the insinuation. Although it was impossible to ignore the way the two of them flirted, she hadn't thought they'd gone any further than flirtation.

"If you'd seen the way they looked last night, you wouldn't have had any doubts left. But," he went on, "it seems that the entities here don't have an issue with the two of them. Maybe they just don't like the psychic energy you and I create together."

"Is that what you call it?" Despite herself, she couldn't help smiling a little at the mental image Michael's words had summoned.

However, he didn't look at all amused. "You didn't feel it that first time we made love? How it felt somehow different from any other sex you'd had before?"

Actually, she'd experienced exactly what he was describing, but at the time she'd thought the intensity of their lovemaking had had a lot to do with the two of them being pretty drunk. Any inhibitions had been checked at the door, thanks to the cocktails they'd consumed at The Bahooka.

"I felt…something," she said slowly. "I just wasn't quite sure what it was."

"I think it's also connected to how we work together so well." His fingers tightened on hers as he continued. "The way we were able to drive the demons away and close the portal at the Whitcomb mansion. Your psychic powers—even if they're just waking up—were able to mesh with mine in a way I've never experienced before I met you. And when we're intimate…the energies that gather around us can be very strong. The demons who've infested this property wouldn't like that at all, so they decided to retaliate."

Audrey looked over at the ruin of the pillow in the corner, sodden feathers scattered across the floor. That was going to be an interesting one to explain. Then again, by this point Edgar and Jackie must be at least somewhat used to these sorts of problems occurring on their property.

"So what do we do now?" she asked, knowing how plaintive the question must have sounded. Her body was throbbing with unspent desire, and she could only imagine how Michael must feel.

"We go to your room," he said, then went on quickly, probably seeing the spark of hope in her eyes, "and we sleep. *Just* sleep. I think it's safer for us to be together."

"At least there aren't any crosses in my room," Audrey remarked, and now he did give her a tired smile.

"You're right—there aren't. I'm not sure if there's anything else in there that might raise their ire, but let's hope that we've beaten them down for now. I'm sure you need a good night's sleep even more than I do."

That was most likely true. Still, she'd hoped to make love with Michael, then sleep the sleep of the just afterward. She was so tired that she'd probably pass out the second her head hit the pillow, but it wasn't the same.

"All right," she said, glad that she'd bought a University of Arizona T-shirt from the clearance pile at the Walgreens where she'd gotten all her other odds and ends. She'd seen it while she was waiting in line to pay for the toiletries she'd picked up there, thinking that it couldn't hurt to have a spare shirt for sleeping or lounging or whatever. Now she could wear it while Michael slept next to her, and maybe it would help that she had something on that was so baggy and unappealing.

Wishful thinking, probably, but she knew they had to behave themselves while they were here. Once they were back in California, though....

Michael looked relieved that she hadn't offered any objections to his plan. "Let me get a few things together, and then we'll head over to your room."

She nodded, and he went into the bathroom. A few minutes later, he came out with a black leather toiletry bag in one hand and a T-shirt and a pair of gray sweatpants in the other. "All right —let's go."

They closed the door to his room, then quickly made their way along the path that led to Audrey's half of what used to be the guesthouse. The other room was unoccupied, so there was no one around to see them slip into her room and lock the door behind them.

"Sorry about the mess," Audrey said, hurrying over to the bed so she could pick up the pieces of discarded clothing she'd left there—outfits she'd decided wouldn't really work for that afternoon's quickie shoot—and hang them back up in the closet. "I was sort of in a rush, since I knew you and Colin were waiting for me."

"It's fine," Michael said. Already he seemed more relaxed, as if he could tell that this room was far less affected by the demons than the one he'd occupied. And while it was decorated in the same sort of subdued Southwestern style as the other rooms in the B&B, there weren't any crosses here, only mirrors framed in talavera tile and canvases of pueblos and outdoor scenes that looked like they were from the Grand Canyon. "I know you weren't expecting company."

No, she wasn't. Whatever half-baked fantasies might have flitted through her mind about her and Michael getting back together, none of them had taken place here, as if they'd both thought of his room as the obvious place for a hook-up.

And there won't be any of that here, either, she thought, both frustrated and angry at the delay. Well, with any luck, they could wrap this up tomorrow and be on their way back to Southern California. This time, she looked forward to the thought of spending all those hours on the road with Michael. Maybe on Yelp she could find some fun, out-of-the-way places where they could stop to eat. After all, what was a road trip without some crazy diner food?

"I still should have put everything away," she said. "Especially since these aren't really my clothes."

"It's all right." He was still holding the items he'd brought over, but now he set the toiletry bag down on the dresser and draped the T-shirt and sweat pants over the arm of one of the chairs. "I was going to tell Colin to let you keep them."

"Really?" Audrey asked, absurdly pleased. Since finances had been tight for a while, she really hadn't allowed herself to do much clothes shopping. The thought of being able to add the pieces Kathleen, their wardrobe person, had carefully picked out to her meager wardrobe was exciting.

"Yes, really." Now Michael grinned, and the worry and strain in his face seemed to disappear. She was glad to see that, not just because he looked so handsome when he smiled, but because she didn't want him to feel so stressed all the time.

At least he doesn't have to hide who he is from me, she thought. *That must be a relief, even if he still has to conceal his identity from the rest of the world.*

"Well, thank you," Audrey said, and went to him and gave him a quick hug, not really much more than a squeeze. She didn't dare do anything beyond that, because even feeling him press up against her for a second or two was enough to remind her body of what it wanted.

Honestly, she knew she didn't used to be this horny. Amazing what the right person could do to you.

He still looked pleased, as if he knew he'd made her happy with the promise of the clothes. And it wasn't all that extravagant, really—four or five jackets, designer jeans, boots and T-shirts and a few blouses. Not much she could use for work, but even her casual wardrobe could use the boost.

After that, they focused on getting ready for

bed, taking turns in the bathroom to brush their teeth and wash their faces. When they climbed into bed, both of them chastely covered enough for a high school sleepover, Audrey almost wanted to laugh. Funny how just an hour earlier they'd been practically tearing each other's clothes off.

Or maybe not so funny. Having Michael make love to her would have helped to erase some of the fear and anxiety of the past twenty-four hours, but she had been denied that relief. Now she had to lie here next to him in the dark, and do her best not to move or brush up against him in case by doing so she set events in motion that they were trying to avoid.

She let out a sigh and told herself, *It's all going to be better soon.*

She just wasn't sure whether she believed that or not.

Chapter 11

MICHAEL WOKE BEFORE AUDREY, THEN allowed himself a minute or so to admire her beauty, the way her thick brown hair spread across the pillow, the fine, graceful outline of her profile as she lay there next to him. Even the tiny little snort she made as she rolled over on her side was too adorable to be called a snore.

His body wanted to respond to her presence, but he knew that wasn't a good idea. The night had been still and quiet, with no sign of any demonic intervention. He'd even woken up at three o'clock, wary that some kind of attack might be mounted then at the devil's hour, but the time had come and gone, and nothing had happened.

Trying to lull him into a false sense of security?

Possibly, but he didn't think so. Although they hadn't yet been able to determine exactly what was infesting the Thunderbird Bed and Breakfast, Michael had the feeling that they were dealing with low-level demons here, the type of entities that liked to cause chaos but weren't really capable of the sort of high-level planning that the Whitcomb-demon had demonstrated.

Just thinking of the spirit that had taken over Jeffrey Whitcomb's body made Michael want to frown, but just as he had pushed away his desire for Audrey a moment earlier, he pushed aside his worries and suspicions for later. Most likely, the demon wouldn't attempt anything while they were all together like this—he'd gone after Audrey because she was alone, and vulnerable. Besides, Fred Peñasco was on the case, and Michael knew his friend would be in contact as soon as he found anything. In the meantime, best to focus on what was happening here at the B&B and hope they'd get some decent footage today, then get this thing wrapped up so he and Audrey could get some much-needed downtime together at his house in Pasadena.

Because of course they'd have to go there. He still wasn't sure whether her house was safe, while his was warded and guarded six ways from Sunday. Nothing would get in there; he'd made sure of it.

Since Audrey was still sound asleep, he carefully slid out from under the covers and went into the bathroom, figuring he would shower and get dressed, and then wander out to see how everyone had survived the night. But no one had come in search of him, and the only noises he'd heard were from the traffic on the street just past the B&B's grounds, which meant that the rest of the crew had probably also passed a peaceful night.

As he turned on the shower, Michael hoped that Colin and Daniela wouldn't look too obviously morning after-ish. That would just be salt on the wound after he and Audrey had been denied that sort of comfort the night before.

Goddamn demons.

He was used to being quick about his showers, so he was in and out and dressed in less than ten minutes. After giving his hair a quick blot with a towel, he went back out into the room, only to see Audrey sitting up in bed and rubbing at her temple.

"Headache?" he asked, concerned. They weren't uncommon in houses that had been infested with demons, but she had seemed fine the night before, had been sleeping peacefully, not restless at all.

"No," she replied at once. "I had a strange dream. Or at least, I think I had one. I can't remember much of it. There were a lot of trees…

but bare…and a stream. It was gray and cold." She shivered. "I'm glad I woke up."

Michael came and sat down on the bed next to her. The description she'd given him could have been one of any number of places, but something about it made an odd little shiver run down his spine. "You don't remember anything else?"

For a second, she didn't reply, as though she was straining to see if she could recall more details of her dream. Then her shoulders lifted. "That's all. I'm sure it was just a dream and didn't mean anything. Maybe I was flashing back to the house in Colorado, but I didn't see any snow. Just all those bare trees."

Which didn't sound much like the forest around the Colorado mansion, since it had been mainly composed of ponderosa pine. But he didn't bother to point that out, mostly because it seemed clear that Audrey couldn't remember any more of the dream right now and he didn't want to press her on the subject. Maybe some more details would surface at a later date, or maybe they wouldn't. Just because the dream had felt odd to her didn't mean there was necessarily anything significant about it.

As Freud had been known to say, sometimes a cigar was just a cigar.

"Well, don't worry about it," Michael said.

"You should probably get in the shower, though—it's almost eight, and we still need to have breakfast and get prepped before we can start filming anything."

"A shower sounds good." She began to push back the covers, so he got up and out of her way, taking a seat in the room's one armchair. After sending him a quick smile, she gathered up some clothes and disappeared into the bathroom…but not before he got a good look at her long legs under the oversized University of Arizona T-shirt she was wearing.

Damn. She really was beautiful, even rumpled and still a little sleepy.

He made himself focus on something else—in this case, the phone he pulled out of his jacket pocket. It was probably way too soon for Fred to have found anything, but Michael found himself hoping anyway. Not because they could use any of that information for the show—he knew in his bones that Whitcomb was connected to something bigger than the random hauntings and infestations that would be showcased on *Project Demon Hunters*—but because he wanted to know what that demon was up to.

Nothing good, he assumed.

But there was nothing from Fred. However, he had a text from Rosemary, letting him know that she was back in Glendora safe and sound, and to let Audrey know as well. *I left her a voicemail,* the text said, *but I just wanted to make sure she got it. Let me know if you need any support from over here.*

He sent a quick reply to tell her he'd pass her message along to Audrey, and also that they'd all survived the night without any disturbances. That was about all he had time for, because Audrey came out of the bathroom not too long after that, scrubbed and glowing, hair damp.

"I need to go back in and blow-dry it," she said. "But that actually takes less time if I let it air dry a little first."

"That's fine," he replied. The shower seemed to have done her a lot of good, because she looked much more relaxed than she had when she'd first woken up. Even if she couldn't remember much of it, that dream seemed to have affected her negatively. "I had a text from Rosemary. She's fine and safely back home."

That information seemed to relax Audrey even more. She sent him a grateful smile and said, "Oh, good. I suppose it was kind of silly of me to have worried, but...."

"But after what happened to you, I can see why you'd be wary." Michael returned his phone to his pocket. "Still, it didn't have anything to do with Susan. The demon just…borrowed…her image."

"I know." A quick glance around, and she frowned. "Doesn't look like there's a coffeemaker in here. I guess we're supposed to get coffee with our breakfast."

He'd noticed that lack as well, but he hadn't worried about it. Although he liked to have coffee in the morning, he'd also trained himself to do without if necessary. "Well, we'll head over as soon as you're ready."

"I'm on it."

She went back into the bathroom, and almost immediately afterward he heard the sound of the blow dryer, raucous and high-pitched. Since they were both dressed now, he figured it was safe to open the blinds a bit and take a look at the day outside. It would have been nice if it were dark and gloomy, like their first couple of days shooting in Glendora, but since this was Tucson, he wasn't going to hold his breath.

When he cracked open the blinds, he couldn't help taking a step backward. Standing right outside the room was a woman he'd never seen before, shining black hair in an exuberant pompadour, wearing a white, high-necked gown of the style popular around the turn of the twentieth century. For a second, her big dark eyes met his, and then she vanished.

"Holy shit," he breathed, and Audrey stuck her head out of the bathroom, expression concerned.

"What's the matter?"

He turned toward her. It looked as though she was done drying her hair, because she was in the process of wrapping the cord around the blow dryer.

"I think I just saw the Thunderbird Bed and Breakfast's resident ghost."

Jackie and Edgar Samuels exchanged a mystified glance. "I know I've never seen her," Jackie said. "Have you, Edgar?"

"No," he answered. His fingers tapped against the coffee mug he held, and he looked more puzzled than worried. "I mean, we'd heard stories about the place being haunted, but we didn't pay much attention to them. Almost any house as old as this one is supposed to have its own ghost. It's actually kind of a selling point."

"I can imagine," Michael said.

Audrey wished she'd seen the apparition, if only because she seemed a lot friendlier than the demons who'd decided to play havoc with her sex life the night before. She was also glad that she and Michael had caught the B&B's owners alone in the breakfast room before the rest of the crew made their appearance. Colin would probably want to try to capture this new spirit on film, even though their focus was supposed to be the demons and helping to get rid of them. After what had happened last night, she wanted to make sure those little bastards were sent straight to hell ASAP, and it would go a lot faster if Colin didn't get distracted by something new and shiny.

"No one ever reported seeing her, either," Jackie said. "We've had a lot of people come and go in this place, as you might imagine. Not one of them ever mentioned anything out of the ordinary…at least not until we started have having our problems last fall."

"Which were demonic in origin, I know." Michael rubbed the scruff on his chin, brows pulling together. He didn't appear angry or worried, though, but merely focused on the problem at hand. "This apparition looked very human, though. She was solid. It was only the way she disappeared that made me realize she wasn't a real person. If any of your guests saw her, they probably wouldn't have even realized she wasn't alive. They might have thought she was a historical reenactor or something, because of the way she was dressed, but…."

"But it probably wasn't strange enough for anyone to mention it," Jackie said. "Especially since we've had living history groups here to take photos from time to time, that sort of thing. If anyone had seen her, they would have thought she was with one of those groups, since we mention it in the brochure we put in all the rooms."

Audrey guessed she wouldn't have mentioned such a sighting, either, especially if the B&B's literature went out of its way to mention that reenactment groups sometimes took publicity photos here. "Why do you think she appeared now?" she asked. "I mean, it seems fairly obvious that she wanted to be seen if she was standing right in front of our—I mean, my—window."

Even as she spoke, she wanted to wince at the slip-up. When he'd recounted the details of the ghost sighting to Jackie and Edgar, he'd made it sound as though he'd seen the apparition as he was coming to meet Audrey for breakfast, and not because he was actually inside the room with her.

Luckily, neither of the B&B's owners seemed to have noticed her gaffe, and instead appeared to be more focused on the answer to the question she'd just posed. "I have no idea," Jackie said, then reached for her mug of coffee so she could take a sip from it. "Maybe she's trying to communicate somehow?"

"I think that's exactly it," Michael said. "My

guess is that the woman I saw is also the blob of light that hangs around the storage shed. She takes on different forms as necessary. Probably the glowing light is easier to maintain for an extended period of time."

"So she was guiding us to the Ouija board?" Audrey asked.

"That seems the most logical explanation."

His eyes met hers for just a second, but that was enough to send a little thrill through her. Her heightened responses to Michael might have had a lot to do with being cock-blocked the night before, and yet Audrey knew she needed to try to play it cool. While she'd told herself that she didn't care whether Colin and Daniela and Susan found out that she and Michael were becoming something of an item, she also knew that it would be easier to keep things somewhat under wraps until they were done filming. His mouth lifted at the corners, a ghost of a smile that seemed to acknowledge her presence while not giving too much away.

"If she's an earthbound spirit that's tied to this location, then having the demons show up would have been extremely disruptive. It would be like having a bunch of noisy frat guys move into your house."

Even though the situation was serious enough, both Jackie and Edgar chuckled a bit at Michael's description. "So the ghost is trying to help us so she can get back to her quiet life?" Edgar asked.

"That seems the most likely explanation," Michael replied.

"Explanation for what?" Colin asked as he came through the door to the breakfast room. Daniela was at his side. If they'd gotten busy the night before, they weren't showing any sign of it—they both looked rested enough, and there weren't any telltale marks on Daniela's throat. Then again, she was a makeup artist. She probably knew plenty of tricks for hiding that sort of thing.

Audrey couldn't tell if Michael was discomfited by the arrival of their producer, because he replied easily enough, "I saw a ghost a few minutes ago. We were just talking about why she appeared to me."

"'She'?" Daniela repeated. "I thought the ghost here was just a blob of light. That's how Colin described it to me."

Michael shrugged. "It could be a different ghost or—more likely—the same ghost using a different form. That sort of phenomenon really isn't too unusual."

Judging by the way Daniela's expertly groomed eyebrows lifted at that comment, Audrey could tell their makeup artist wasn't completely buying that explanation, but she didn't say anything.

"Where did you see her?" Colin asked, his tone eager. "Was it anywhere near one of the motion-sensing cameras I set up?"

"Outside Audrey's room," Michael replied. "So no—the closest camera is a few yards away and pointed in the other direction. Anyway, the ghost was just standing there and not doing anything, so I'm not sure she would have set off the motion detectors anyway."

Jackie seemed to recall her duties as hostess then, because she got up from where she'd been sitting and told Daniela and Colin, "There's fresh coffee and hot water for tea, and pastries to hold you over until I get the strata out of the oven. Actually, I should go check on it now."

She excused herself, and Edgar rose and went with her, saying she would need some help. As Daniela poured herself some coffee and Colin looked over the tea offerings, Michael said, "I'm not sure how well this ghost would read on camera anyway. She looked like a regular person, or at least a regular person in clothing from a little over a hundred years ago."

"Pretty?" Colin asked, his tone sharpening with interest.

One-track mind, Audrey thought, but she remained silent and pretended to be absorbed in sipping her coffee.

Michael's mouth twitched, but he answered

Colin seriously enough. "Yes, she was attractive. Young, probably in her mid-twenties. Very dark hair and eyes, so I have a feeling that whoever she was, she had either some Mexican or some Native American blood."

Which probably wasn't so strange, considering the locale. Audrey wished she'd been able to see the ghost for herself, because Michael hadn't mentioned much about her expression. Had she been frightened? Or did she look more pleading, as if she knew how hard it was to get her message across to anyone who could help her?

"Maybe she'll show up again," Daniela suggested. She'd gotten some coffee and a cherry danish, and was now sitting in the chair Jackie had occupied up until a few minutes earlier.

"It'll be interesting if she does," Michael said. "But she shouldn't be our focus. We need to concentrate on drawing out the demons and dispelling them."

This suggestion made Colin give an indelicate snort. "Demons, my ass. I slept like a baby last night. No disturbances. Even though we found that Ouija board yesterday, there hasn't been a damn thing going on."

"Well, something tried to drive a wrought-iron cross through my head last night, so there's definitely some kind of presence here," Michael said, tone so casual, he might have been mentioning that he found a spider in his bathtub.

"It what?" Colin had been dunking a teabag of Earl Grey in and out of his mug and carefully eyeing the color of the liquid inside, but now he stopped dead.

"The cross in my bedroom—it's been moving around a lot, turning upside down, then going back in place. But this was the first time it actually pulled itself off the wall."

Audrey held back a shiver, because of course she'd been there to see the whole thing. However, since she and Michael were trying to be discreet, she thought it better not to mention what the two of them had been doing the moment when the cross launched itself across the room.

"Bloody hell," Colin said. "What did you do?"

"Well, Audrey and I were talking when it happened, so I grabbed one of the pillows from the bed and used it to shield the two of us. After the cross got stuck in the pillow, I doused it with holy water, and that seemed to calm it down." Now that he'd related the story, he picked up his coffee and drank some. With a shrug, he added, "There haven't been any occurrences after that one, though."

"It sounds like that should be plenty," Daniela remarked. "I would have run screaming into the night."

"Well, as demon attacks go, I've suffered worse."

Now Colin looked almost annoyed. "If you'd only let me put a motion-activated camera in your bedroom—"

Michael sent him a glance that managed to be both disbelieving and annoyed. "Sorry, I had to draw the line somewhere. The world doesn't need to see me walking around in my underwear."

Privately, Audrey thought the show's ratings could only improve with the addition of a few shots of Michael in just a pair of boxer briefs, but she kept that opinion to herself. Thank God he'd managed to dissuade Colin from having those damn cameras *everywhere*—they were all entitled to a little bit of privacy, after all.

Colin didn't seem inclined to respond to Michael's remark, and instead made a sound halfway between a snort and a growl before stepping over to the trash can in the corner so he could dispose of his used teabag.

"Anyway," Michael went on, now that it seemed as though their producer wasn't going to force the issue, "like I said yesterday, Audrey and I should smudge the place, try to see if that will draw out the demons. They're obviously still here, but they're engaging in classic demon infestation behavior by attacking, then backing off. Their whole game is to put us as off balance as possible, so we need to make sure we all stay on our toes."

"I'll be on my toes," Colin grumbled. "But I'll be happier about it if they give me something filmable. Your little blob of light in the shed yesterday was decent, but I'm not sure if that was spectacular enough for the viewers at home."

Would anything be? To the jaded types who would call everything some kind of CGI trick, maybe not. But everyone here knew what they were seeing was real.

"Well, here's hoping they fling some more crosses at my head," Michael remarked, his tone now noticeably caustic. "I won't try to block them this time—I'm sure your audience would get off on some blood and mayhem, wouldn't they?"

Colin didn't rise to the bait. "It would make for a good episode, that's for sure."

Luckily, Jackie and Edgar reappeared then, she with a large casserole dish of strata, and Edgar with a plate of bacon in one hand and a bowl of freshly cut fruit in the other. The sight of the food apparently was enough for everyone to agree to a temporary ceasefire, because Colin sat down next to Daniela, and for a minute or two, all was quiet as the food was dished up.

After he'd set down the bowl of fruit, however, Michael looked up at Jackie and Edgar and said, "After breakfast, we're going to smudge the house.

We figure that's a good way to force the demons out."

"'Smudge'?" Jackie repeated, looking dubious. "Is it going to leave marks on my walls?"

"No," Michael said. "There'll be a scent of burning sage, but I promise, it won't hurt anything, and the odor will disappear after an hour or two. We just figured it would be a good way to provoke the demons into appearing?"

Edgar spoke then. He seemed vaguely alarmed. "Is that really necessary?"

"It's the best way to draw out the demons," Michael replied. "These ones are kind of cagey. I think they like it here and don't want to run the risk of coming across someone who can dispel them."

That response got a rueful shake of the head. "Should I be honored?" Edgar asked.

"Probably not." After breaking a piece of bacon in two, Michael said, "Did you have any luck checking your records around the time you found the Ouija board?"

Jackie volunteered that information, saying, "We weren't very busy in late August—peak season around here starts in October. But we had at least fifty-percent occupancy for most of the month, so it's going to be hard to know for sure who might have left the Ouija board here."

"I think it was those damn kids," Edgar said,

sounding so grumpy, he might as well have been a character in an old Scooby Doo cartoon.

"What kids?" Audrey asked. They must have done something to make Edgar respond so negatively. Up until that moment, she'd thought he seemed fairly even-tempered, especially when you considered that he'd been dealing with demonic disturbances for the past six months.

"A group of college kids from California," Jackie said. "I think they were from San Diego, someplace like that."

Well, that made some sense. Even up in the San Gabriel Valley that was her home, Audrey had heard what a party school San Diego State was supposed to be. If a bunch of students from that school had descended on the Thunderbird B&B, she could see why they might have left a trail of destruction in their wake. Why they would choose a sleepy bed-and-breakfast like this one and not a bigger hotel where their antics might be overlooked, she didn't know. However, her question was answered in the next moment.

"I think it was partly my fault," Jackie said. "I was trying to bring in more business during the summer, which is always slow for us. So I did one of those Groupon things. That's how they found us."

"There were six of them," Edgar put in. "They were here for three nights, and we were definitely glad to see the last of them. Drinking every night—"

"Smoking pot, too." Now Jackie looked almost as annoyed as her husband. "It took days to get the smell out of those rooms, and we had to replace all the bedding. That may be legal in California, but it isn't here—"

"And all our rooms are nonsmoking, so it's not like they didn't know they weren't doing anything wrong," Edgar said. "They left all kinds of trash behind, and I suppose they could've dumped the Ouija board out back when we weren't looking. They seem like the most likely suspects, anyway."

Audrey was inclined to agree. She'd attended a few wild parties in college, but they'd all taken place in student housing, not in someone's carefully maintained historic bed-and-breakfast. Even at her most disaffected, she would never have taken those kinds of liberties with someone else's property. Glancing over at Michael, she said, "Do you think there was any kind of malicious intent in their leaving the Ouija board here?"

He was eating the second half of the piece of bacon he'd broken in two. After he was done chewing, he replied, "I suppose there could have been, but I don't think so. It sounds as if they were just being careless. They probably thought it would be funny to get high and play with the thing. Maybe they got some answers that spooked them, and they dumped it rather than take it back with them to California."

This explanation seemed plausible enough. She was still learning to read Michael's expressions, but now he seemed almost disappointed, as if he'd hoped the abandoned Ouija board might point them to some sort of larger conspiracy. Instead, they'd gotten a group of hard-partying college kids who probably hadn't wasted a second thought on what might happen if they left something so dangerous behind.

"So, dead end," Colin announced cheerfully. He'd seemed halfway bored with the conversation, and probably had been framing shots in his mind and hoping for something really spectacular from the demons instead. "Finish eating, everyone—we need to get to work."

Both Jackie and Edgar appeared a little startled by his cavalier attitude, but Audrey knew it was just Colin being Colin. Since she'd been steadily making her way through a large slice of Jackie's excellent strata while everyone was talking, she was almost done with her breakfast anyway. After spearing the last sliced strawberry from her plate and eating it, she put down her fork and said, "I'll just go and brush my teeth. Daniela, will you come by when you're ready?"

"Sure." There was still a large chunk of strata on her plate, along with a healthy pile of fruit, but she looked resigned to not being able to eat it all. "I'll be there in a few minutes."

Audrey gave her an encouraging smile and then headed out, glad of the warm sunshine and the bright blue sky overhead. It was hard to believe that demons and ghosts inhabited this property, what with the quiet splash of the fountain in the courtyard and the brightly blooming geraniums and pansies and petunias.

A whisper of movement caught her attention, and she looked over at the guest house where she'd been staying. There, next to one of the stucco-coated pillars, was the woman Michael had described seeing earlier that morning. Yes, she was very pretty, with her shining black hair and warm-toned skin, which contrasted nicely with the lacy white gown she wore.

Her expression was strained, however, and she pointed upward with one hand, indicating the rough-beamed ceiling of the covered walkway. Audrey followed the movement and then sucked in a breath as she realized what was sitting on the roof there.

She might have even noticed it as she walked over here and dismissed it, thinking the small, grotesque shape was only a statue of a gargoyle. The garden had several statues scattered here and there, although they were the sort of thing you'd expect to see in such a place—a graceful girl with a watering can, a gnome peeking out from underneath some elephant's ears.

This wasn't a girl or a gnome, however. It wasn't even a gargoyle.

No, as her eyes met its red ones, she realized she was staring up at a demon.

Chapter 12

THE DEMON WAS MUCH SMALLER THAN THE
terrifying, shadowy beings Audrey and Michael
had battled in the basement of the Whitcomb
mansion in Glendora. Crouched up there on one
of the beams that supported the adobe structure's
roof, it really did look like a gargoyle—not quite
three feet tall, with black scaly skin and bat-like
wings that beat slowly against the warm air.

As their eyes met, its mouth opened in a wide
grimace of a smile, revealing several rows of
yellowish, pointed teeth. Before Audrey could
even begin to react, it launched itself from its
perch and dived directly at her, small hands with
their curved black talons reaching out toward her
face.

A scream escaped her lips, and she flung
herself to the ground, thinking in her panic that

maybe a quick tuck and roll might send her out of range of the creature's claws. But even as she smashed into the concrete walkway, something wickedly sharp slashed across her shoulders, shredding the cotton shirt she wore.

From somewhere behind her, she heard a confusion of shouts, of running feet. And then there was Michael's voice, crying out, "You will not touch her!"

Something wet splashed against her cheek, and Audrey realized he must have deployed one of his bottles of holy water, since the miniature demon let out an ungodly screech. As she pushed herself back up to her feet, she saw it zoom across the courtyard and then disappear into thin air.

At once Michael was at her side, his hand on her arm. "Are you all right?"

"I'm okay," she gasped, then pulled in a breath to steady herself. "But that thing scratched me."

He touched the shoulder of her torn shirt, pulling the torn edges away so he could get a better look at her wound. "We'll need to get that cleaned up at once."

Then Edgar was next to her, saying, "We have a first aid kit in the kitchen. Let's go back to the breakfast room, okay?" He seemed more concerned than shocked, which made her think he hadn't seen the actual attack, only the aftermath.

Somehow, Audrey was able to nod. With Michael steadying her, she managed to stumble back to the room where they'd all been sitting just a few minutes earlier. The cuts along her shoulder felt like they were on fire and throbbed with each step. Dimly, she realized that Colin and Daniela were tagging along as well, Colin with his phone out for some reason.

Oh, right. He didn't have the big video camera with the Steadicam unit, but he could still get all the action on his iPhone.

Jackie pushed a glass of cold water into her hands. "Drink this. Do you want some aspirin or ibuprofen?"

The ibuprofen would help with any swelling, so she asked for that, and Jackie left the room to fetch the analgesic. In the meantime, Edgar had reappeared with the first aid kit and began to dab at her wounds with some alcohol-soaked pads.

Audrey couldn't help but let out a hiss of pain, because the antiseptic only made the demon's scratches hurt that much more.

"Sorry," Edgar said, "but we need to get these cuts cleaned out."

Gritting her teeth, she nodded in reply. He went back to work while she clutched the glass of water and tried to tell herself that it really didn't hurt as much as she thought it did.

Colin and Daniela were now huddled over his

phone, apparently watching the playback of the video he'd just shot. Maybe he'd decided he didn't need a long, drawn-out sequence showing her wounds getting tended. At any rate, he exclaimed, "Bloody brilliant! I caught almost the whole thing!"

"Colin, that goddamn thing tried to kill her," Michael bit out, sounding as if he was ready to commit mayhem himself.

"Just scratches," Colin scoffed. "Anyway, she's getting patched up. You're all right, aren't you, Audrey?"

"Fuck off," she said distinctly, wishing there was something stronger than water in the glass she held.

Daniela chuckled, then went silent as Colin directed an evil glare in her direction.

A soft touch on Audrey's arm, and Michael said quietly, "Edgar's cleaned out the wounds, but I need to pour some holy water on them…just in case. You understand?"

She nodded. "Is it going to hurt?"

"Probably."

"Do it. Just get it over with."

He gave her arm a gentle squeeze, as if to offer what reassurance he could, then drew a glass vial from his jacket pocket. For a second, he hesitated, probably worried about the pain he was about to cause her. Then he tipped the contents of the vial onto the scratches the demon had carved into her right shoulder.

Oh, God, it was like fire, like acid. The glass of water she was holding slipped out of her hands and fell to the floor, luckily landing on the area rug and not on the Saltillo tile. With both hands, she gripped the edge of the wooden tabletop and felt tears of pain sliding down her cheeks and dripping onto her ruined shirt.

"Audrey." Michael's voice, urgent, next to her ear. "I know it hurts. You have to ride it out. The water is working. It's cleaning out the demon's poison. Just let it do its job, and you'll be okay."

Easy for him to say—he wasn't the one who had trails of glowing coals slashed across his upper back. But because it hurt too much to talk, she only continued to hang on to the table, her teeth gritted, sweat dripping down her brow and mingling with the tears on her cheeks.

At last, the pain began to subside again. She pulled in a breath, then another, and one more after that, and now the searing agony in her shoulder was dulling down to a throb, and then not much more than a twinge. Voice a harsh whisper, she said, "I think it's going to be okay."

Michael nodded at Edgar, and he stepped forward, then began to tape down an antiseptic pad to cover her wounds.

Standing off to one side, Daniela said, her

tone dubious, "Shouldn't we take her to the emergency room or urgent care or something?"

"No," Michael replied at once. "They wouldn't be able to do anything more for her than we did here. The wounds have been cleaned out now, so it's only a matter of giving them time to heal."

Listening to this exchange, Audrey felt oddly disconnected, as though they were talking about someone other than herself. In a way, it helped, because she could more easily be detached about what had just happened. She couldn't remember the last time she'd experienced pain like that, but Michael was right—a hospital couldn't help her. The supernatural first aid he'd just applied to her wounds would do much more to assist in her healing than any emergency room visit might.

She cleared her throat and said, "It's okay—my tetanus booster is up to date."

A pause, and then Edgar and Colin both gave an uneasy chuckle, as though they weren't quite sure what else they should do. Right then, Jackie reappeared with another glass of water and a bottle of generic ibuprofen in her hands. She glanced around, looking curious, but apparently decided it wasn't worth asking what had just occurred. Instead, she handed the water to Audrey, then opened the bottle and tipped a couple of tablets into her palm.

"Here you go," she said, handing the

ibuprofen over. "Is there anything else we can do for you?"

"I think I'm going to be okay," Audrey replied. And really, it wasn't as though they had much of a choice. Obviously, the demons were already on the attack, and the only thing to do now was make sure they got banished to the pit of hell where they belonged. A glance over her shoulder told her that her shirt was now only fit to be used as rags. "I'll need to change before we start filming anything, though."

"You should rest—" Michael began, but she shook her head.

"No. We need to get this over with."

He opened his mouth, clearly about to protest, and Colin overrode him, saying, "That's the spirit! And she's right—the sooner we get this infestation handled and on tape, the sooner we can all go home. Right?"

For a moment, Michael didn't say anything. He only stood there next to Audrey, gazing down at her, obviously trying his best to gauge her mood…and her determination. At last he gave one small nod, as if confirming for himself what she'd already told him. "Okay. Daniela, you help Audrey out of that shirt. Colin, you and I can walk the grounds and see if any more of those things are hiding anywhere."

This prospect didn't seem very appealing to

Edgar and Jackie, both of whom looked shaken and pale. When Edgar spoke, it was in the tones of a man who knew he was in way over his head. "What should Jackie and I do?"

"You haven't had any demonic activity in your part of the property, have you?" Michael asked.

Jackie replied at once, "No. It's always been quiet there. That's part of the reason why we had such a hard time at first—we didn't want to believe anything was wrong here because we'd never witnessed anything for ourselves. But after a month or so of complaints, I finally saw a vase of flowers from the garden rise up into the air and smash on the floor, and I realized people weren't making these things up." She waved a hand, as if trying to dismiss her early skepticism that something was terribly wrong at the Thunderbird B&B. "Anyway, our wing doesn't seem to have been affected."

"Then go there and stay there until either I or Audrey lets you know that it's safe to come out."

Edgar crossed his arms. "I don't feel good about hiding while you do the work."

Michael's expression, which had been downright stern, softened a little. "It's not about 'hiding,' Edgar—it's about letting the experts handle things. There really isn't much you could do. You'll have to trust me on this."

A few seconds passed, and then Edgar gave a

reluctant nod. "All right. As you said, you're the experts. But we'll be here in case you need anything."

"And thanks for that." Michael paused for a moment, surveying everyone else in the room. "All right, people—let's send these demons back to hell."

───────

He didn't like to let Audrey out of his sight, but Michael told himself that she would be fine, that she'd be back at his side as soon as she'd changed her clothes. In the meantime, he and Colin had work to do.

"Where the bloody hell is Susan, anyway?" Colin scowled as he and Michael began their sweep of the property, starting with the covered walkway where the demon had been perched. There was certainly no sign of it now, which didn't necessarily mean anything. "She never showed up for breakfast, but I thought she was just sleeping in. Even if she was asleep, though, that commotion in the courtyard should have brought her running. That scream your girlfriend let out sounded like an air raid siren going off."

"She's not my girlfriend," Michael said absently. Most of his energy was being directed toward feeling the air around him, trying to see if he could get any sense of a demonic presence here. Even so, he'd retained enough presence of mind to try to deny there was anything going on between him and Audrey. Of course, there was, but Colin didn't need to know that. Especially not now.

"If you say so. But we should go check on Susan. I need her working, not getting her beauty sleep."

"I'd just keep filming with your cell phone camera," Michael suggested. "It'll make this part of the show seem less staged."

"It's not staged," Colin retorted.

"Well, you know that and I know that, but you have to remember how all this will look to the audience at home."

This argument seemed to hit its mark, because although Colin made a grumbling sound, he didn't offer any further protests. And because they had to check out the entire property anyway, Michael figured it couldn't hurt to go to Susan's room first.

At least they didn't have to worry about smudging the place after all, since it was fairly obvious that the demons were already here...and on the attack.

Acutely aware of Colin's iPhone capturing everything—his producer had pulled it back out of his pocket and now held it up in front of his face—Michael headed for the room that Susan and Daniela were supposed to have been sharing and which Susan now occupied alone, thanks to Daniela quite openly shacking up with Colin. They seemed like an improbable pair, but maybe all either one of them was looking for was a good time…and possibly someone to share their bed so they wouldn't be alone at night. Even someone as unabashedly enthusiastic about this project as Colin appeared to be might have experienced a few midnight heebie-jeebies after everything they'd seen so far.

The blinds to Susan's room were still shut, but that didn't necessarily mean anything. Michael hadn't opened his, either, mostly because he'd gotten distracted by the apparition of the young woman just outside his window.

Reaching up with one hand, Michael rapped on the door. "Susan? You in there?"

Dead silence. He glanced over his shoulder at Colin, who made a spinning gesture with the fore-finger of his right hand, clearly urging Michael to provide some verbal context for their future television audience.

"We're checking on Susan now," he said to Colin's cell phone camera. "You all just saw the attack on Audrey—an attack noisy enough to bring us all running to her rescue. She's fine and will be joining me in a moment, but we realized we hadn't heard anything from Susan Loomis, our sound person. That's why we're here at her room…to make sure she's okay." Once again, he knocked on the door. "Susan?"

Then her voice, so faint Michael could barely hear it through the thick pine door. "Don't come in. There's a…a thing standing by the door."

Cold rushed down his spine, but he made himself ask calmly, "A demon?"

"I think so."

Michael glanced over at Colin, who gave him a thumbs up and mouthed, *Brilliant!*

Of course, this would be brilliant to him. He wasn't the one trapped in a room with a demon blocking the door.

There was one vial of holy water left in Michael's jacket pocket. He had a few more back in Audrey's room, but he hadn't realized he would run through them so quickly.

Well, theoretically, one should be enough.

"Stay away from the door, Susan," he said, but left it at that. The last thing he wanted to do was telegraph his intentions to the unholy being guarding the threshold to her room.

"No worries," came the reply, and Michael felt his lips twitch a bit. Trust Susan to remain calm no matter what the situation.

The door was sturdy enough that he didn't know for sure whether or not he'd be able to break in. Besides, Jackie and Edgar Samuels had already dealt with enough—they didn't need to add a ruined door to the tally of damage caused by the demons. No, Michael had something less messy in mind.

He got out his lock picks and bent toward the key hole, Colin's cell phone tracking his every movement. Luckily, the doors here still had old-fashioned locks and not the electronic kind found in most modern hotels. It only took a second or two for him to lift the tumblers out of the way and disengage the lock. He paused to look back at Colin and gave a slow nod, indicating that he was about to go in.

His producer wore a shit-eating grin and gave another thumbs up gesture.

All right. Time to do this.

Michael put away the lock picks, trading them for his remaining vial of holy water. Then he pushed the door inward.

At once, something screeched toward his head, the sharp, thin sound tearing at his ears. He ducked and caught a quick glimpse of Susan flattened against the far wall, while a dark form about the same size as the demon that had attacked Audrey paused in midair, wheeled, and came back toward him.

He'd been waiting for a maneuver like that. Lightning fast, he splashed some of the holy water on the creature, catching it mid-flight. It howled in pain and anger, the light from the open doorway showing how the demon's dark flesh smoked where the water had hit it. However, the blessed liquid didn't seem to be enough to stop the creature, because it came at him again, red eyes blazing with fury, clawed hands outstretched.

Another splash of holy water, and it screamed once more, screamed so loudly that across the room, Susan let out a startled gasp. Sensing he now had the upper hand, Michael intoned,

"*The light of God surrounds me;*
The love of God enfolds me;
The presence of God watches over me;
Wherever I am, God is!"

And with one last screech, the demon flashed out of existence while still in flight. The silence that followed its departure was so intense, Michael's ears rang at the contrast.

Then he looked over at Susan. She was still flattened against the far wall of her room, face pale with shock.

"Did it hurt you?" he asked.

She shook her head. "No. I was just about to come out and meet you all for breakfast when suddenly that thing popped into existence right there above the door. Since my cell phone was on the table"—she pointed to a small round table and set of two chairs by the window—"I couldn't even call for help."

"Well, luckily, we were wondering where you were, so your room was our first stop on a sweep of the property," Michael said. Even as he spoke, though, he wondered why the demon had singled out Susan of everyone in their little group. Because she had been on her own, and they were easier to attack when they were alone or even in small groups?

The thought was enough to get his pulse speeding up from worry. Audrey could handle a lot of things, but if she had been attacked again—

"We need to check on everyone else," he said quickly, not giving Susan a chance to speak. "Let's get out of here and make sure Daniela and Audrey are okay."

Since it was Susan, she didn't argue or waste time with questions. A brief, brisk nod, and she was following Michael out of the room, Colin bringing up the rear, still with his cell phone camera recording everything. Hopefully, it had started out with a full charge this morning.

But they didn't even make it all the way to Audrey's room before they saw her and Daniela approaching, Audrey with her hair brushed and her makeup repaired, and wearing a wine-colored leather jacket. Probably the jacket was too hot for the mild Tucson weather, but then again, the leather would offer some protection against demons that the cotton shirt she'd been wearing earlier wouldn't.

As soon as her eyes met Michael's, Audrey's brows creased with concern. "Is everything okay?"

"It is now," Susan said. "These two just rescued me from a demon that decided to take up residence in my room."

Audrey looked shocked, and Daniela muttered something in Spanish that probably would end up getting bleeped out. "What was it doing?" Audrey asked.

"Blocking the door." Susan ran a hand through her fair hair; for the first time, Michael realized it was falling down loose on her shoulders rather than pulled back into a ponytail the way she usually wore it. Maybe she'd been about to put it up when the demon appeared. "I don't know why."

Often, what went on in a demon's mind was inscrutable at best. Michael addressed the whole group then, saying, "I don't know what its other intentions were, but I think it was trying to keep us split up if possible. Makes sense—there's strength in numbers. So we all need to stay together as we go over the property. Audrey, I'll need to get more holy water. It's in the bag I left in your room."

He spoke matter-of-factly, but from the way Daniela's mouth pursed and Susan sent a quick, speculative glance at the two of them, it was fairly obvious that the two women had immediately picked up the context behind the request. Luckily, he couldn't see much of Colin's expression, since his face was partially blocked by his phone.

Although the bright morning sunlight picked up a flush of color on Audrey's cheeks, she responded without missing a beat. "Sure. I think it's still sitting on the floor by the dresser."

Without saying anything else, she turned back toward her room, with everyone else following. Michael wished he could go up and walk beside her, but he thought it prudent to stay where he was and allow Daniela to stay at Audrey's side.

And I'll be glad when this damn show is over, he thought, *and I don't have to hide anything from anyone.*

Not that they'd been doing all that great a job of hiding anything, when you got right down to it.

As they approached the door to Audrey's room, however, several black figures blotted out the sun for a moment. As Michael looked heavenward, he realized those figures were anything but heavenly.

"There are more of them!" he shouted. "Take cover!"

Unfortunately, his words didn't seem to have much effect. Daniela raised her hands over her head, as if thinking that would help to protect her in some way, and bolted for the dubious cover of the walkway. Susan didn't move at all, while Colin continued to record the scene with his phone.

And there was Audrey at his side, face taut with worry but showing no signs of panic. "Should I try for the water?" she asked.

"No, there's no time," he replied. Even if there had been, he worried this might all have been a trap, that there might be more of the creatures waiting for them inside her room.

And, just as he had said, there was no time. The demons dived for them, claws outstretched. Michael wasn't quite sure how she did it, but suddenly, Audrey had wriggled out of her leather jacket and was using it like a flail, swinging it this way and that. One blow caught a demon across the midsection and sent it tumbling for a good ten seconds before it recovered itself. Another whip of the jacket, and it hit a second demon right between the eyes.

Where she'd learned how to do that, he had no idea. But, resourceful as she was, he knew she wouldn't be able to hold them off for much longer, not with more demons popping into exis-tence to join their fellows. He could use the prayer to hold them back, but they needed a more permanent solution, one that would send the demons packing once and for all.

Then his gaze fell on the garden hose that was coiled neatly in the garden bed off to his right. They might not be able to reach the vials of holy water now trapped inside Audrey's room, but here was a way for him to have an unlimited supply.

Another screech from a demon, and he saw that Susan had picked up the garden gnome statue he'd seen the day before and was wielding it like a club. The statue smashed into a demon's head and shattered the pointy hat the gnome had been wearing, but there was still enough left to make an effective weapon.

No more time to waste, though.

Michael lunged for the hose, grasping it with one hand while he reached for the spigot with the other and turned it on. At once, a steady stream of water flowed out, but it didn't quite have the range he needed. Positioning his fingers over the end of the hose, he flattened the flow of water into an arc that shot out a good ten feet from where he stood. The water splashed Audrey and Susan, both of whom paused in their demon swatting to give him indignant looks.

However, as soon as he began to speak, comprehension dawned on their faces—and terror entered the shrieks of the demons.

"I exorcise thee, creature of water, in the name of God the Father almighty, in the name of Jesus Christ, his Son, our Lord, and in the power of the

Holy Spirit. Put to flight all the power of the enemy, along with his fallen angels, through the power of our Lord Jesus Christ, who shall come to judge the living and the dead and the world by fire!"

The water sluiced through his fingers, newly purified, and where it struck the demons, they smoked like the hellfire they'd come from. Their wings turned to shreds, and one by one, they turned to ash and scattered on the wind, until they were all gone and the courtyard was quiet again.

For a second, no one moved. Then Audrey put a hand to her damp hair and grinned, her gaze meeting Michael's with a warmth that was impossible to ignore.

"Well, that's one way to kick a demon's ass."

Chapter 13

THEY WALKED ALL THE COVERED PORTALS OF the Thunderbird B&B, explored all its rooms. And in every one, Audrey couldn't see or feel a single trace of the demons that had once lurked here. Even so, this time she and Michael performed the smudging ceremony as they went, just to make sure that all evil was driven from the property and that it would be returned to its original light and hospitality.

When they were done, and were taking the smudge stick and its bowl back to her room, she caught a glimpse of the B&B's ghost standing near the fountain in the courtyard. A brisk breeze had sprung up, but neither her hair nor her dress moved. She raised a hand, as if in gratitude—or possibly farewell—and then vanished.

"You saw her?" Michael said in a murmur, and Audrey nodded.

"I did. I think she's at peace again—or as much at peace as any ghost can be. I wonder who she is."

"We could probably figure it out. We'd just need to take some time to research the history of this place."

Maybe so, and yet Audrey thought it might be better to let the spirit remain anonymous. She clearly had no malice in her—in fact, if it hadn't been for her help, the *Project Demon Hunters* crew might have had a more difficult time dispelling the demons who'd decided to infest the property.

A shake of her head, and Audrey replied, "No, that's all right. Frankly, I just want to go home."

Michael reached over and took her free hand, squeezing her fingers gently. "Soon. Less than eight hours from now, we'll be back in Southern California." A brief pause, as if he wasn't quite sure how to phrase the question, and then he said, "But whose home? Yours isn't really safe, is it?"

She'd managed to push all that mess out of her head for a while, but now she realized she still had a lot of unfinished business to manage back in Glendora. "I—I'm not sure. I mean, we closed the portal in Whitcomb's mansion, but he's clearly free to come and go as he pleases, isn't bound to any one place. The last time I was in my house, it looked as though it had been cleaned up, but maybe all that was just an illusion. I haven't had a chance to go back and check."

"We'll look together," he said. "But still…."

Audrey knew what he meant. "I'd rather go to your place first, just to be safe. Then we'll see what's going on at my house. If it still really is trashed, at some point I'm going to have to get started on cleaning it up."

"I know. First things first, though. We'll get back and figure out what to do next. We have a few days, since we don't need to be in Santa Barbara until Monday."

"'Santa Barbara'?" she repeated, a little startled. "I thought that location had fallen through."

"So did I, but I guess Colin worked on them a little more, and now the shoot is back on." Michael smiled down at her, a welcome warmth in those gold-lit gray eyes. "Much better than having to go back to Colorado, isn't it?"

"Definitely," Audrey said, her tone vehement. It would be a long time before she felt it was safe to set foot in Colorado again. Not that anything of what had happened to her was the state's fault, but she still thought it would be better to stay far, far away, just to be safe. After all, she had no idea where the Whitcomb-demon had gone, or where he'd turn up next.

Hopefully, not back in Glendora. But he had no real reason to be there any longer, not with the portal destroyed and his former home now owned by strangers. He had to have gone somewhere else to regroup. With any luck, he'd be sufficiently distracted that he wouldn't bother them until after they were done filming the show.

They went into her room and put away the abalone shell and the smudge stick, both of them carefully wrapped in plastic. Everything else was already packed, and they'd made their farewells to a very grateful Jackie and Edgar Samuels. Susan and Daniela and Colin had left about twenty minutes earlier, all of them clearly eager to get back to home base as well.

Still, Audrey couldn't help feeling a small pang as she got into Michael's rented SUV and they headed toward the freeway. Even though the demons had been vanquished and the property was safe enough now, she couldn't quite rid herself of a nagging feeling, as if they'd left something unfinished.

"What's the matter?" Michael asked as he pointed the Grand Cherokee north on the 10 Freeway. "That was a job well done. And you and Susan were pretty magnificent, fighting those demons. You should've seen the grin on Colin's face as he was getting all that on his phone."

"I'm not really sure," she confessed. "Just that

something feels…off. You're right—the Thunderbird B&B seems as though it will be fine, and I can't really think of what else we might have done, but…."

He lifted his right hand from the steering wheel and laid it on top of hers. Just for a few seconds, but it helped to feel his touch. "You've had a harrowing few days. I'm not surprised that you feel a little off balance."

Audrey nodded, but she still had this niggling sensation inside her, as if her newly awakened spider sense—or whatever you wanted to call it— had picked up on something her conscious mind couldn't quite comprehend. Well, just like a word that evaded memory or a name that didn't immediately surface, there was no use in trying to force the situation. Either she'd figure it out, or she'd realize that she really was just having the heebie-jeebies for no particular reason. Right now, she was still trying to get used to these newfound powers of hers, and it wasn't always easy to tell what was a true psychic twinge and what was just regular garden-variety anxiety.

Leaning her head back against her seat, she said, "That's probably all it is. And it'll be good to have some time off before we have to go up to Santa Barbara. What's the story on that one?"

"Another old house," Michael replied. "It has a long history of paranormal activity—the daughter of the original builder committed suicide there when her parents stopped her from eloping with the son of their head gardener."

"Lovely."

He didn't exactly smile, but she noted a twitch at the corner of his mouth. "In general, happy houses are not the ones that are haunted, or that become infested. Negative energy draws negative energy."

"So we're dealing with another haunting?" Once again, Audrey thought of the spirit who lingered in the Thunderbird B&B. She couldn't have been more than twenty or twenty-one when she died.

"Not exactly. Or rather, the ghosts in Langdon House are well documented, and were disclosed to the current owners when they bought the place. California law." His gaze flickered sideways at her. "But I suppose you already knew that."

"Yes," Audrey said. Not every state had that sort of law on the books, but in California, buyers had to be informed if a property they were interested in had any kind of documented spirit activity. "The ghost clause," her father had once jokingly called it when they were talking about their own hundred-year-old house and its complete lack of any kind of ghosts or spirits. "So what's the story?"

"The house's present owners have been there

for five years. During that time, their daughter has gotten increasingly obsessed with black metal music and the occult. At first, they didn't try to intervene, because they thought she was just going through an exploratory phase, was just being a teenager. But things have gotten worse."

This all sounded far too familiar to Audrey, and not in a way she appreciated. Frowning slightly, she said, "I hope you're not trying to imply that the kind of music she listens to has pushed her over to the 'dark side,' or whatever you want to call it."

"No." His tone was even, and he didn't look away from the road. "I was a punk rock kid during high school, and look at me now."

Audrey's eyebrows lifted. "Seriously? I would never have guessed." Mostly because his over-long hair seemed such a part of him that it was hard to imagine it buzzed short or worn in a mohawk or something.

"Hardcore. My hair was dyed blue for a while. You can imagine how much my parents appreciated that." Now he chuckled a little, although his expression grew sober again soon enough. "Anyway, Kayla's parents made sure to express to Colin and me that they didn't believe the music had anything to do with it. They were more worried about the books she was reading. Sometimes her mother could hear her reading the rituals aloud in her bedroom, which of course is a very dangerous thing to do."

"Like playing with a Ouija board," Audrey said, thinking of the one they'd found in the Thunderbird B&B's storage shed.

"Except even worse. Ariel, Kayla's mother, said she's heard strange noises inside the walls, like something's moving around in there."

"Rats?"

"She called an exterminator. They couldn't find anything. One night, she saw a black form moving down the upstairs hallway, but Kayla was in bed, and her son Aidan was also asleep." Michael's fingers tapped on the steering wheel, as if the movement somehow helped him remember all the details of the case. "Actually, it's been so bad this past week that Ariel's husband Luke has moved out and taken Aidan with him. Kayla wouldn't leave the house, basically threw a hysterical fit when her parents tried to get her to go with them to a hotel. So Ariel and Kayla are there alone. I think that's why Ariel got in touch again —she really didn't want the publicity of being on the show, but now she's willing to do it because she's afraid for her daughter."

Audrey could understand that. Raising children was hard enough. Trying to deal with one who might or might not have called a demon into the house put matters on an entirely different level. "The situation does sound pretty dire. Just please tell me that we don't have to actually stay in the house this time. I don't feel like having to dodge flying crosses when I'm trying to sleep…or do other things."

This time he smiled for real, eyes crinkling at the corners behind the sunglasses he wore. "No, I put my foot down on that one as well. We have rooms at the La Quinta Inn in Santa Barbara—nice and normal and definitely not haunted."

"Well, thank God for that." She was quiet for a moment, watching the early spring desert landscape—surprisingly green here, just north of Tucson—pass by outside the car window. However, her thoughts were far away, with a troubled girl in a California coastal city. "Do you think you'll have to do an exorcism?"

Michael shot her a surprised glance. "I'm surprised a psychologist would suggest something like that."

"I'm not suggesting. I'm asking what you plan to do."

He didn't reply at first, although once again his fingers tapped against the steering wheel, indicating that he wrestled with an inner conundrum. At length he said, "Until I meet her and see how bad the situation is, I'm not going to say yes or no. When I talked to Ariel, I told her that it might be a possibility, just to see whether she would be open to the suggestion. The family isn't religious in any way, so at least Ariel said she would be all right with me handling the duties if it turns out to be necessary."

"Have you ever performed an exorcism?" Audrey asked, genuinely curious. As a psychologist, she knew she should be fundamentally opposed to the practice, and yet there were accounts that seemed to show that an exorcism had worked, even if it had only done so via the placebo effect.

Well, that was what she'd once thought. Now she knew that demons were real, and so exorcisms by extension were a necessary evil. At least they were a rite of last resort, one undertaken only when all other options had been ruled out and it was clear that mental illness wasn't involved.

Michael expelled a breath, then reached for one of the bottles of water that sat in the center console cupholders and took a drink. Then he said, "I assisted with one once. It was…grueling."

"Did it work?"

"It seemed to, yes. The man I worked with—a Unitarian minister—gave me updates on the subject for a year afterward, said he appeared to have made a complete recovery."

This revelation comforted Audrey somewhat. If they had to take such a drastic step, Michael had some experience in the matter and wouldn't be going in completely blind. Spurred on by something he'd said, she asked, "You're a Unitarian minister, too, right?"

"I was ordained in that church, yes, but I don't practice."

Obviously, because instead he was busy giving lectures on the supernatural and chasing down demons. Somehow, that thought seemed uncharitable, and she pushed it away. Good thing he was an ordained minister, or that encounter with the demons at the bed-and-breakfast might have gone very differently. "Was it because of what happened with your brother?"

He didn't bother to ask her what she meant. Voice level, he replied, "If you mean because I realized he'd been possessed by a demon, well… yes. At the risk of sounding corny, I needed to be able to fight on the side of the light. We weren't all that religious a family, either, and the Unitarian church appealed to me for a lot of reasons. Partway through my education, though, I realized I would never be a minister with a congregation. Getting ordained was just part of my toolbox, so to speak."

It seemed that he'd had a goal early on in the process. Audrey knew she couldn't have said that for herself, had bounced from history to English lit in college before she settled on psychology as her major. Why, she really couldn't have said for sure, except that she'd spent so much time seeing shrinks after her parents were murdered, she felt as though she was already pretty familiar with the field. The jump from psychology to parapsychology might have seemed strange to an outsider, but the strange, paranormal events that had occurred in her life told her there was more to this world—or at least the human mind—than met the eye.

He glanced over at her again. "I hope you don't mind getting involved with a minister. Some people have hang-ups about that sort of thing."

"Are we involved?"

A lift of his eyebrows. "You tell me."

For a few seconds, she hesitated, not sure of the best way to respond. "We're doing something. I haven't quite figured out what it is, though. But, either way, let me set your mind at ease—I don't have any problem getting 'involved' with you. It's not like Unitarian ministers have to take a vow of celibacy or anything, right?"

"God no," he replied, so emphatically that they both laughed outright, although Audrey wasn't sure whether she would have been able to explain to an outside observer exactly what she found so funny.

After that, they drove in silence for a while, but it was a friendly sort of quiet, one where they both could take comfort in the other person's company and yet not feel any need to chatter about empty topics. Once again, Audrey could only smile inwardly at how easy she felt around Michael, and how she would never have believed such a thing was possible if someone had suggested it to her a few days earlier.

They reached the outskirts of Phoenix's sprawling suburbs and kept on driving, having agreed that they'd stop someplace less crowded for an early dinner, maybe Quartzsite or Blythe, near the Arizona/California border. And that was exactly what they did, stopping at a hole in the wall called the Bad Boys Café, where they dined on French dips and Reubens and got back on the road, comfortably full, in less than a half hour.

There was still the stretch of California desert to get through, and the sprawl of the Inland Empire as well, but eventually they were back in places Audrey knew, Redlands and San Bernardino, and then Rancho Cucamonga as they jogged north to get on the 210 westbound and close up the short distance that remained until they got to Pasadena.

As they passed Glendora and the Grand Avenue exit, Audrey couldn't quite help but send it a longing glance, knowing they were passing by her home without even pausing. Michael seemed to sense her distress, because he said, "We'll go back there first thing tomorrow."

"I know," she replied automatically. "And it's fine. I told you I wanted to go to your place. It just feels…strange."

He nodded. "I can see why you must feel sort of adrift. But we haven't heard anything from Rosemary, which I assume must be good news. She said she'd be in contact if anything happened in Glendora that felt odd."

Yes, that was good news. Maybe now that the Whitcomb-demon had been flushed out, he wasn't going to bother with Glendora or her house any longer. At least, she could hope for such an outcome, even while she told herself not to get her hopes up too much.

At last they pulled off the freeway at Hill Avenue and headed toward Michael's house. And there it was, lamps glowing behind the blinds at the front of the place.

Audrey cocked an eyebrow at him, and he said briefly, "Timers. My schedule is irregular enough that it's just safer to have some things automated."

That made sense. And also, she was oddly relieved to be coming home to a lighted house. Or maybe there was nothing all that odd about her relief, considering she'd been dodging demons in one form or another for the past few days.

They got out of the car and took their luggage inside, Audrey carrying much more than she would have if Daniela hadn't told her to go ahead and take all her wardrobe items home with her. Between those pieces and the items she'd picked up at Walgreen's, Audrey figured she had enough to keep her going for another three or four days. At that point, she could retrieve some of her things from her house, or go shopping.

But all that was in the future. For now, it was enough to drop her bags at the foot of the staircase next to Michael's things, and to have him pull her into his arms and give her a hearty, satisfying kiss, something she'd been wanting for hours.

"It's nice to be able to do that without worrying about Colin catching us," he said, and Audrey snuggled up against him and released a happy sigh.

"I know. I've been thinking about kissing you since Tempe."

His mouth twitched. "Only there? I've been thinking about it since the moment we pulled out of the driveway at the B&B."

She chuckled. "I guess I have more restraint than you do."

"Hmm." He went into the library, where he got a pair of crystal snifters out of the cupboard, along with a decanter of brandy. "I don't know about you, but I could use some of this."

Although she really wasn't a brandy drinker, that sounded like a great idea. Just a little bit to take the edge off. They'd had such a big meal in

Quartzsite that she wasn't hungry at all, even though that had been almost four hours ago now.

"Sounds great."

She took one of the snifters from him and swirled its contents, the warmth of the amber liquid echoing the golden light given off by the room's Tiffany lamps. While this wasn't her home, she still felt safe here, protected by all the wards Michael had set in place to make sure no demons could ever venture within its walls.

For some reason, they both remained standing. Maybe it was because they'd spent so many hours on the road that the last thing either of them wanted to do was sit back down again.

The brandy was surprisingly good, not nearly as sharp as a brand she'd tried a few years ago, mellow and smooth. She took another sip, and let its heat travel down her throat to warm her insides.

"Better?" Michael asked.

"Yes," she said. "That is, the car trip was fine. But it feels good to be back, even if I know we'll have to hit the road again over the weekend."

"That drive should be a lot easier. Santa Barbara is less than four hours away."

True. But she realized she didn't want to talk about Santa Barbara, or what might be waiting for them there. They should have a few days' peace here—well, as long as Colin left them alone—and

Audrey knew she needed that, needed the chance to take a breath and put everything that had happened in Colorado behind her.

She made a noncommittal sound, and Michael seemed to understand, because he was quiet for a moment, standing next to her as they drank their brandy.

"Do you ever get used it?" she asked abruptly.

He was quiet for a moment, then gave a small lift of his shoulders. "If you mean, does it ever get easy…well, not exactly. Every situation I've encountered has been a little bit different. But also, you need to realize that even for me, this sort of pace isn't usual. Most of the time, I'll investigate six or seven cases in the space of a year. They won't all be crammed together like this. I understand why Colin scheduled it this way, but it can be grueling." Offering her a smile, he added, "And after we're done in Santa Barbara, we'll be halfway there."

Well, that was something. Not that the Santa Barbara case sounded like a cakewalk, but as long as they took it one step at a time, they should be all right.

Hopefully.

She sipped more of her brandy, let it help smooth out some of the tension in her neck and shoulders, allowed herself to take in deep breaths and try her best to relax. When she was done—

and when Michael had swallowed the last sip in his glass as well—he took the empty snifter from her and set it on a side table next to his, and took her by the hand. Bending close, he touched his lips to her cheek, then asked, "How tired are you?"

"Not that tired," she replied, knowing the warmth stirring in her belly had only a little bit to do with the brandy she'd consumed.

His eyes glinted. "I was hoping you would say that."

Their ascent up the stairs was very different this time. While they weren't completely sober, neither were they as stumbling drunk as they'd been the first time they'd done this. Audrey held Michael's hand as they went, and knew very well what was about to come next. Which was fine, because they'd only been delayed because of those interfering demons, something they certainly wouldn't have to worry about here.

The mica-shaded lamp on the bedside table glowed rich amber, giving them just enough light to see what they were doing. She undid the buttons of his shirt, and he slipped off her leather jacket and pulled her T-shirt over her head, tossing it to the floor. Their shoes and jeans were next, and then they were falling to the bed, now only in their underwear, bare skin against bare skin, warm despite the relative coolness of the room.

That didn't matter though, because their mouths were seeking one another, tasting the spicy heat of the brandy they'd just drunk. Michael unhooked her bra, his hands closing over her breasts, and she moaned at his touch, her body craving the release she needed so badly right now.

He seemed to understand, because he removed her bra, then slid his fingers under the elastic of her panties so he could pull those down as well. And he was kissing her, moving from her breast down her stomach, tongue moving slowly over her, languorous yet intense, as she buried her hands in his hair and held on to him as he made love to her with his mouth.

She didn't know how long she floated on those cresting waves of pleasure, but she could feel the climax building in her, taking her away from the pain and the worry and the fear of the past forty-eight hours. And when she did come, and cried out, he held on to her for a moment, pressing his face against her stomach before he shifted, moving so he could enter her, so she could feel him hard and ready inside.

Then they sped up, moving faster as they seemed to realize this was what their bodies needed now—a furious culmination of the need that had been growing in them for more than a day. Michael came first, his groan wrenching through the stillness of the night, but Audrey's climax hit soon afterward, flooding through her as she clung to him and rode it out, knowing this was exactly what she had needed, this affirmation that they were here for each other, no matter what this world—or the next—might fling at them.

He held her close afterward, his hand stroking her hair. Neither one of them spoke; Audrey knew what she held in her heart, but she wasn't sure whether this was the right time to speak the words. It was all new, this closeness they shared, and she didn't want to risk what they had by being too hasty.

So she snuggled closer, and let her eyes close, knowing he would be there in the morning.

He just had to be.

Chapter 14

Yes, this was much better than waking up at the Thunderbird B&B, when his body had ached for her and he'd known he couldn't do anything until the demons were contained somehow. Now they were dispelled, and he was safely home, with the woman he loved asleep at his side.

A strange feeling, knowing that he'd come to love her in the brief time they'd spent together, that even now he wasn't sure what he would do without her. Long ago, he'd resigned himself to a mostly solitary existence, since he knew his vocation was not one that would be appealing to most women. But now, like a miracle, Audrey Barrett was here for him.

Then again, he had to admit that Audrey Barrett was not "most women."

They'd fallen asleep after making love, both of

them probably more exhausted by the drive than either of them wanted to admit. His mouth was a little gummy, but overall, he was aware of a soothing sense of well-being, something he hadn't experienced in a very long time…if ever.

She stirred, stretched, and then smiled up at him. "Good morning."

"Good morning." He bent and placed a soft kiss on her forehead. "Sleep well?"

"I did." Blinking, she sat up, sheet clutched against her bare breasts, and squinted at the clock on the mantel. "Is it really almost eight-thirty?"

"It is, but since we don't have any real plans for the day, does it matter that much?"

A shadow of a frown touched her brow, but then she shrugged. "Well, we do need to go check on my house—"

"Which we will," he assured her. "Let's go downstairs and get some coffee, and then we'll get dressed and go for breakfast. Flappy Jack's again, since we're headed back to Glendora?"

"That sounds great." She slid out from underneath the covers and pulled on her panties, T-shirt, and jeans, but remained barefoot.

Michael also retrieved his underwear, but didn't bother with the clothes that lay discarded on the floor, instead getting some sweatpants and a clean T-shirt from his dresser. Belatedly, he realized that Audrey was getting back into her clothes from the day before because all her luggage was still waiting down at the bottom of the staircase.

Well, they could bring all that up after they'd had their coffee. They made their way downstairs and into the kitchen, where Audrey sent a wary glance toward the window that overlooked the backyard. He lifted an eyebrow, and she gave a not very convincing laugh.

"Just making sure the ghost of Jeffrey Whitcomb isn't hanging around out there. If that really even was his ghost."

"I think it was," Michael said as he slipped a filter into his coffeemaker. "I think he was trying to warn us about his doppelgänger, although at that point, neither of us had actually encountered him—it—yet."

Audrey sat down in one of the kitchen chairs and tilted her head slightly, as if doing her best to decipher what he'd meant by that statement. "His soul is trapped here because the demon's in his body?"

"It's probably more complicated than that. His human body couldn't have survived all these years, even with a demon inhabiting it." After pouring ground coffee into the filter and flipping on the machine, Michael turned back toward her. She was frowning a little, obviously still trying to wrestle with the conundrum of the Whitcomb-demon. "It's more like…after so many years of inhabiting Jeffrey Whitcomb's body, it was easy for the demon to take on that shape permanently. They're not really like us—although demons have what you would call their 'natural' form, for lack of a better word, they can change and shift as needed. It wouldn't require any more effort for this particular entity than it would for you to wear your hair in a different style."

"Well, that's comforting."

She looked so perturbed, he couldn't help going to her so he could bend down and place a kiss on her neck. Her hand reached up to take his, and for a moment they remained like that, fingers twined together, his lips pressed against the smooth flesh of her throat.

"I know it can be disconcerting to realize they can look like humans if they want to, but it does take some energy. Besides, they can't come and go from this world at will. They have to be invited."

"Or have a friend of theirs open a portal," Audrey said darkly.

"Well, that," he acknowledged. "Still, it's not something that happens every day. After all, how much of your life did you live before you were confronted by the reality of demons?"

This question seemed to make her pause, because she sat there quietly for a moment before she gently let go of his hand and he straightened, moving with some reluctance away from her.

"Pretty much all of it, I guess," she replied. "I guess I can see your point. But it's still not a very comfortable feeling to know they're out there."

"No, it's not. I'd like to say it gets easier to deal with as time goes on, but I'm not sure about that."

The coffeemaker beeped, and Michael went over to fetch a pair of mugs and pour coffee for both of them. He remembered that Audrey took a scant teaspoon of sugar in her coffee, and he doctored it before he handed the mug to her.

"Thank you." She wrapped her hands around the mug as though needing its warmth. The kitchen was a comfortable temperature, but he thought he understood why she would still need something to warm her.

"As for Jeffrey Whitcomb's ghost," he went on. "I think he's probably doing his penance for inviting the demons into this world. I'm not sure what it would take to get him to achieve peace and be able to move on."

"Obviously, closing the portal wasn't enough to do it," Audrey remarked. "Or else I wouldn't have met the real Jeffrey on the astral plane." She paused, then shook her head. "It still feels so strange to even say that out loud. And here I was supposed to be the rational one."

"You're completely rational," Michael assured her. "You've just had some…unusual experiences."

A chuckle, and then she sipped some of her coffee. "I guess that's one way to put it. Awful as it sounds, I'm not going to expend too much effort on figuring out how to allow Jeffrey to forgive himself and move on. It's his fault we're in this mess in the first place."

Michael didn't bother to contradict her, because he knew she was mostly correct. If it hadn't been for Whitcomb's desire for material wealth and success—and a certain amount of ruthlessness—he would never have explored the dark paths that led him to invite the demon into him. And without the demon controlling his actions, he would never have opened the portal in the Glendora mansion. Forgiveness might be divine, but it also didn't mean that you had to forget everything a person had done.

"Well, we're slowly cleaning it up," Michael said. "But, just to be sure, after breakfast I want to go to the mansion and make sure it's all still quiet there. I have no reason to think it won't be, but I'm ready to splash some more holy water and put up a few wards if necessary. After we're done at the Whitcomb place, we'll go to your house and check on it, too. Does that sound all right?"

Her mouth pursed slightly, but after a moment, she gave a reluctant nod. Clearly, she had no desire to return to the Whitcomb mansion, even as she understood why it was important to make sure that what they'd done hadn't been only a temporary fix.

"It's fine," she said. "Here's hoping everything will be okay."

Breakfast was good—even on a Wednesday morning, Flappy Jack's was crowded and noisy, but Audrey didn't mind. In fact, the restaurant's relentless ordinariness helped to calm some of the butterflies in her stomach. She honestly didn't know which prospect worried her more—going to the Whitcomb mansion and possibly getting attacked again, or returning to her house, only to find that it really was still trashed, that the demons had only made it look as though it had been cleaned up.

But better to face the worst and get it over with, and try to move on from there, no matter what had happened.

Besides, she was still experiencing some pretty fine afterglow from the sex last night, and that seemed to be helping to smooth out the worst of her anxiety. It wasn't completely gone, because she still had plenty to worry about, but the world didn't seem like quite as terrible a place when she could look across the table and see Michael sitting there, every smile, every glance an affirmation that he was exactly where he wanted to be. This was definitely not a wham-bam, see-you-later kind of situation.

Which she knew in its own way was fraught, although honestly, probably the worst repercussions they would face if they were found out would be Colin either doing his best to exploit their relationship to increase the tension on the show, or possibly teasing them without mercy. Never mind that he and Daniela were clearly an item, at least for the duration of the shoot. That wasn't the same at all.

No, it wasn't. Neither Colin nor Daniela showed any signs of being head over heels, but rather amusing themselves for now without any care for what the future might hold. Audrey knew that she wasn't amusing herself. There wasn't anything funny about falling hard for someone, which seemed to be what had happened to her.

Luckily, Michael seemed to have done his share of falling as well.

If they survived all this—and Audrey still didn't know if they would—then it would be time for the two of them to have a serious discussion about what was going to come next. For now, though, it was enough to be with him, to know that he was looking out for her. Probably she'd be much more worried about her house if she didn't have Michael's place as a fallback. Truth be told, she really had no desire to go home, except to get the things she needed. Otherwise, she was just fine with staying at Michael's house indefinitely, which she knew signaled a sea change in her feelings. Once upon a time, the house her parents had left her had been nearly the most important thing in her life, the only thing that felt truly permanent.

They finished their breakfasts, and Michael paid the check. Then it was time to get in the rented Grand Cherokee—he had it for the duration of the shoot, and so was using it to avoid putting more miles on his already ancient Land Cruiser—and drive over to the Whitcomb mansion.

The day was mild and sunny, with not a cloud in the sky, but Audrey couldn't help imagining a dark cloud hanging over the huge house, even though in reality it was bright and tranquil behind its screen of palm trees. They pulled up into the driveway, which looked odd without all the vehicles of the other crew members crowding it.

As they approached the front door, she said, "I'm surprised you still have a key. Aren't the owners coming back so they can move in?"

Michael didn't look too concerned. "Next week, supposedly. Colin told them they could pick up their keys at the production office, but they said they were going to have a locksmith out to re-key the place, and then they're having a new security system installed. So they don't really care about the keys they gave us."

It seemed sort of paranoid to her to have a state-of-the-art security system put in for a house in sleepy Glendora, but then, Audrey had never had much that was worth stealing. She supposed that people who could afford a multi-million-dollar home would have expensive jewelry and high-end electronics, maybe valuable art as well, although that sort of thing was a lot harder to fence.

About all she could do was say, "Oh," and then follow Michael inside after he opened the door and went in. The interior was dim and gloomy, but only because all the curtains had been pulled shut. And the air felt stale, but again, that was probably just because everything had been closed up tight after they finished the shoot.

Michael stood inside the foyer, eyes shut, hands held palm up in front of him. "I'm not getting anything. What about you?"

Feeling vaguely ridiculous, Audrey did the same, doing her best to quiet her inner voice so she could focus on the building that surrounded her. She breathed in and out, waiting for that jangle of screechy voices to start up again, or to be enveloped in a cold that couldn't be explained, or to smell something that shouldn't be there.

But she experienced none of those phenomena. All she could sense was the house around her, the faint *tick-tock* of a clock in another room, the slightest of creaks as the sun shone down on the structure and the wooden frame expanded a bit.

There was nothing here. Nothing except her and Michael.

Opening her eyes, she shook her head. "I can't feel a damn thing, but then again, it's not as if I really know what I'm doing. Maybe we should have called Rosemary and asked her to meet us here. She's really the expert."

"No, I don't think that's necessary. If there was anything here, you and I should have felt it." He paused, chin up as he tilted his head toward the ceiling. "But let's still do a walk-through, just to be sure."

So they left the foyer and went over the entire house, in rooms she'd never seen before—the secondary bedrooms upstairs, the family room, the library, the exercise room off the kitchen. In every single one of them, Audrey had the same experience—or rather, non-experience, since she couldn't sense a single thing that shouldn't be there.

When they went back downstairs, Michael paused at the door to the basement. "You know we have to check down there."

Despite how placid the house felt, revisiting

the basement was probably the last thing she wanted to do. "I don't see the point," she protested. "I think we've already established that the house is clean."

"Famous last words," he remarked with a glint in his gold-flecked gray eyes. "Haven't you ever seen *Poltergeist?*"

She stuck her tongue out at him. "Smart ass."

And—probably because they were alone—he reached out and pulled her to him, then gave her a hearty kiss. It might have been inappropriate, given their surroundings, but the embrace was very, very welcome. Audrey just wished they were at his house so the kiss could be followed up by something even more delicious.

As it was, she stepped away after a moment, then straightened her jacket, which had gotten a bit askew. "It's like you're daring the demons to do something."

"Or just trying to prove to you that they aren't here."

Before she could say anything else, he'd put his hand on the knob and turned it. The door opened inward with a faint squeak. Audrey wasn't sure what she'd been expecting to happen next— possibly a horde of imp demons like the ones that had attacked her in Tucson to come pouring out —but it was definitely anticlimactic, since nothing happened at all. Michael glanced back at her, eyebrow cocked slightly, and she planted her hands on her hips.

"Fine. But you go first."

"I would never suggest we do otherwise."

He flicked on the light from the switch beside the door, then began to make his descent. Audrey followed immediately behind him, shoulders tensed, waiting for something to pounce. However, all remained quiet, and within a moment or two, they stood at the base of the stairway.

"Wow, what a mess," she remarked.

That was putting it mildly. The floor remained torn up, scraps of the ugly '60s-vintage carpet and the wood flooring underneath pushed off to the sides and corners, the concrete substrate underneath an ugly pinkish-gray hue, most likely the diluted remnants of the paint that had once been used to write the summoning spells on the floor. There were also stains on the wall, some the same unpleasant pink shade, others darker. She didn't want to look at any of them too closely.

Michael didn't look very concerned by any of this. "The owners are going to have everything cleaned up and redone. They were talking about turning the basement into a wine cellar."

"That would work," Audrey said, although she wasn't sure she'd want to drink any wine that had been stored down here. Somehow, she had the feeling that the noxious energy that had dwelled in the basement for so long would manage to seep into the very bottles themselves.

But that could all just be her imagination. As she stood there, letting her newly discovered sense reach out into the space around her, once again she felt nothing at all. The portals were closed, the demons that had come through them banished. There really was nothing left except a mess that was not her responsibility.

She turned toward Michael, shoulders lifting. "Okay. You were right. It's just…a blank space. But can we please get out of here?"

To her relief, he didn't argue, only replied, "Sure. It's not a place where I'd want to hang out, either. I just wanted to make sure that we weren't leading the owners astray by telling them it was okay to move back in."

"I think they're safe." Privately, after what she'd experienced within these walls, she didn't think she could have lived here, would have quietly put the house on the market and then looked for the newest-construction home she could find, but she realized she was probably being a little irrational.

"Good. Let's go."

They climbed the stairs and closed the door behind them, then went outside and locked the front door. Within a few minutes, they were back in the car and headed over to Audrey's house. She clutched her purse in her lap, hoping that her own place would be as blank and decidedly not demon-infested as the Whitcomb mansion…and not sure what she would do if it wasn't.

From the outside, the house looked fine. She'd switched over to a digital *L.A. Times* subscription years ago, so it wasn't as though she had to worry about papers piling up in the driveway. And most of her utility bills were paperless, so a bulging mailbox wasn't an issue, either. The grass looked a little patchy—the timer for the sprinkler system had obviously failed again—but that seemed to be the extent of the damage.

From out here, anyway.

Michael parked in the driveway, and they both got out. Automatically, she reached in her purse to get out her keys—and realized her hand was shaking a little.

He put a hand on her arm. "Do you want me to open it?"

She really should be able to do this. After all, she'd come back here with Rosemary, and it hadn't been a problem. But that was before she realized everything she'd seen could have been an illusion. It had been bad enough to witness the destruction the first time. Going through that all over again….

They're just things, she told herself. *It's just a*

house. The house where she'd grown up, the only home she'd ever really known, but....

"No," she said to Michael. "I'm fine."

And she turned the key.

The smell was worse this time, probably because the house had been closed up for days. All the wreckage was still there—the furniture strewn around, banged-up and torn and completely unusable. Even though Audrey had steeled herself against this moment, still the totality of the destruction took her breath away.

At once, Michael's arm was around her waist, steadying her. "I'm here," he said. "It's going to be okay."

She didn't know whether that was really true or not, but right then, it was enough for him to say the words, to be there to offer her some reassurance. "Sure," she replied, surprised that her tone was so even. "At least I don't feel anything here—whatever did this came and went days ago."

He went still, breathing deeply. How he managed that, when it stank so badly inside, Audrey didn't know, but she supposed he had more experience with this sort of thing than she did. After a long moment, he nodded. "I agree. I can't sense any dark presences here."

Well, that was something at least. She said, "Let's go upstairs and see if there's anything salvageable there."

"Of course."

They had to weave around the pieces of furniture that had been shoved through the spindles of the stairway railing, but eventually they made it to the second floor. Up here, Audrey couldn't see any obvious signs of destruction; the little table in the hallway with its vase of silk flowers was intact, as was the painting that hung above it.

The relief that coursed through her as she went into her bedroom and saw that it, too, was intact made her knees a little weak, but she told herself she didn't have time for that.

"Well, this will make the clean-up easier," she told Michael, who still had a supportive arm around her waist. "It looks like we only have to worry about fixing up the downstairs."

He offered her an encouraging smile. "See? It's not as bad as you thought."

She couldn't quite return the smile, but she did nod as she headed over to the walk-in closet and opened the door.

The clothing inside had been slashed to ribbons. Her shoes and purses had been torn apart, looking as though a wild animal had ripped them open with its claws. Audrey stared at the destruction for a moment, soundlessly cataloguing every ruined jacket, every mutilated purse, each mangled shoe. Only things, true, but ones she'd carefully collected over the past few years, waiting for sales, shopping on eBay, whatever it took to get the best deal possible in order to justify spending the money at all.

She hadn't realized he had moved over next to her, but, very gently, Michael placed his hand on the door and pushed it shut.

"It's okay," he said quietly. "You have the wardrobe from the show for now, and I'll get you anything else you need."

The lump in her throat was too big for her to reply, so she only nodded and went into the bathroom, fully expecting to find her makeup and toiletries strewn all over the place, or possibly floating in the toilet bowl, knowing how the demons delighted in inventive destruction.

However, those terrible creatures either hadn't come in here at all or had decided that it wasn't worth despoiling a tube of toothpaste or a pack of floss, because everything looked untouched, neat and orderly in its various drawers and cupboards.

"Well, that's something," she said at last. "I don't know how I'm going to carry this stuff out of here, though—all of my purses and tote bags are destroyed."

"Do you have any trash bags under the sink?" he asked.

Actually, she did. Audrey crouched down and retrieved one, then began tossing a bunch of random items into it—eye shadow palettes, extra tubes of lipstick, toothpaste, a box of tampons, and so on and so on. Eventually, she had everything she thought she would need, and she wearily straightened back up again.

"I think that should hold me. We can go."

He watched her for a moment, expression concerned. "You don't want to check the other rooms?"

"Not really," she replied. As he began to frown, she added, "What's the point? There's nothing in there I really need. My desktop computer is ancient, and I took my laptop with me when I came back to get my things the last time I was here. Either the stuff in those rooms is destroyed, or it isn't. I can deal with that when I have the insurance people come inspect the place."

"Colin's insurance people," Michael said grimly. "Because we know what did this…and why."

"Good luck explaining that to the adjusters." Right then, she honestly didn't care. She just wanted to get out of there.

He seemed to recognize her mood, because he didn't put up any further arguments, but only said, "Okay. Let's go, then."

They went back downstairs and Audrey locked the door, although she didn't quite know why she bothered. There certainly wasn't anything left worth stealing in her house, that's for sure.

For a few minutes after they got in the rented Jeep, neither of them said anything. It wasn't until they were back on the freeway and headed toward his house that Michael spoke. "I'm very sorry about your house, Audrey. That was a very vindictive set of demons we were dealing with…but they're gone now."

"All except Whitcomb." All right, she knew it wasn't really Whitcomb, was instead a demon wearing his face, but right then she didn't have the energy to call him anything else.

"True, but I'm not sure he was directly involved in that destruction. From what you've said about him, he seems to be a little more subtle than that."

Audrey wasn't sure she wanted to give the demon even that much of the benefit of the doubt. She clutched her one remaining purse where it sat in her lap, and tried to recall how calm her world had been before Michael Covenant entered it, how downright mundane. It was hard to believe that less than two weeks had passed since the day he came into her office.

And yet…despite everything that had happened, she wouldn't want to roll back time to that world before he entered it. As she'd told herself earlier, things could be replaced. But there was only one Michael.

"And they tried to make me think the house was fine because…?"

He sent her a quick sideways glance, then looked back at the road. They were past the morning rush hour, but westbound traffic on the 210 Freeway was still very heavy. "They wanted you there, alone, vulnerable. Possibly only to frighten you enough that you would quit the show, stay away from me, but maybe to hurt you. I won't lie, Audrey. Demons have hurt people, have killed them. Not necessarily in a way that could be ever be connected to them, but if you frighten someone enough that they run from their room in the middle of the night and fall down the stairs and break their neck, you're still responsible. Rosemary was very wise to make sure you didn't stay there, and instead went to stay at a property that was protected."

This revelation made the blood in Audrey's veins suddenly feel more like liquid nitrogen. Yes, she'd known she could have been in danger if she'd been stubborn about the whole thing and had refused Rosemary's offer of hospitality, but hearing Michael state the risks so baldly made her realize how closely she'd flirted with death that night.

Thank God for Rosemary.

Audrey let out a gust of a breath and told herself it was okay, that she wasn't about to take a risk like that again. Probably she'd encounter a new and exciting set of risks, judging by what had happened over the past few weeks, but at least she wouldn't have to face any of them alone.

"So, what now?" she asked.

"We prep for the Santa Barbara trip," he replied. "And I'll do whatever I have to in order to keep you safe. That's a promise."

And Michael Covenant kept his promises.

"Okay," she said. "Onward and upward."

Chapter 15

WHILE IT FELT STRANGE TO KNOW SHE wouldn't be going home any time soon, that she'd have to be camped out at Michael's place for the indefinite future, Audrey was still comforted by the way he tried to make the situation a little less awkward, making sure she knew that the room she'd first stayed in was hers for the duration and that he wasn't expecting her to immediately move into the master bedroom with him. Not that she really would have minded—she had a feeling she'd be sleeping in there with him every night, even if the arrangement wasn't formal—but it was also good to know she had her own space if she needed it.

In the meantime, she and Michael went back to her house once more, just to get pictures and video of all the destruction. He told her that he'd passed copies of everything on to Colin, although he was conspicuously quiet about how their producer had responded to the images and whether he was, in fact, going to contact the insurance company about getting her reimbursed. In the back of her mind, she harbored a sneaking suspicion that Michael had already resolved to pay for the repairs if necessary. How she'd be able to tell him he shouldn't do any such thing, Audrey wasn't sure, but she figured she'd leave that argument for sometime in the future.

Right now, she had to focus on meeting with her clients on Saturday—and taking a small break in the middle of the day to meet Rosemary for lunch. As soon as she heard that her suspicions about Audrey's house had been correct, she managed to somehow look both triumphant and worried.

"I knew it," Rosemary said as she dug into her salad. "I just kept getting the weirdest feeling about it, like what we were seeing wasn't vibing with what I sensed when I was inside the place."

"Well, you were right," Audrey replied. "I'm glad I listened to you. Eventually, I'll get the house straightened out, but that's probably going to have to wait until we're done filming. There's no way I can oversee repairs when I have to be out of town so much."

"Which is why you're shacked up at Michael's house."

Protesting the phrase would have been useless. She could pretend she was only staying in the guest room, but the actual situation was really quite a bit different…and she had a feeling Rosemary knew that just as well as she did.

"Yes, I'm staying with him," Audrey said, her tone studiously neutral. Even so, she thought she could feel her cheeks flush a bit despite herself. What she hadn't expected was how natural it felt to be with Michael, to wake up in his bed, to have coffee in the morning and discuss their plans for the Santa Barbara shoot, to go out to eat, even see a movie. And the way he'd driven her to Glendora so she could see her clients, even though she'd made a half-hearted protest about not wanting to waste his time and that she could have just called an Uber instead. She'd never lived with anyone before, had never allowed herself to get that close to a man. Her longest relationship had lasted about five months, and in all that time, she'd never once allowed the man she was seeing to leave so much as a toothbrush at her place.

In a way, it was almost frightening to think about how connected she and Michael already felt, even though she'd only been staying with him for a few days. It couldn't always be like this, could it? Sooner or later, the other shoe would have to drop.

"Hmm," was all Rosemary said, but it seemed obvious enough that she knew there was a lot more going on than Audrey wanted to admit. But then she lifted her shoulders, as if admitting to herself that it was best to leave all that aside for now, and asked, "So…you're off to Santa Barbara tomorrow?"

"Yes," Audrey replied, glad of the change of subject. Not that a haunted house with a possibly possessed teenage girl living in it was all that reassuring, either, but at least it didn't involve any discussions about her personal life. "You're still sure you don't want to come?"

"Absolutely," Rosemary said, her tone leaving no room for argument. "Possessed people just aren't my thing. And frankly, I've had enough demons to last me a lifetime. I'm surprised you haven't."

Audrey sipped some of her iced tea, then said, "Well, of course I have. But it's not really negotiable, is it? I signed a contract and need to see this thing through."

This comment made Rosemary lift an eyebrow. "You're seriously telling me that lover-boy wouldn't let you out of your contract if you asked?"

Ignoring the "lover-boy" comment, Audrey

responded, "It's not really up to him. The contract is between me and Colin's production company. And Colin was already telling me that walking wasn't an option when we had only one episode shot. Now that two are done, there's no way I'm leaving."

And she really didn't think she would have left the show even if she didn't have Colin's threats hanging over her. She knew she wouldn't walk out on Michael like that. No matter what happened, she was sticking with him.

Rosemary seemed to pick up on some of this —for all she knew, Audrey was "sending" her emotions strongly enough that even someone who wasn't psychic might have received them—and so she gave a fatalistic shrug. "I didn't think you would. But I'm worried…about both of you. So far you've escaped unscathed, but how long will your luck last?"

"I wouldn't call having my house ruined and getting kidnapped by a man who's been dead for a century 'unscathed,'" Audrey pointed out.

"But you're still okay. It's horrible what happened to your house, yes, but no one got hurt. Same with the Whitcomb thing. It's creepy, but you came out the other side just fine."

There wasn't much point in arguing with Rosemary's comment, because she was right. There had been frightening moments, definitely, but Audrey realized she could have been much worse off.

"Well, I'll just have to make sure my luck continues to hold on," she said lightly. "Anyway, I have a feeling Michael is going to do most of the heavy lifting on this next trip. I'll just be there to provide moral support."

"Is he up to it?"

Audrey smiled, although she had a feeling she did so more to reassure herself than to convince Rosemary. "Of course he is."

And time would tell whether she was right.

It was a beautiful day, warmer than average for late February, with a few clouds scooting along, propelled by a brisk sea breeze. Even though the drive would take longer, Michael had decided to follow I-10 all the way to Pacific Coast Highway, then wind along the coast through Santa Monica and Malibu until the highway turned north and intersected with the 101 in Oxnard. Although he probably wouldn't have admitted it to anyone but himself, he realized he was enjoying his rented Grand Cherokee, all the bells and whistles and the smooth ride. He'd had his ancient Land Cruiser since high school—bought with earnings from his part-time job as a bag boy at the local grocery store in his hometown—and had nursed it along for fifteen years now, but maybe it was time to rethink his chosen mode of transportation.

And it was good to have Audrey there in the passenger seat, her big brown eyes taking in the sights as they went. "I haven't been to the beach since high school," she said as they passed Palisades Park. "I'd forgotten how beautiful it is."

"Well, cross your fingers that everything will go smoothly in Santa Barbara," he replied. "We have our hotel rooms for four nights, so maybe we'll have time to stay afterward and visit the beach there."

"That would be nice." A small frown touched her brow as she added, "Unfortunately, these cases don't seem to be all that smooth, if you know what I mean."

Yes, he knew exactly what she meant. Dealing with the demon world meant bracing yourself for the unexpected. However, they'd still gotten the Tucson infestation managed in record time, and had also been ahead of schedule in Glendora. Whether their luck would hold out in Santa Barbara was in fate's hands, however.

"We'll just have to see," he said, not wanting to engage on the topic right now. In fact, he didn't want to think about demons or hauntings or what might lie ahead of them, but only about the woman who rode in the vehicle with him, and the beautiful day outside. He knew it was important to focus on what beauties he could, since so much of what he had to confront in these cases was dark and ugly.

Audrey seemed to realize he didn't want to discuss the case further, and so she returned her gaze to the landscape outside the window. They drove for a while without speaking after that, except for her asking if he wanted any of the grapes they'd packed in a cooler for the drive. Both of them had agreed to wait until they got to Santa Barbara to have lunch, and so they'd brought a few snacks to hold them along the way.

He accepted a cluster of grapes from her, then held them loosely in his left hand while at the same time maintaining his grip on the steering wheel. By that point, they were well past Malibu and nearing the outskirts of Oxnard, and the traffic had lessened a bit. Still, enough cars shared the road with him that he had to pay attention to what he was doing. In a way, that was good, because Audrey was quiet as they ate grapes and made their way to the connection with the 101 Freeway.

It wasn't that he didn't enjoy talking with her, but more that he wanted to let himself be as relaxed, as free-floating, as possible by the time he got to Santa Barbara. During the past few days, he'd realized that he wanted Audrey to stay with him, that he didn't want her to return to her house, even though that day by necessity had to be some time off in the future. Any rational person would have realized this was far too early in the game to even be thinking about moving in together, but there he was.

Did she feel the same way?

Did he dare even ask?

Better not to say anything at all.

They passed through Carpinteria and then on to Santa Barbara proper, making their way up State Street to their hotel. Its exterior was very mid-century, like something out of a 1960s sitcom, but the rooms were sleek and modern, very different from the house they would be visiting the next day.

Since it was only one-thirty in the afternoon, their rooms weren't ready yet, but that wasn't a problem; only a few blocks away there was a Mexican restaurant with a beautiful patio that was still serving brunch, and Michael and Audrey were given a table outside near a brightly painted fountain, where they could see a beautiful Spanish-style theater with a cupola across the street. A cool ocean breeze flowed around them, but Audrey had brought a sweater and he wore his ubiquitous jacket, so they were both quite comfortable.

They'd walked, and technically wouldn't be "on duty" until the next morning, when they were scheduled to meet with Ariel Vargas and her daughter, so Michael figured it was safe to order a margarita. Audrey's brown eyes laughed at him from across the table, but he noticed that she also asked for a drink, margarita on the rocks with a shot of Cuervo on the side.

"Feeling adventurous?" he asked as the waiter departed to fetch their drinks.

"I guess so." She leaned back in her chair and shut her eyes for a moment. The breeze caught at a few strands of her long brown hair, playing with the ends.

God, she was beautiful.

After releasing a deep breath, Audrey opened her eyes and looked at him. She wasn't smiling, not exactly, but something about her regard still made him feel warm inside. "I suppose I'm feeling like this is the calm before the storm. I might as well let myself enjoy it."

"True," he said, halfway wishing he'd ordered a shot of tequila as well. But he could always ask the waiter for one when he ordered his second drink. Michael had a feeling they probably wouldn't stop at just the one.

However, they'd need to be a little careful. He really didn't know when Colin and Daniela and Susan were supposed to show up at the hotel, but they'd be arriving at some point, and he recalled that Colin had requested their rooms be adjacent if possible. To make coordinating their comings and goings a bit simpler, was the explanation. Anyway, Michael guessed that too much tequila might lead to him spending the afternoon in Audrey's room, or vice versa, and it would be a little awkward if any of the other people on the crew spotted them coming out of the door to said room at exactly the wrong time.

Besides, he couldn't exactly say he was feeling deprived, since he and Audrey had slept together every night since she'd come to stay at his house. It was more that, every time he looked at her, he wanted to experience her all over again.

The waiter came back with their drinks, and they ordered their meal—huevos rancheros for him, a breakfast burrito for her. A moment or two passed as they sipped at their margaritas and breathed in the fresh sea air.

"It's beautiful here," Audrey said.

"You've never been to Santa Barbara?"

"No. I mean, I think we passed through once on a road trip up to San Francisco, but we didn't stop because we had lunch in Ventura or Oxnard. I was only eight, so I don't remember exactly."

"Well, then, I'm glad this was our destination, rather than Colorado."

Her nose wrinkled a bit, an expression so adorable, he wanted to lean across the table and kiss her. Fingers fidgeting with the straw in her margarita, she said, "No, I think it's going to be a long time before I'm comfortable going back there. Maybe in the summer, when there's no chance of snow."

Or demons seemed to ring in the air between them, but luckily, she hadn't said the words out loud. Michael had to force himself to remember that they were here on a dark and dangerous task, and that Santa Barbara, just like every other town, had its own secrets and sinister undercurrents. It would be much better to pretend they were here only as tourists and nothing more, but that was certainly not the case.

"I've only been there in the autumn, which is spectacular," he said.

"Except for your recent rescue mission," Audrey reminded him.

"Well, that. But since I was there for a grand total of about four hours, I'm not sure I can really count that visit."

Her expression darkened for a moment, and she leaned forward to pick up her margarita. "I wish I didn't have to."

Yes, so did he. While no one could have foreseen what had happened at the Tucson airport—or afterward—Michael still couldn't quite forgive himself for letting her be taken like that. He should have put aside his worry that she would rebuff him on sight after their quarrel and gone to pick her up himself. Then none of that would ever have happened.

But you also might not know everything you know now, he thought, and he had to admit, with some reluctance, that this particular insight was nothing more than the truth. Harrowing as that experience had been, if Audrey hadn't been kidnapped by the Whitcomb-demon, they would have even less information to work with than they currently did.

"It's over," he said gently. "Nothing like that is going to happen again."

Now her lips curved in a smile, and she reached for the shot of Cuervo and poured it over her drink. "No, probably not," she agreed. "Since you've barely let me out of your sight since then."

"You say that like it's a bad thing."

His remark made her chuckle. She swallowed a mouthful of Cuervo-laced margarita and said, "No, it's not a bad thing at all. Quite the contrary. I'm just pointing out that we've been kind of joined at the hip the past few days. Whitcomb would have to be pretty clever to pry us apart."

"I honestly don't think we need to worry about him," Michael told her, although he couldn't really say what prompted him to make that particular statement.

"You sound pretty sure of yourself." Audrey lowered her glass and sent him a speculative look.

"Have you heard from your friend Fred? The one who was supposed to be checking on Whitcomb's properties?"

"Not really. That is, he sent me an email yesterday saying he was still working on it but really didn't have anything concrete yet." Which was about what Michael had expected. He guessed that Whitcomb probably owned a number of properties, but it wouldn't be his name on any of those deeds. Trying to follow all those tenuous threads and unravel them would take time. Very likely, discovering exactly what that demon in human form had been up to all these years would be a project to be tackled later, after the more immediate logistics of *Project Demon Hunters* had been handled.

"Just as well, probably," Audrey remarked. "I'm not sure all that is really within the purview of the show."

Just about what Michael had been thinking, and once again he had to marvel at how often their thoughts seemed to run along the same lines, especially when you considered that their first meeting hadn't exactly been cordial.

"No, we have other things to focus on right now," he agreed.

Once again, her expression darkened, but she perked up as the waiter came back with their food and set it before them. For a time, they were quiet, concentrating on their meal—it had been almost six hours since they'd last eaten—and he was okay with that. He could tell Audrey didn't want to discuss any of the particulars of the case that awaited them here, probably she wanted to enjoy this time in the sunshine while she could, and also because there were still a few other diners out here enjoying a late brunch as well. Luckily, everything the two of them had discussed had been broached in fairly vague terms, with no real mention of demons, but it never hurt to be careful.

That first set of margaritas segued into another as brunch stretched out well past two o'clock. Eventually, though, they finished their meal and wandered along State Street in a pleasant tequila buzz, looking in shop windows, enjoying the air. At last it was time to check in; as Michael got the electronic keys for both their rooms, he glanced around the lobby but didn't see any sign of Daniela or Colin or Susan.

"Have the other members of my group shown up yet?" he asked the front desk clerk, an attractive Hispanic woman probably a few years older than he.

"Yes, about twenty minutes ago," she responded. "Their rooms were ready early, so they're already all taken care of."

"Thank you." Michael gave Audrey a significant gaze, and she replied with the slightest of nods. Good thing they'd stopped after that second margarita…and good thing they'd decided to wander State Street as they worked off their buzz. This way, everything looked above board, more or less.

They took the elevator up to the second floor and got off, bringing with them the luggage they'd left in the back of the Grand Cherokee. An older woman wearing a loose caftan over her bathing suit wandered past them and into the elevator, but she was the only sign of life on the floor.

Luck stayed with them, because Michael was able to go with Audrey into her room and give her a quick kiss, then head next door to deposit his suitcase in his own room. He sent a quick text to Colin—*Audrey and I are here and checked in*—and waited for the reply. It came back faster than he'd expected.

Good. We can all amuse ourselves tonight, and then we'll meet at the Vargas house at 10 a.m. tomorrow. You have the address?

Yes.

See you there.

And that was it. He had the evening free to do as he pleased, which he assumed would include taking Audrey out for dinner at some point.

But that's all, he told himself. *You need to be sharp for the filming tomorrow.*

That was all the admonishment he needed. He and Audrey had already determined to be circumspect, and he would stick to that plan. Besides, if it turned out that Kayla Vargas really did need an exorcism, then he couldn't be expending his energy on the physical, would have to make sure he was as mentally and spiritually agile as possible, especially since he knew he would have to do this alone. True, Audrey would be there for moral support, but the burden of carrying out the ritual would fall on him. And while he had assisted in an exorcism before, this would be his first time flying solo, so to speak.

He could only hope he would be up to the task.

Chapter 16

Ariel Vargas was a very pretty woman in her early forties, and her sixteen-year-old daughter Kayla showed echoes of that prettiness as well, in her big brown eyes and sculpted little cupid's bow of a mouth. However, both of them looked as though something had been slowly draining their lifeblood and energy away, eyes smudged with dark circles, faces pale.

Audrey and Michael sat opposite mother and daughter at the big oak table in the dining room of the Vargas house, surrounded by antiques that matched the Italianate splendor of the large Victorian home. While not as big as the Whitcomb mansion, in many ways it felt far more gracious, possibly because it was obvious that Ariel and her husband—who was conspicuously absent from this meeting—had put a great deal of care into making sure their home retained its original character, while at the same time doing their best to keep it from feeling like a museum.

"We had another bad night, I'm afraid," Ariel said.

Colin was off to one side, back using his expensive video camera rather than the makeshift of his iPhone, and Susan stood next to him, boom mike angled toward the table. Even though she really didn't need to be there, Daniela stood on Colin's other side, taking longhand notes on some paper held down on a clipboard. She did make the whole setup seem more professional, so Audrey supposed there was some point to her presence.

Thin fingers with bitten-looking nails played with the handle of her coffee mug as Ariel went on, "The knocking just goes on for hours and hours. And then there's the moaning—"

Kayla broke in abruptly, saying, "Mom, I don't feel well. Can I go upstairs and lie down?"

Her mother hesitated, looking over at Michael. He said, his tone very gentle, "Kayla, I'd really like to hear from you before you go and rest. Can you give us just five minutes?"

Watching him, Audrey had to be impressed by his patience, the way his eyes met the girl's in a friendly, yet concerned manner. There was something about him that seemed eminently trustworthy, and she wondered whether the Vargas women had been told that he was a minister.

Kayla's fingers clenched on the edge of the tabletop, but then she shrugged. "Okay."

"Do you hear the same things your mother does?" Michael asked.

Another lift of her thin shoulders. Her hair had been bleached and then dyed a sort of magenta purple, but it had clearly been growing out for some time, since it showed about two inches of dark roots. "I hear the knocking sometimes. And then kind of a howling, like a dog that's been left outside too long and is crying to be let in. But there's no dog—our dog Missy died last year."

Audrey wondered whether the dog's death had anything to do with the demonic infestation. It wasn't the sort of question she thought prudent to ask, however, and so she remained silent.

Michael's eyes had narrowed for just a moment, though, which meant more or less the same thought had probably crossed his mind as well. His voice was still mild as he said, "But you don't hear the moaning?"

"No." Now Kayla looked almost petulant, as if she was being accused of something she knew she hadn't done. "My mother thought I was up there having sex with someone, but that's just stupid.

My boyfriend and I broke up two months ago and I haven't been with anyone else."

"Well, what was I supposed to think?" Ariel said. "You can hear it all over the house when it starts up. Then I thought maybe she was watching porn somehow, even though we locked down her laptop after we discovered she'd been looking up all those rituals online, ordering all sorts of crazy books through our Amazon account."

As soon as these words left her mother's mouth, Kayla's face twisted in anger, distorting so terribly that Audrey had to force herself not to recoil. It was as though something inhuman was trying to tear its way out of her, forcing skin and muscles to perform incredibly unnatural contortions, turning them alien.

Daniela gasped, but Susan's boom mike never wavered, and Colin kept filming.

Probably just glad he was able to get that on tape, Audrey thought, and the mundane observation helped to calm a little of the fear that had flared in her heart.

Or maybe it was only the sight of Michael, who still looked at Kayla with that concerned but friendly expression on his face and hadn't even blinked, that helped Audrey to steady herself. Somehow, as long as he didn't seem worried, she couldn't be all that worried, either.

"That fucking bitch shouldn't have touched

my stuff," Kayla said, although that didn't sound like her voice, either, guttural and rasping and nearly an octave lower than her regular intonation.

"It's hard when someone messes with your things, I know," Michael told her without missing a beat. "What happened to your books?"

No reply, except the table began to rattle. Looking more weary than afraid, Ariel lifted her coffee mug before it tipped over, and Audrey did the same with both her water glass and the one that sat in front of Michael. He didn't move, however, but only sat there calmly, fingers steepled in front of him, his whole aspect rather like that of Mr. Spock from *Star Trek,* even though he didn't resemble the character at all.

"Did your mother throw them away?"

Now the shaking spread throughout the room, making the chandelier above them dance and the china in the cabinet rattle so much that Audrey feared it might shatter into pieces at any second. Even though Kayla's mouth was clamped shut in anger, a low growling emerged from her throat, guttural, something that sounded like no human being should have been able to produce it.

Audrey forced herself to sit still, trusting that Michael knew what he was doing. It was one of the hardest things she'd done yet, because fight-or-flight hormones surged in her blood, telling her that she needed to get the hell out of there.

"Ah," he said at last. Only that one syllable, and yet it seemed to be enough to break the tension. The growling abruptly stopped, and Kayla stared at him in confusion for a moment, as if she couldn't quite recall who he was or what he was doing there.

Then she turned and fled the room. The pounding of her feet on the stairs sounded very heavy for someone so light and thin.

For a long moment, no one spoke. Audrey was acutely aware of the red light on Colin's camera, telling her that he was still filming, that he wasn't about to miss a single moment of any of this.

At last, Michael turned toward Ariel Vargas. "I think I need to see upstairs now."

———

He didn't quite know why he was prolonging this. The scene in the dining room had already told him that Kayla was clearly possessed. The growling, the way a face that didn't seem to be quite hers had emerged from her thin features, the way she'd made the room shake—they were all classic signs of a demonic infestation that had moved on to possession.

However, he'd also seen the fear in her mother's face, the worry that he was about to tell her possibly the worst news she would ever hear. It couldn't hurt to walk around the house a bit more, get a feel for what he would have to do here. Even if he told Ariel on the spot that he would have to perform an exorcism, it wasn't as though he could turn around and do it right then. He was working on his own and not formally sanctioned by any church, but there were still rituals he needed to follow to prepare for the ordeal. The soonest he could possibly do anything would be the following morning, and even that might be pushing things.

He went upstairs, Ariel immediately behind him, Audrey and the others bringing up the rear. Michael knew he couldn't allow himself to think about Audrey too much, because he couldn't allow any thoughts but those focused on Kayla and the current situation to occupy his mind. Audrey had already proven that she could handle herself in a crisis situation, and so he had to trust she would do the same here.

The house was truly magnificent, with its high stained-glass windows and dark moldings and reproduction wallpaper. A William Morris design, he thought, slate gray picked out with gold and crimson, but beneath the surface beauty of the place, he could feel the pulsing heart of something dark and evil, something that wanted to bring pain and suffering and destruction to this house. Even though she might not consciously be able to sense these things, they clearly weighed on Ariel; her footsteps seemed to drag the closer they got to the upstairs hall, as if some unseen force was doing its best to keep her away.

Michael sensed it as well but kept going. It was too late to back out now, and even if he could, he wouldn't do that to the woman whose daughter had been overcome by a force older than the world. Who else could she turn to? The Catholic church was reluctant to help even its own parishioners in these sorts of cases, let alone someone who was at least agnostic if not an outright atheist.

Well, that was something she'd have to work through on her own eventually. People caught up in demonic struggles like this rarely remained atheists.

The door to one of the rooms on this floor was shut. He looked over at Ariel, and she nodded.

"Yes, that's Kayla's. Maybe I shouldn't let her shut the door, but the sounds were so awful when I tried to keep it open—I stuck a chair under the knob a few days ago, and I didn't sleep at all that night, what with all the banging and the howling and moaning."

"And your husband?" Michael asked, his tone

very quiet, although he knew the boom mike probably picked up the question anyway. He knew something of the particulars, and understood why Luke Vargas would have taken his son with him and gotten the hell out of here, but one would have thought he might have at least attempted to take turns watching Kayla so his wife wouldn't be trapped here day in and day out.

Ariel made a sound of disgust. "He says he's keeping Aidan safe. Which, I get it, but Aidan's in school most of the day. Luke could come back here and help me out, since he can do his job from home, but—" Tears glittered in her eyes, and Michael saw how she swallowed to keep herself from breaking down completely. "Kayla's not his, you know. She was two when we got married, and he's always said he thought of her as his own, but I guess when push comes to shove, it's a whole different story. Anyway, forget about getting any kind of help from him."

"I'm sorry," Michael said, knowing how inadequate those words must have sounded. This kind of ordeal was difficult enough to manage with someone by your side. Having to do it alone —"We're here," he went on. "I won't leave until your daughter is well again."

She managed a tremulous smile. "Thank you, Mr. Covenant. And now"—her thin shoulders squared, as if she was steeling herself against what was coming next—"now we'd better go inside."

Her hand turned the knob, and the door opened.

Even though he had some idea of what to expect, Michael couldn't help recoiling at the stench that boiled out into the hallway. Trash left rotting in the sun for days, feces, vomit—it was as though they had all been thrown together in some sort of infernal cauldron and brought to a boil. Behind him, he could hear Audrey and Colin and Daniela gagging and coughing, but he couldn't worry about them right now. There was a bathroom down the hall; they could go in there and throw up if they needed to.

As bad as the smell was, though, what he saw in that room was worse. Runes and sigils had been scratched into the lovely molding and expensive wallpaper, and others had been painted on top of them in what he thought was probably fingernail polish, dark shades of maroon and gray and black. The air here was icy cold, at least thirty degrees colder than it had been in the rest of the house, and he saw his breath billowing white in front of him. Unfortunately, the cloud of his breath wasn't quite thick enough to obscure the sight of Kayla writhing on the bed.

Her eyes had rolled back in their sockets, showing only white, and fresh scratches had appeared on her forearms and cheeks. Worse, though, was the way her T-shirt had been pushed up to show the plain white bra she wore underneath, the swell of her small breasts. The pale skin of her belly seemed to undulate in a grotesque fashion, as if unseen fingers were caressing her. That was probably why she moaned the way she did, as if caught in the throes of some unholy pleasure.

It was the most obscene thing he'd ever had the misfortune to witness. Next to him, Ariel put her hand to her mouth, but she didn't move, didn't speak, as if she no longer had the strength to cry out against the thing possessing her daughter.

Michael turned away—not because he didn't have the strength to see what was happening on the bed, but because he knew this was not something Colin should be recording. "Turn the goddamn camera off," he told him.

His producer looked offended. "Are you having a go? This is amazing."

"Turn it off, or I'm going to fucking break the damn camera."

For a second, their eyes locked. Colin was the first to break the contact; he gave an awkward shrug and said, "Okay, mate. Don't get your knickers in a twist." And, reluctantly, he toggled the switch to put the camera in standby mode.

Standing behind him, Audrey looked stricken, Daniela nauseated. And Susan had quietly switched off the mike so none of the conversation would be recorded.

Kayla appeared oblivious to all this. Michael knew she was caught in the thrall of the thing that now inhabited her body, that her consciousness was so far subsumed that she could have no idea of what was going on around her. That was some comfort, but not much.

"I've seen enough," Michael said. "We can go back downstairs now."

Ariel Vargas turned a pair of shocked eyes on him. "Aren't you going to do something?"

"I am…but not today. This sort of thing requires preparation—I could splash some holy water on her, try to shock her out of it, but that would only put the demon on the attack, something that could have dire consequences for your daughter. And there are some matters we need to discuss before I get started."

"We can't leave her like this—"

Unfortunately, they had to. Whatever Kayla was suffering now, it would only be made much worse if he went off half-cocked, so to speak. "How long do these episodes last?"

A deep breath, and then Ariel replied, "Sometimes as much as an hour. But not longer than that."

It could have been worse. He'd read of cases where the victim of a possession had been caught in this kind of a demonic assault for twelve hours at a time. But Kayla would come back to herself, and probably wouldn't remember anything of what had happened, except that she would be exhausted and physically aching from the abuse her muscles had just suffered.

But alive. That was the important thing.

Rather than try to convince Ariel of that, Michael only said again, "Let's go downstairs," and backed out of the room, forcing her to follow —and forcing the rest of the crew to get out of their way. He allowed himself a single glance at Audrey, saw how white she was, how the pinkish-brown lip gloss she wore stood out against her pale skin.

There was no point in telling her that this would get easier over time, because it never did.

By unspoken agreement, they all went back to the dining room and sat down. Colin was still sulking, but at least he kept quiet, for once understanding that he was out of his element here.

This next part would be hard, and yet it was necessary. He said quietly, "Daniela, do you have the paperwork?"

She nodded, then lifted the top paper of her clipboard so she could get to the release form underneath, then handed it and her ballpoint pen to him. "Here you go."

He took the paper and pen from her, then put them down on the dining room table and pushed them toward Ariel.

"What's this?" she asked, looking down at the form in front of her.

"It's a release form."

Her brows pulled together. "I already signed one of those. Your producer"—she gave Colin a single contemptuous look—"emailed it to me, and I signed it and scanned it and sent it back."

"That was the standard release form," Michael explained. "It allows us to film in your house, and it also allows us to use your image and your daughter's image on the show. But this...I wasn't going to ask you to sign it until I knew for sure."

"Knew what for sure?" Ariel asked, although, judging by the way her voice trembled, Michael thought she knew exactly what he was talking about.

"Knew that your daughter was possessed by a demon." He folded his hands on the tabletop and tried his best to look capable but nonthreatening. "I'm going to perform an exorcism on her, Ariel, but before I do that, you need to sign a waiver releasing me from any liability. I will be as careful as I know how. I will do everything to free your daughter from the control of this entity. But there is no guarantee—the exorcism might not be successful. The demon might hurt her as it desperately clings to her body. And…."

The next two words came out in a whisper, as if she knew what was coming but didn't want to acknowledge that terrible possibility. "And what?"

"And there is the chance that she may die." Michael wished he didn't have to be so blunt, but he knew that Ariel needed to understand the risks they were taking. "It's happened before. Not in my personal experience," he added hastily, "but the precedent is there. This isn't like getting a tooth extracted. The process carries a great deal of risk with it, but it's the only way for you to get your daughter back."

Silence then, as Ariel stared at him, so pale he wondered that she didn't faint, and he tried not to look over at Audrey, at the stricken expression on her face. Surely she must have known how dangerous an exorcism could be, even if demonology wasn't her particular field of expertise.

Still in a whisper, Ariel asked, "What happens if I don't have you perform an exorcism?"

Somehow, Michael had known she would ask such a question. He pulled in a breath, then said, "These outcomes can vary from case to case—"

"I don't care about that," she cut in. "Just tell me the worst-case scenario."

"Worst case, she'll still die," he said bluntly. "The demon will continue to use her, drain her energy, until her body can no longer take the abuse. That's the worst case. Otherwise, she could survive, but her mind would break, and she would no longer have any lucid periods like the one I saw this afternoon. You would have no choice but to institutionalize her."

Tears glittered in Ariel's eyes, but none of them fell, instead seemed to get tangled in her lashes. She pressed her lips together and looked away from Michael, up toward the ceiling, as if visualizing her daughter in her bedroom above them. Then, mouth still compressed, she picked up the pen and signed the form.

"When will you be back?" she asked next, her voice calmer now, as though she'd confronted the worst and made her peace with it.

"Tomorrow morning," he replied. "Between nine and ten. I need tonight to prepare myself."

"How long will it take?"

There was no real way to answer that. So much depended on how strong a hold the demon had on the girl—and how strong the demon itself was. There were exorcisms that had taken days, weeks…in some cases, months and months. He wouldn't know until he got started, and possibly not even then.

"I can't say," he told her, hoping she would

take his frankness at face value. "The time required varies from case to case. I hope—I very much hope—that it won't take more than a few hours, or a day at the most. But you should probably prepare yourself for a long ordeal."

"Whatever it takes to get my girl back," Ariel said. Now she looked fierce, ready to do battle.

Only she wouldn't be the one fighting this particular battle. That task would fall on his shoulders, and his alone.

"I'll do my very best." Since there wasn't anything else he could do now, he rose from his seat. "We'll be back tomorrow. Try to get some rest if you can."

Once again she slanted a look upward, as if she knew that her ability to get any sleep depended wholly on how much of a disturbance the demon would cause tonight. "I'll do my best."

"Good. We'll see you then."

He nodded toward the *Project Demon Hunters* crew, indicating that it was time to get going, and they all rose from the table as well. Audrey sent Ariel a sympathetic smile before she followed Colin, Susan, and Daniela out of the room and then the front door.

Once they were out on the sidewalk in front of the house, however, Colin shot Michael an annoyed glance. "Are you going to keep interfering with me like that?"

"If I have to." He really didn't want to get into this now, but if Colin wanted a confrontation, so be it.

"What's that supposed to mean?"

Audrey opened her mouth—probably trying to act as peacemaker—but Michael gave her a subtle shake of the head. To his relief, she didn't argue, but crossed her arms and waited to see what would happen next.

"It means," Michael said, "that while you can film the procedure, if things start to get too out of hand, then you have to stop. I don't want to exploit this poor girl."

This argument didn't seem to have any effect on Colin. Still scowling, he retorted, "If that was the case, then you shouldn't have chosen to come here at all. We had other options."

Yes, they did, but the quiet urgency of Ariel Vargas' most recent phone call, coupled with his desire to stay the hell out of Colorado for the immediate future, had been enough to convince Michael that this needed to be their next case file. "We can record enough to show that exorcisms are scary, scary things. You'd have to edit the hell out of the thing anyway to get it to fit into a forty-two-minute run time, so there's no need to film every damn second. All right?"

For a second, Colin didn't reply. Then he gave an elaborate shrug that Michael didn't buy for a second and said, "Sure, mate. Whatever." He turned toward Daniela, "Let's go. We're done for the day, right?"

"Right," Michael replied. In that moment, he felt very tired, but he knew he didn't dare give in to his weariness. He still had a great deal to do. "I'll call you tomorrow morning when I'm ready to leave the hotel."

"Looking forward to it."

With that, Colin got into his Porsche SUV and Daniela followed suit, although her expression was considerably more apologetic. Susan, calm as ever, just said that she'd be ready, and climbed into her car as well.

"Let's go," Audrey said. She waited a few feet away, and he wished he could take her in his arms, hold her so he could breathe in her sweetness and warmth. However, he couldn't allow himself that kind of distraction, not now with so much on the line.

When this was all over with….

He had to cling to that belief. Because the one thing he hadn't told Ariel Vargas was that it wasn't just her daughter's life on the line.

His hung in the balance as well.

Chapter 17

IT WAS HARD TO REMAIN QUIET ON THE DRIVE
back to the hotel, but Audrey did so for Michael's
sake. There was something taut and cold about
him right then, something that made her feel as if
he was doing everything he could to put a safe
distance between them. She hadn't interrupted
back at the house because this was his field of
expertise, not hers; what she'd seen in Kayla
Vargas' room had been both tragic and deeply
disturbing. While she'd dealt with several case
studies during the time she was getting her degree
that, on the surface, were almost as unsettling, this
was different. Although she couldn't say precisely
how she was able to sense such a thing, she could
tell that Kayla's behavior was not something
caused by the troubles inside her own mind, but

some terrible outside influence that made her behave as she did.

There was no sign of Colin or Daniela when Audrey and Michael rode up in the elevator; she guessed that Colin had probably gone in search of the nearest pub to nurse his woes. She couldn't really blame him for doing such a thing, because Audrey thought she could have used a drink as well. However, she also knew that she needed to be on top of things when they went back to the Vargas house the next day, and that meant no alcohol and a good night's sleep.

If she'd be able to sleep after the things she'd seen that morning.

As she was about to slip her key card into the lock, Michael spoke.

"I'm sorry," he said. "I wish—I wish I could spend a normal day with you, take you out to dinner. But I can't do any of those things. I have to prepare myself as best I can, and that means solitude and prayer…and fasting."

"You can't eat anything?" she asked, feeling slightly alarmed. "I'm not sure it's a good idea to tackle this kind of ordeal on an empty stomach."

Her concern made him smile, and for a second, she thought he was going to bend down and kiss her. However, he seemed to take control of himself, and he shook his head. "Unfortunately, this is exactly the sort of thing that needs to be faced on an empty stomach. It's all about purifying myself, making sure that I'm a vessel for God's power when I face the enemy tomorrow."

"'Enemy'?" Audrey repeated. "She's just a girl. She's barely old enough to drive."

This time he touched her hair—just for a moment, so gently she couldn't even feel the brush of his fingertips against the strands that fell around her face. "I'm not talking about Kayla. I mean the thing inside her. The war with their kind has been going on for millennia."

Cold moved over Audrey's body, and she wished he would take her in his arms. Since she knew that wasn't going to happen, she set her jaw and waited for the shiver to pass. "I think I'm a little freaked out, Michael."

His gray eyes met hers. "You should be. Or at least, let yourself be freaked out now. I'm going to need your strength tomorrow."

"My strength?" she faltered. "I thought you said you had to do this on your own."

"Up to a point," he replied. "In the Catholic faith, two priests perform the ritual, with one in an assisting role. I need you to be my assistant, Audrey, to bring me water, to lend your will to mine if I begin to show any signs of flagging. Can you do that?"

Could she? The very thought of having to spend hours in that room, watching as Michael wrestled with the devil—or at least a demon—made her stomach knot up. But then she realized they'd all be there, or at least Colin and Susan would, because they had to record the exorcism. If Daniela were smart, she'd stay far away…and Audrey guessed she would. It wasn't as if any undying love existed between her and Colin, just a casual attraction. Looking in from outside, someone else might have said the same thing about her and Michael, but Audrey knew that wasn't the case. She loved him, even if she hadn't yet been brave enough to utter the fateful words, and she knew she wouldn't abandon him when he needed her most.

"I can do that," she said firmly. "And I will." After a pause, she asked, "Do you want me to drive tomorrow?"

The smile he offered her now was very genuine. "Yes, that would help. Come and knock at eight-thirty tomorrow—I'll be ready."

"Okay." She squeezed his fingers briefly—somehow she knew that was the only contact he'd allow—then went into her room and closed the door behind her.

Michael had said he would be ready…but she sure as hell didn't know whether she would be.

This was only a hotel room, with nothing personal about it, but maybe that was for the best. For a moment, Michael touched the wall that separated his room from Audrey's, wishing fiercely he could be there with her, knowing that was impossible. Then he put her out of his mind, because he had work to do.

Water, lots of it, ordered from room service. The kid who brought the pallet of bottled water up to the room looked a little confused by the request, but he obviously had been trained not to ask questions, because he took the generous tip Michael offered him and then beat a hasty retreat.

Michael cracked open one of the bottles and drank down half of it in one long gulp. Then he set the bottle down on the dresser, went to his luggage, and got out his cross and his Bible. His purpose now was merely to clear his mind of any extraneous worries or weaknesses, anything the demon might use against him. He could not think of his clash with Colin, or his need for Audrey. For a moment, he wondered if he was asking too much of her to be present during the ritual, but he needed someone there. At least as a trained psychologist, she would have plenty of experience being around those who'd been tortured by the demons of their own minds, and so—he hoped— she would be less likely to be shocked by what she witnessed.

But no, he needed to put her out of his mind. Audrey was strong; Audrey could do this.

He needed to put his own house in order.

Kneeling on the carpet in front of the cross where it stood on the dresser, he recited the opening words of the Lord's Prayer for the first of what would be many times that night.

"Our Father, who art in Heaven
Hallowed be thy name…"

All was silent on the other side of the wall. Audrey didn't know what Michael was doing in there, but he certainly wasn't making any noise.

Praying?

Probably.

She wished she could. Maybe it would help.

But she hadn't been raised to think of a higher power in anything but the abstract. In a way, she was a little amused at herself for falling for someone who so clearly was a man of faith, even though he didn't advertise that he was a minister, didn't go out of his way to show that it was more than an interest in the supernatural that had led him to hunt demons.

No, it was his way of trying to restore the natural balance of things.

It was only the early afternoon, and for a

moment Audrey thought that she should go out for a while, see something of Santa Barbara, get some fresh air. Maybe with Susan, who was probably also wondering what to do with herself until the next morning. However, engaging in those sorts of activities seemed unfair to Michael, who clearly was determined to lock himself up in meditation and fasting until, like some prophet of old, he emerged ready to do battle with one of the Devil's minions.

Audrey didn't think she had it in herself to do that. She could, however, get down on the carpet and do some yoga exercises, eat lightly, go to bed early. Part of her wanted to call Rosemary, just so she could talk to someone who knew a little of what was going on, but no—no one on the crew was supposed to talk to outsiders about the particulars of any of the cases being covered on *Project Demon Hunters.* Michael had bent that rule more than once, but he was one of the show's producers and had more leeway. Colin was already on a rampage; the last thing Audrey wanted to do was give him a convenient scapegoat.

So she put on some yoga pants and a tank top, did a few simple exercises, watched a little television, stretched some more, and ordered a light dinner of Asian chicken salad and some green tea. As she was getting ready for bed—at the ungodly hour of 8:45—her phone pinged.

She picked it up, hoping against hope that the message might be from Michael, that he'd decided contacting her this way wasn't breaking the rules, but it turned out the text was from Rosemary.

Only two words.

Be careful.

Hand shaking a little, Audrey set down the phone. She wouldn't bother to ask how Rosemary knew she and Michael and the rest of the crew were walking into the lions' den the next morning, because Rosemary was the sort of person who just knew things. Clearly, she was feeling some uncomfortable vibes, or at the very least had managed to pick up Audrey's worry across the miles.

"Be careful," she said to herself as she went in to brush her teeth. Of course she was going to be careful. What exactly that would entail, she didn't know, but she understood that she had to be on her guard at all times during the ritual, even if she wasn't the one who would be going toe to toe with the demon…or demons. Sometimes they traveled in packs.

When she was done in the bathroom, she came back and picked up the phone and typed, *I will,* then hit "send."

That was all. She wasn't about to give Rosemary anything other than that. But, being Rosemary, she probably knew already.

Time to turn out the light and go to sleep. However, as her fingers touched the pushbutton control for the bedside lamp, she hesitated. True, Michael was on the other side of the wall, and Susan and Colin and Daniela were just down the hallway. Even so, Audrey realized she didn't want to go to sleep in the dark. She knew better than anyone else that things lived in the darkness, or at least used it to hide their movements.

Slowly, she withdrew her hand, then pulled the covers up to her chin. It seemed awfully quiet in there, the only sound the faint hum of the climate-control system.

Maybe she should turn on the TV?

No, better not. It wasn't that she expected the "TV people" to come howling out of the screen, the way they had in *Poltergeist*…but what if they did?

Instead, she picked up her phone from where she'd left it charging on the nightstand, then opened the Pandora app and started streaming one of her favorite stations for background music, the one that focused on acoustic guitar solos, no vocals. That seemed the safest, and with the phone plugged into the charger, she didn't have to worry about the battery draining out sometime in the middle of the night.

Doing her best to ignore the glare of the bedside lamp, she rolled over and went to sleep.

And, once again, she saw those empty hill-sides, the place with the gray sky and the chill wind. She supposed she shouldn't have been surprised to see Jeffrey Whitcomb there, either, walking up the slight rise to where she stood.

He came to stand next to her, his heavy, gray-streaked dark hair ruffled by the wind. "You're losing the thread, you know."

"What thread?" Even in the dream she was cold, arms hugged around herself. Or maybe it was simply the chill of seeing him again, knowing that she spoke to someone long dead and not merely a dream-figment.

"The thread of me, or what used to be me. Everything else is a distraction."

"We have to help her," she protested, not stop-ping to wonder whether the astral Jeffrey would know who she meant by "her."

"You think you do." A pause as he looked away from her, deep-set black eyes surveying the gray horizon. "But she's not important."

Audrey's dream-self experienced a wave of anger. Who was this man—or what was left of this man—to tell her who was and wasn't impor-tant? The first time she'd encountered him, she'd almost felt sorry for him, despite what he'd done when he was alive. Now, though, she saw clearly the arrogance that had led him to invite dark energies into his life. He'd thought he could control them, but they had ended up becoming his masters.

"We can pick up that thread when we're done here," she said firmly. "Not before. If we start trying to say one life is more important than another, then we're just as bad as the things you've let loose in this world."

His lip curled. "I suppose I shouldn't have expected you to understand."

"I understand completely. You want us to help you because you want to be free to move on, rather than being bound to this world. And we will help you—but we have to help Kayla first."

As Audrey had expected, these words didn't appear to sit well with the astral-Whitcomb. His black eyes glittered, and he said, "She's beyond help."

"No one's beyond help," Audrey said, then added, "Not even you."

Even as the words left her mouth, a gale of a wind came out of nowhere, catching at the skirts of his long jacket, picking him up and blowing him away from her so he floated like a black kite against the gray skies. Audrey reached out to grab his coat before he was out of reach, but the heavy fabric slipped through her fingers and she was left grasping empty air.

And then he was gone, and she woke up, gasping, to her hotel room and the music playing through the tinny speakers of her cell phone, and the soft light from her bedside lamp. Everything appeared calm here, utterly still, and yet she felt cold sweat dripping down between her shoulder blades, and her heart wouldn't stop pounding.

You know, these damn dreams can stop anytime, she thought, then reached for the glass of water she'd left on the nightstand so she could swallow a few mouthfuls.

The problem was, she knew they weren't really dreams. She couldn't let this latest encounter rattle her, though; she had to get as much sleep as she could.

Because as frightening as that dream…projection…whatever it was…had been, Audrey knew she would be facing something much more terrifying the following day.

Dawn came, and Michael allowed himself the luxury of a long, hot shower, even though he'd denied himself any other comforts during the long night he'd just endured. He didn't know whether he felt purified, but he did feel damn tired.

The pounding of the hot water helped some, as did his morning rituals of yoga stretches and deep breathing. He looked longingly at the little basket of various teas and coffees that had come with the room. Unfortunately, they were forbidden to him. Only water would pass his lips until he had come safely through the ordeal he was about to face.

On the other side of the wall, he thought he heard the faint sound of the shower in Audrey's room starting up. Apparently, she hadn't slept much later than he. Perhaps her night had been restless, although he didn't think he'd done anything that could have been heard through the hotel's admittedly somewhat thin walls. No, she'd probably just been worried about what was to come the next day.

That was all he'd let himself think about, though, because Audrey was a distraction he couldn't afford right now. It would be difficult enough to have her in the room with him as he was performing the ritual, but her presence was necessary. He needed someone to assist him, if only to bring him water when he needed it, or to help him recite the Lord's Prayer. Did she even know the words? That was something he'd forgotten to ask her; he knew her family hadn't been religious, that she'd never really gone to church, but the words of the prayer were such common knowledge that he had to hope she'd committed them to memory at some point.

Even though he'd told her to knock on his door at eight-thirty, he still startled a little at the sound. Just to be sure, he glanced at the clock radio on the nightstand. Yes, it was now eight twenty-nine. For some reason, knowing that Audrey had been so prompt reassured him. She must be frightened and nervous, but she hadn't tried to avoid the inevitable.

When he opened the door, he was as struck by her beauty as he'd been the first time he saw her, even though now she looked pale under her makeup. It wasn't as heavy as when Daniela applied it, so Michael guessed Audrey had put herself together on her own this morning, probably understanding that thick eyeliner and too much lip gloss really didn't have any place at an exorcism.

She managed to smile as she looked at him, but her expression was hesitant. He knew he looked like hell, with dark circles under his eyes and the lines on his brow standing out more than ever. There wasn't much he could do about that, however. Actually, Colin would probably like the effect—it would make the exorcism seem that much more dramatic.

Not that it really needed any assistance.

"How are you doing?" she asked.

"I'm fine," he said shortly. He understood why she was worried about him, but he couldn't allow her concern to stand in the way of what needed to be done. "Where's everyone?"

A quick glance over her shoulder, although there wasn't anyone else in the hallway. "The three of them went out to grab a quick breakfast. They'll meet us at the Vargas house. Or rather, Colin and Susan will. Daniela said she was going to sit this one out…they're going to drop her back here and then head out from there."

Michael wished he could have said he was surprised by Daniela's defection, but he wasn't. Not really. Unlike the other two, she was a fairly devout Catholic and probably wanted to stay far away from the kinds of entities they'd soon be facing. Anyway, her presence wasn't really necessary, although it might have been helpful to have another person of faith on the premises while he performed the ritual.

"Okay," he said, then reached in his pants pocket and got out the key fob for his rented Grand Cherokee. "Are you still willing to drive?"

"Of course," Audrey replied immediately.

That was a bit of a relief. He handed the fob to her, then came out into the hall and shut the door behind him, hearing it lock. All he had now was a satchel with a few spare water bottles stowed in it, along with his Bible and cross. A Catholic priest would have brought his stole with him as well, but Michael didn't own one, would have to do without several of the trappings of a more traditional ritual.

"Let's go."

She gave him a brief nod and headed toward the elevator. Inside were a man and a woman clearly planning on an early morning swim, since they wore flip-flips and T-shirts over their bathing suits. Their gaze moved over him and Audrey, vaguely curious. He supposed that the two of them didn't look much like tourists, him in head-to-toe black, Audrey in dark jeans and a black T-shirt and sweater. At least he wasn't wearing his clerical collar; while he had every right to that symbol of his ordained status, he always felt like a fraud when he put it on, since he didn't have a congregation or a church.

But he had to put that thought away, because the very last thing he should be thinking right now was that he was a fraud, or unworthy in any way to perform the ritual that lay ahead of him. Demons were tricky things, ready to exploit any weakness, prey on any doubts.

Apparently sensing his mood, Audrey was quiet as she walked with him to the hotel's under-ground parking garage and his rented SUV. She climbed in behind the wheel, took a few minutes to adjust the seat, and then pulled out of the parking space. Sooner than Michael would have liked, they had reached the Vargas home, some ten minutes from the downtown area where he and the rest of the *Project Demon Hunters* crew were staying.

Today was gray and overcast, the sky obscured by fog and clouds drifting in off the ocean. A chill went through him as he looked up at the house, which seemed to loom over them where it stood on a slight rise. To anyone else, it probably would have looked picture perfect, with its green, cream, and brick-red color scheme and beds of orderly roses, but even from the curb he could sense the rot within, the darkness coiled inside the perfectly preserved structure.

As he and Audrey got out of the Grand Cherokee, Colin's Porsche SUV pulled up and parked behind them. Susan emerged first; she gave them a small wave, then headed toward the rear of the vehicle. Colin got out next, frowning ferociously. Michael didn't know whether his current expression was due to Daniela's defection, or whether his producer was still angry at him after their exchange the day before. Not that it mattered. He couldn't afford to expend any mental energy on Colin's current mood.

Once Colin and Susan had gotten their equipment out of the car, Michael nodded at them, indicating it was time to go. They fell in behind him, Audrey first, then Susan, then Colin. As they walked up to the front door, Michael had to wonder what the neighbors thought of this little spectacle. Did they know anything of what had been going on in the Vargas household, or had Ariel done her best to keep her daughter's condition a secret from everyone around them?

It probably didn't matter one way or another. Once this show aired, they would find out anyway.

He had just put his finger on the doorbell when the door opened and Ariel Vargas looked out at them. Today she appeared even more exhausted than before, shadows under her eyes so dark, they looked more like smudged makeup than a natural consequence of her overall weariness.

"Come in," she said, stepping out of the way so they could all enter the foyer. Almost at once, Michael could hear the growls and screams coming from upstairs, and a thin finger of worry trailed its way down his spine.

"She's taken a turn for the worse?" he asked, and Ariel's teeth caught on her lip for a moment before she gave him a reluctant nod.

"It was bad last night," she said. "Actually, it was so bad that I called Luke and told him he had to come over. She was thrashing around, and we were both worried she was going to hurt herself. So...we tied her to the bed. I know that sounds awful, but—"

"No, that was a very good idea," Michael cut

in. "I would have had to restrain her anyway, and so you've made my work here a little easier."

Some of the tension in Ariel's face eased itself. Not all, but enough that she didn't look on the verge of collapse. "Oh, good. So…."

"So," Michael said. "We might as well get started."

"Do I—do I really need to be there? I don't know how much I'll be able to help."

While he could understand Ariel's reluctance, he knew it was imperative that she be present. Kayla needed someone there who loved her, who would give her a reason to fight the alien presence that had taken up residence within her. "I'm afraid you do," he replied gently. "But it's all right— Audrey will be with us as well, and of course Colin and Susan will be recording the ritual. We'll all work together."

Ariel's gaze flickered toward Audrey, who gave her an encouraging smile. "Yes, I'll be there through the whole thing," she said. "It will be fine."

"All—all right." Ariel winced as a particularly ear-piercing shriek sounded from above.

That seemed to be the signal he needed. Michael glanced back at Colin and Susan, then over at Audrey, who appeared pale but composed.

"Then let us begin."

Chapter 18

Audrey wasn't sure how she managed to put one foot in front of the other, to force herself up that long staircase. Maybe it was only Michael moving them all along by the sheer strength of his will. Whatever the case, she kept going, even though the horrible sounds emanating from Kayla's bedroom kept getting louder and louder, so loud that she wondered how Michael would even make himself heard over those screeches and howls and guttural moans.

They went inside the room. Once again, it was bitterly cold, but even the cold wasn't enough to mask the stench inside. As Ariel had said, Kayla was tied to the bedposts, not with ropes, but with what looked like torn-up sheets. Her gray T-shirt and leggings were soaked, although with sweat or urine—or possibly both—Audrey couldn't tell for sure.

And her face had contorted again, looking like nothing from this world, eyes staring, mouth open in a snarl. As soon as Michael entered the room, she started to laugh, horrible, harsh laughter that didn't sound as if it possibly could have come from a fifteen-year-old girl's throat.

"Going to play exorcist?" she asked, and laughed again, foamy spittle flying from her mouth. Her gaze moved to her mother, shifty, eyes glinting with unholy amusement. "You do know he doesn't know what the fuck he's doing, right?"

Everyone ignored her. Colin and Susan had taken up their positions in one corner of the room, a spot where they had a good vantage point but were well out of range of the girl...the thing...on the bed. In a low tone, Michael instructed Audrey and Ariel to stand slightly off to one side. As they moved to the spot he'd indicated, he got a Bible and several vials of holy water out of his satchel and set them down on the trunk at the foot of the bed, then took out a wooden cross, kissed it, and placed it on top of the dresser, which was located a few feet away from where Kayla lay.

At the sight of the cross, she began squirming on the bed, pulling at her bonds. Luckily, they seemed to be holding, for all their makeshift nature. Despite herself, Audrey couldn't help staring at Kayla, at the alterations in her face. Honestly, if she hadn't known this was the girl she'd met the day before, she would never have guessed they were the same person.

"We ask your protection, O Lord, for this girl and those who attend her," Michael said. Somehow, his voice sounded deeper, richer than it did in ordinary conversation…but then, Audrey realized this was about as far from normal conversation as you could get.

He then sprinkled holy water on Kayla, and she screamed and writhed, doing what she could to get away from the liquid, which, judging by the sounds she made, appeared to be burning her like acid. Ariel made an incoherent sound of dismay and began to step forward, but Audrey caught her by the arm.

"Don't," she said in a murmur. "You can't interrupt him. You have to let him do what he came here to do."

Stricken, Ariel replied, her voice also pitched low, "I don't know if I can."

Audrey wasn't sure whether she'd have the strength to stand by and watch her own child be tormented in such a way, but she made herself say, "Yes, you can. Just follow what Michael says, and it'll be all right."

He glanced back at them. His face was so

stern, he, too, was almost unrecognizable. "Let us say the Lord's Prayer."

Thank God—no pun intended—that she knew the words. Only because they'd sung it in choir when she was in high school, but Audrey figured that was good enough. To her surprise, Ariel chimed in as well, the trio of their voices joining, gaining strength, as Kayla hissed and squirmed on the bed, clearly becoming more uncomfortable with each syllable.

When they were done, Michael didn't stop, but recited more words that Audrey guessed must be a Psalm, although she'd never heard it before. Something about God being a tower of strength, along with an invocation of holy protection. Halfway through, Kayla began laughing again, a high-pitched giggle that made Audrey want to cover her ears.

"That'll never work," she said in between giggles.

Undaunted, Michael went on, "Unclean spirit! Whoever you are, and all your companions who possess this servant of God. By the mysteries of the Incarnation, the Sufferings and Death, the Resurrection, and the Ascension of Our Lord Jesus Christ; by the sending of the Holy Spirit; and by the Coming of Our Lord into Last Judgment, I command you: Tell me, with some sign, your name, the day, and the hour of your damnation. Obey me in everything, although I am an unworthy servant of God. Do no harm to this girl, or to my assistants!"

Had he taken those words from the Catholic ritual? It seemed he must have, because they seemed too formal for a Unitarian minister. For all she knew, Unitarians didn't even believe in exorcisms, although it was clear enough that Michael did.

Now the thing on the bed writhed and howled, twisting its head so it wouldn't have to look at the man who stood over it and invoked the power of God. Audrey couldn't help thinking of the possessed girl as "it," because it really didn't even look human, red fire glaring from its eyes, limbs contorted, face now completely unrecognizable. Once again, Michael sprinkled it with holy water, and again it screamed and thrashed against the sweat-soaked sheets.

"Tell me your name!" he thundered, but more of those grotesque howls emerged from its throat, and not any words that could be distinguished as such.

Ariel grasped Audrey's hand and clamped down on it so hard that the bones seemed to grind together. A little gasp of pain escaped Audrey's lips, but she didn't take her hand away, knowing that Ariel needed something to hang on to as she watched her daughter be tortured.

No, not her daughter, Audrey thought. *The thing that's reacting…that's not Kayla.* She could only hope that Kayla's real spirit—her mind, her soul—was someplace far away, wasn't feeling every splash of holy water against her skin, or the way Michael pulled a silver cross from his pocket and placed it against her forehead.

Another screech, one cut off by Michael demanding once again, "Tell me your name!"

More howls, so unearthly that Audrey had to shut her eyes for a moment, because she didn't want to believe they'd come from a human throat.

"Tell me your name!"

This went on for what felt like hours. After reciting more Bible verses, Michael said in a quick aside, voice rough as sandpaper, "Water, Audrey."

She let go of Ariel's hand and fetched one of the bottles from the satchel he had brought, then brought it over to him. He unscrewed the cap and drank most of it in one gulp before handing it back to her. Without missing a beat, he grasped a new vial of holy water and splashed it on Kayla's face.

"Tell me your name!"

"*Aaaaaaaalastor!*"

The syllables sounded as if they'd been ripped from Kayla's throat. The room went deadly still.

Then Michael spoke again, a note of triumph in his voice. "I exorcise you, Alastor! In the name of Our Lord Jesus Christ, be uprooted and expelled from this creature of God. Christ commands you, he who ordered you to be thrown down from the highest Heaven into the depths of Hell!"

The girl squirmed. For just a moment, Audrey caught a glimpse of her normal face, eyes wide with fear, before it contorted again. "She is mine! *Mine!*"

Michael seemed to be expecting this, because he said, "I exorcise you, Alastor! God the Father commands you. God the Son commands you. God the Holy Spirit commands you!"

Each of these commands was accompanied by more splashes of holy water. And each time, the girl writhed...and Audrey could see her true self more and more each time.

Ariel clearly saw it, too, because she took a step forward. At once, Michael shook his head and she stopped, uncertain.

"Not yet," he said in the barest of whispers.

"Be gone, Alastor! Be gone!"

Kayla sat up—or at least tried to. Her arms struggled against the sheets that held her in place, and her mouth opened. From it emerged a horrible greenish cloud the color of bile. Without flinching, Michael flung the remnants of the vial of holy water at the cloud and it disappeared, leaving behind a terrible stench.

Audrey coughed, and he reached for yet another vial of holy water, sprinkling it over the bed and the girl who lay there. For the first time, she didn't flinch, but only remained where she was, shivers wracking her thin form.

No one moved. Out of the corner of her eye, Audrey was vaguely aware of the red light on Colin's camera, that he'd been capturing the entire process while Susan held the boom mike overhead, but they both seemed peripheral, like shapes from another world.

Very slowly, Michael spoke the words of the Lord's Prayer again. Or rather, he began, and Ariel and Audrey chimed in once more, their voices growing stronger with each syllable. And Michael bent and dabbed holy water on Kayla's brow, and her eyes opened.

"What happened?" she asked.

Ariel broke into relieved laughter—although that laughter had a tinge of hysteria to it, and tears rolled down her cheeks. She moved toward the bed, but Michael raised a hand.

"One last thing," he said. "I need to bless the room and everyone in it, so we know the demon is truly gone. Then it should be safe to untie your daughter."

A nod. "Of course," Ariel whispered. "Whatever you need to do."

He gave her a reassuring smile, then sprinkled

holy water on the bed again, and touched a few drops to Ariel's forehead, just as he'd done to her daughter. She let out a relieved breath, as if she'd been worried that the demon had decided to jump to her next.

And, to be honest, Audrey couldn't help but experience some of that same relief when Michael came to her and placed a finger on her forehead, smearing some holy water there. He stood very close, and more than anything, she wished she could reach out to him, even though she knew this was not the place or time. For now, she'd have to be content that he was all right, that he had come out okay on the other side of this, just as Kayla Vargas had.

Michael went over to Colin, who rolled his eyes but submitted to the same ritual placement of the holy water. Then he turned to Susan, who sent him a rueful smile.

"I really don't think that's necessary," she said.

"But it is," he told her. "Even if you don't think so."

Her smile grew a little tight. "Is that purified water? Because I have really sensitive skin—almost everything makes me break out in a rash."

"Susan, it's just a dab. Here." And before she could utter another protest, he reached over to her and touched his fore- and middle finger to her forehead.

Her response was immediate. A terrible scream tore itself from her lips, too like the ones Kayla had been uttering just a short time earlier to be a coincidence. Even as Michael took a step back in shock, Susan hurled the boom mike at him, catching him full in the chest with such force that he staggered backward and fell to the floor.

And then she fled the room.

Audrey had stood there for a few seconds, frozen in shock, before she realized what must have happened. The demon had left Kayla's body…only to take up residence in Susan's.

Without thinking, she grasped the remaining vial of holy water and ran after the possessed woman. There she was, pounding down the hall toward the staircase. Her foot was already on the top step.

"Stop!" Audrey shouted.

Just for a second, Susan paused. Or rather, the thing that had taken control of Susan paused. Her mouth twisted in a snarl, and a terrible reddish light glowed from her hazel eyes. "You can't stop us, fool. We always win."

Instinct drove Audrey forward. She didn't even know exactly what she planned to do. From behind her, she heard a jumble of voices—Colin shouting, Michael calling out for her to wait. But she couldn't wait. Even now the Susan-thing had turned away and resumed its flight down the stairs. There was no way they'd be able to catch up with her before she reached the bottom of the steps and freedom.

Audrey had only this one chance.

With shaking fingers, she pulled the stopper from the vial, then leaned over the banister and flung the holy water downward at their possessed sound operator. The thing inside Susan shrieked in pain, clawing at her eyes, then stumbled and went down, tumbling over and over until her body hit the floor at the bottom of the steps and was still.

No…oh, no….

Audrey pounded down the stairs, vaguely aware that Michael and Colin were now in the hallway and coming toward the staircase as well. When she got to the bottom, she knelt next to Susan. With icy fingers, she reached toward Susan's throat to see if she could feel a pulse, even though her neck was twisted at such a terrible angle, there was no way…there was no way….

Suddenly, Michael was crouching beside her. "Wait," he said. From an inner pocket, he drew out yet another vial of holy water. Hand shaking, he sprinkled some of the vial's contents on Susan's body. She didn't move, didn't stir.

It was hard to breathe. Tears blurred Audrey's eyes, and then Michael was helping her stand, pulling her away so she could sit down on an antique bench placed up against the wall next to the stairwell. Colin was there as well, leaning down to close Susan's eyes, which stared sightlessly up at the chandelier that hung in the foyer. When he stood back up, his expression was curiously blank, as if he didn't quite know how he was supposed to react to all this.

"Bloody hell," he said at last. "She's dead."

———

Audrey and Michael's story concludes in *Unholy Ground.*

Also by Christine Pope

PROJECT DEMON HUNTERS

(Paranormal Romance)

Unquiet Souls

Unbound Spirits

Unholy Ground (April 2019)

———

THE WITCHES OF CANYON ROAD

(Paranormal Romance)

Hidden Gifts

Darker Paths

Mysterious Ways

A Canyon Road Christmas

Demon Born

An Ill Wind (May 2019)

Higher Ground (August 2019)

———

THE WITCHES OF CLEOPATRA HILL*

(Paranormal Romance)

Darkangel

Darknight

Darkmoon

Sympathetic Magic

Protector

Spellbound

A Cleopatra Hill Christmas

Impractical Magic

Strange Magic

The Arrangement

Defender

Bad Blood

Deep Magic

Darktide

Books 1-3 and Books 4-6 of this series are also available in two separate omnibus editions at special boxed set prices. Chronicles of Cleopatra Hill includes the series' two "back in time" novellas, *Bad Blood* and *The Arrangement*.

THE DJINN WARS

(Paranormal Romance)

Chosen

Taken

Fallen

Broken

Forsaken

Forbidden

Awoken

Illuminated

Stolen

Forgotten

Driven

Unspoken (June 2019)

Books 1-3 and Books 4-6 of this series are also available in two separate omnibus editions at special boxed set prices!

THE WATCHERS TRILOGY*

(Paranormal Romance)

Falling Dark

Dead of Night

Rising Dawn

THE SEDONA FILES*

(Paranormal Romance)

Bad Vibrations

Desert Hearts

Angel Fire

Star Crossed

Falling Angels

Enemy Mine

Get the first three books of this series in an omnibus
edition, or read the complete six-book series in one
super-low-priced boxed set!

TALES OF THE LATTER KINGDOMS

(Fantasy Romance)

All Fall Down

Dragon Rose

Binding Spell

Ashes of Roses

One Thousand Nights

Threads of Gold

The Wolf of Harrow Hall

Moon Dance

The Song of the Thrush

Snow Fall (Second half of 2019)

Books 1-3 and Books 4-6 of this series are also available in two separate omnibus editions at special boxed set prices.

———

THE GAIAN CONSORTIUM SERIES*

(Science Fiction Romance)

Beast (free prequel novella)

Blood Will Tell

Breath of Life

The Gaia Gambit

The Mandala Maneuver

The Titan Trap

The Zhore Deception

The Refugee Ruse

Books 1-3 of this series are also available in an omnibus edition at a special boxed set price!

———

STANDALONE TITLES

Hearts on Fire

Sympathy for the Devil

Taking Dictation

Night Music

Golden Heart

* Indicates a completed series

About the Author

USA Today bestselling author Christine Pope has been writing stories ever since she commandeered her family's Smith-Corona typewriter back in grade school. Her work includes paranormal romance, fantasy romance, and science fiction/space opera romance. She makes her home in Sedona, Arizona.

Christine Pope on the Web:
www.christinepope.com

facebook.com/ChristinePopeAuthor

twitter.com/ChristineJPope

pinterest.com/ChristineJPope

www.ingramcontent.com/pod-product-compliance
Lightning Source LLC
Chambersburg PA
CBHW020516260626
47156CB00006B/2026